TONI CADE BAMBARA
DEEP SIGHTINGS AND
RESCUE MISSIONS

Toni Cade Bambara is the author of two short-story col-
lections, *Gorilla, My Love* and *The Sea Birds Are Still
Alive,* and a novel, *The Salt Eaters.* She edited *The Black
Woman* and *Tales and Short Stories for Black Folks.*
Bambara's works have appeared in many periodicals and
have been translated into several languages.

DEEP

SIGHTINGS

AND

RESCUE

MISSIONS

DEEP

SIGHTINGS

AND

RESCUE

MISSIONS

Fiction, Essays,
and Conversations

TONI CADE BAMBARA

EDITED AND WITH A PREFACE BY
TONI MORRISON

VINTAGE CONTEMPORARIES   VINTAGE BOOKS
A DIVISION OF RANDOM HOUSE, INC.   NEW YORK

Grateful acknowledgment is made to the following for permission to reprint
previously published material:

Five Colleges, Inc.: "Language and the Writer" by Toni Cade Bambara *(Contributions in Black Studies).* Reprinted by permission of Five Colleges, Inc.

Hatch-Billops Collection: "How She Came By Her Name," an interview by
Louis Massiah with Toni Cade Bambara *(Artist and Influence,* Vol. 14). All
rights reserved. Reprinted by permission of the Hatch-Billops Collection.

Routledge: "Reading the Signs" by Toni Cade Bambara from *Black American
Cinema* edited by Manthia Diawara (1992). Reprinted by permission of the
publisher, Routledge: New York and London.

Stewart, Tabori & Chang, Publishers: "School Daze" by Toni Cade Bambara,
from *The Films of Spike Lee: Five for Five.* Copyright © 1991 by Forty Acres
and a Mule Filmworks, Inc. Reprinted by permission of Stewart, Tabori &
Chang, New York.

The Library of Congress has cataloged the Pantheon edition as follows:
Bambara, Toni Cade.
Deep sightings and rescue missions : fiction, essays, and conversations /
Toni Cade Bambara / edited and with a preface by Toni Morrison.
p. cm.

1. Afro-Americans—Social life and customs—Fiction. 2. American fiction—
Afro-American authors—History and criticism—Theory, etc. 3. Afro-
American women in literature. 4. Afro-Americans in literature. I. Title.
PS3552.A473D44   1996
813'.54—dc20   96-18637

Vintage ISBN: 0-679-77407-6

Book design by Deborah Kerner

www.randomhouse.com

Printed in the United States of America

CONTENTS

PREFACE

Deep Sightings and Rescue Missions is unlike other books by Toni Cade Bambara. She did not gather or organize the contents. She did not approve or choose the photograph on the jacket. She did not post a flurry of letters, notes and bulletins on the design, on this or that copy change, or to describe an innovative idea about the book's promotion. And of her books published by Random House (*Gorilla, My Love, The Seabirds Are Still Alive* and *Salt Eaters*) only this one did not have the benefit, the joy, of a series of "editorial meetings" between us. Hilarious title struggles. Cloaked suggestions for ways to highlight, to foreground. Breathless discussions about what the whores really meant. Occasional battles to locate the double meaning, the singular word. Trips uptown for fried fish. Days and days in a house on the river—she, page in hand, running downstairs to say, "Does this do it?"

Editing sometimes requires re-structuring, setting loose or nailing down; paragraphs, pages may need re-writing, sentences (especially final or opening ones) may need to be deleted or re-cast; incomplete images or thoughts may need expansion, development. Sometimes the point is buried or too worked-up. Other times the tone is "off," the voice is wrong or unforthcoming or so self-regarding it distorts or mis-shapes the characters it wishes to display. In some manuscripts traps are laid so the reader is sandbagged into focusing on the author's superior gifts or knowledge rather than the intimate, reader-personalized world fiction can summon. Virtually none of that is applicable to editing Bambara's fiction.

Her writing is woven, aware of its music, its overlapping waves of scenic action, so clearly on its way—like a magnet collecting details in its wake, each of which is essential to the final effect. Entering her prose with a red pencil must be delicate; one ill-advised (or well-advised) "correction" can dislodge a thread, unravel an intricate pattern which is deceptively uncomplicated at first glance—but only at first glance.

Bambara is a writer's writer, an editor's writer, a

reader's writer. Gently but pointedly she encourages us to re-think art and public space in "The War of the Wall." She is all "eyes, sweetness and stingers" in "Luther on Sweet Auburn" and in "Baby's Breath." She is wisdom's clarity in "Going Critical," plumbing the ultimate separation for meaning as legacy.

Although her insights are multiple, her textures layered and her narrative trajectory implacable, nothing distracts from the sheer satisfaction her story-telling provides. That is a little word—satisfaction—in an environment where su-perlatives are as common as the work they describe. But there is no other word for the wash of recognition, the thrill of deep sight, the sheer pleasure a reader takes in the com-pany Bambara keeps. In "Ice," for example, watching her effortlessly transform a story about responsibility into the responsibility of story-telling is pure delight and we get to be in warm and splendid company all along the way.

I don't know if she knew the heart cling of her fiction. Its pedagogy, its use, she knew very well, but I have often wondered if she knew how brilliant at it she was. There was no division in her mind between optimism and ruthless vig-ilance; between aesthetic obligation and the aesthetics of obligation. There was no doubt whatsoever that the work she did had work to do. She always knew what her work was for. Any hint that art was over there and politics was over here would break her up into tears of laughter, or elicit a look so withering it made silence the only intelligent re-sponse. More often she met the art/politics fake debate with a slight wave-away of the fingers on her beautiful hand, like the dismissal of a mindless, desperate fly who had maybe two little hours of life left.

Of course she knew. It's all there in "How She Came By Her Name." The ear with flawless pitch; integrity embedded in the bone; daunting artistic criteria. Perhaps my wondering whether or not she realized how original, how rare her writing is is prompted by the fact that I knew it was not her only love. She had another one. Stronger. As the Essays and Conversations portion of this collection testifies, (especially after the completion of her magnum opus about the child murders in Atlanta) she came to prefer film: writing scripts, making film, critiquing, teaching, analyzing it and enabling others to do the same. *The Bombing of Osage Avenue* and *W. E. B. Du Bois: A Biography in Four Voices* contain sterling examples of her uncompromising gifts and her determination to help rescue a genre from its powerful social irrelevancy.

In fiction, in essays, in conversation one hears the purposeful quiet of this ever vocal woman; feels the tenderness in this tough Harlem/Brooklyn girl; joins the playfulness of this profoundly serious writer. When turns of events wearied the gallant and depleted the strong, Toni Cade Bambara, her prodigious talent firmly in hand, stayed the distance.

Editing her previous work was a privilege she permitted me. Editing her posthumous work is a gift she has given me. I will miss her forever.

"She made revolution irresistible," Louis Massiah has said of her.

She did. She is. Irresistible.

TONI MORRISON
June 1996

Special thanks to Ms. Toni Morrison
and Mr. Louis Massiah
for their help in
pulling this collection together
and keeping my Mother's voice alive.

KARMA BENE BAMBARA
June 1996

DEEP
SIGHTINGS
AND
RESCUE
MISSIONS

FICTION

GOING CRITICAL

I

One minute, Clara was standing on a wet stone slab slanting over the drop, a breaker coming at her, the tension tingling up the back of her legs as though it were years ago and she would dive from the rocks to meet it. And in the next minute, the picture coming again, brushing behind her eye, insistent since morning but still incomplete. Then the breaker struck the rocks, the icy cold wash lifting her up on her toes, and the picture flashing, still faint, indistinct. Teeth chattering, she flowed with it, tried not to understand it and blur the edges, but understood it beneath words, beneath thought. The brushing as of a feather, the wing-tip arrival of the childhood sea god who had buoyed her up from the deep when she'd been young and reckless in the waters. A feather brushing in the right side of the brain, dulled by three centuries of God-slight neglect, awakened in Clara at the moment of her daughter's conception.

Nineteen eighty, middle-aged woman in dated swimsuit and loose flesh, sliding perilously on moss slime stone, image clustering behind right eye, image-idea emerging from the void, a heresy in one era, a truth in the next, decaying into superstition, then splashing its message before returning to the void. The water sucking at the soles of her feet before sliding out again to sea, she saw it and shivered.

And then she was running, forgetting all her daughter had taught her about jogging. Running, she pushed her chilled body through an opening in the bushes as though heading toward a remembered site—a clearing, a desert nearly, where the bomb test was to be conducted. They'd been told through memos, at briefings, and over the PA system that they were in no danger providing, so long as, on the condition that, and if. No special uniforms or equipment had been issued, not even a shard of smoked glass. They were simply to take up their positions in the designated spots where the NCO rec hall was to be built. Line up, shut up, close the eyes—that was all, once the incomprehensible waivers had been signed.

Cold and damp, Clara plunged through the green, seeing in memory remnants of the ghost bush, seeing the open-mouth Lieutenant Reed, a gospel singer in civilian life, crash through the bush at the last minute, leaving a gaping wound. The twigs and leaves trying to squeeze to, trying to knit closed, trying to lock up before the blast. Their straining prying Clara's eyes open. And in that moment, the deep muffled thunder of the detonation. And the ground broke and the light flared and her teeth shook in the jellied sockets of her gums. Her heart stopped, but her eyes kept on seeing—Lieutenant Bernice Reed a shadow, an X-ray, the twigs and leaves transparent too, showing their bones.

Clara passed through the bushes out of breath and exchanged her swimsuit for a towel, wondering if the bush still quaked on the flats in Utah. Had it ever closed, had it ever healed? And did Bernice Reed still sing in the choir in Moultrie, Georgia, or had she left her voice there in the wounded green?

II

"Ya know, Mama, the really hip part of the fish and loaves miracle?"

Clara watched her daughter squat-walk across the sandy blanket, thinking fishes and loaves, the Piscean age, Golden Calf, the Taurean. Wondering too, would the girl ever get it together and apply her gift in useful ways in the time of the Emptying Vessel?

"There were no dishes to wash, no bottles to sterilize or nipples to scrub. And no garbage to put out, Mama. That was the miracle. Hell, feeding the multitudes ain't no big thing. You and Aunt Ludie and women before and mamas since been doing that season in and season out."

Season in and season out. To feed the people, Clara muttered, pulling her overall strap over her shoulder and hooking it. What crops would be harvested from the contaminated earth?

"But of course, it was probably a classic case of the women doing the cleaning up. So quite naturally all that non–high drama escaped the chronicler's jaundiced eye."

"I knew you were going to say that," Clara said. She stumbled into her clogs, watching Honey bury a lump of potato salad in the sand.

Honey shrugged. "How boring it must be for you to always know what I'm going to say."

"Not always. I don't always know, I mean."

Clara stuffed garbage into a plastic sack while her daughter gathered up the casting stones. The bone white agate Honey always used as the control was slipped into the leather pouch she wore around her neck. The two pebbles she'd found on the beach, the yes and no for the impromptu reading, Honey tossed into the picnic hamper.

"You were able to help them?" Clara knew Honey would merely glance toward the couple she'd read and shrug. The arguments over the proper use of Honey's gifts had been too frequent and too heated of late. Honey could not be lured into a discussion just like that. Clara ignored the press of time and softened her voice all the more. "You saw something for them?"

They had walked right up, the couple, tracking sand onto the blanket, ignored Clara altogether as though she were already gone, and said to Honey that they'd recognized her from the Center and would she read their cards, or read their palms, or throw the cowries, or "Give us some money," the woman had joked not joking, "Cash money in the hand," karate-chopping the air and baring her teeth. And Clara had done a quick aura-scan, first of the couple, swarmy and sparkish, then of her daughter, a steady glow.

"They seemed bad news to me," Clara said, still not expecting an answer, but searching for a point of entry. And saying it for the sake of the phrase "bad news," in preparation for the talk they'd come to the old neighborhood beach for but thus far had skirted. "Vampires," Clara said flatly. Honey did not take up the challenge, but went right on gathering up their things, her beaded braids clinking against her earrings.

Clara squatted down and folded the towels, wondering if Honey'd had a chance to rest, to recharge after the command-performance reading. She leaned over to dump the towels in the hamper and too to place her hand on her daughter's nerve center.

"Was there anything helpful you could tell them, Honey, about, say budgeting for the future?" Clara heard it catch in her throat, "the future," and felt Honey hearing it in the small of her back.

They both sat silent for a moment, gazing off in the direction of the couple arguing and wrassling their beach chairs as far from the water's edge as they could get.

"But then, what could you tell them? Hard to make ends meet when you've got your ass on your shoulders," Clara said, and was immediately sorry.

"Mama," Honey made no effort to disguise her annoyance, "I will gladly pay you back for the wedding. I will tell Curtis not to bug you any further about a loan. And damnit, I will pay for the parking."

"I didn't mean . . ." Clara didn't bother to say the rest of it, that she was only trying her hand at a joke. Her ears, her tongue, her heart were stinging.

III

They shook the sand out, then began folding the blanket, remembering how they used to do the laundry together, each backing up till the bedspread or sheet pulled taut—the signal to begin. Sometimes, flapping it flat, they'd dance to meet in the center, doing precise minuet steps, their noses pointed toward the basement ceiling, their lips pursed in imitation of a neighbor lady who complained of their incense, candles, gatherings, "strange" ways. Or, clicking across the ceramic tile of the laundry room, grimacing in tortured Flamenco postures, they'd olé olé till Jake, overhead in his den, hollered down the heat duct to lighten up and hurry up with supper. Sometimes, as part of their put-down of the school PE program, they'd clog, doing the squarest square dance steps they could muster. Yodeling, they'd bring each other the corners of the sheet, their knuckles knocking softly when they met, blind, each hiding behind her side of the raised-high fabric to prepare a face to shock the other with, once Clara, clasping all the corners and twanging in a hillbilly soprano, or Honey, nesting her hands in the folds to get the edges aligned, signaled the other to lower the covers in the laundry basket, their howls drawing stomps from overhead.

In those free times before the lumps appeared and the nightmare hauntings began, Clara would hold on to a funny face remembered from a Galveston carnival mask, while Honey, bending, would smooth the bedspreads down her mother's body to save her time at the ironing board. But then came the days when their signals went awry, when Clara, breathless with worry and impotence, and Honey, not yet reading the streaks in her mother's aura or the netted chains in her palm's mercury line, were both distracted, and the neatly folded tablecloth would wind up a heap on the basement floor. "I thought you had it, damnit. I thought you were going to take it. Shit." And Jake, husband/father, would avoid the loyalty trap by giving both bristling women wide berth for the course of the day.

There were the hot, silent times too, Clara racing feverishly through lists of healers yet to be seen, Honey searching for some kind thing to say now that radium and chemotherapy had snatched huge patches out of Clara's hair and softened her gums, ruining a once handsome jawline. The covers between would get ironed flat by the heat of mother and daughter clinging to the spread, touching through terry cloth or wool or chenille, neither letting go. Overhead, Jake, his face pressed against cold iron, breathing in burnt dust from the grate and cat hairs in the carpet, weeping into the ashes, would pray they'd let go of each other before the time.

"I've got it," Clara said finally, when she could bear it no longer, neither the strain of the silence, the memories, nor her daughter's presence too close and too intense. "Let go, Honey," as though the sun that Honey's young body had soaked up all day were searing her now through the wool. "Let go."

Clara draped the blanket over Honey's outstretched arm, dropped it really, as though it had singed her, as though she wanted to be done with blankets and outings and Honey and all of it quickly and get away, race back to the rocks, to the ice-cold waters that had known her young and fit and with a future.

"Mama, are you alright?"

Her daughter whispering as in a sickroom with shades drawn and carpets muffling; Honey slow-motion bending to lay the blanket in the hamper, slow and quiet as in the presence of the dying. Clara grabbed up one handle of the wicker hamper, and Honey took up her end. And now they could go. There was nothing to keep them there except what was keeping them there. But how to begin? Honey, your ole mama's on her last leg and needs to know, you won't be silly . . . My darling, please promise not to abuse your gifts . . . Before I kick off, Sweetie, one last request . . . ? Words tumbled moist and clumsily in Clara's mouth, and she rejected them. For now she wanted to speak of other things—of life, food, fun—wanted to invite her daughter, her friend, for a promenade along the boardwalk on the hunt for shrimp and beer, or quiche and a nice white wine.

"The lunch was lovely, Honey, but I'm hungry for more. For more," she said, veering closer to the subject that held them on the sand. But she could get no further into it and was grateful that Honey chose that moment to turn aside and hook-shoot the garbage sack into the dumpster some three feet away from the arguesome couple. Clara longed to touch her again, to trace with the tip of one finger the part in the back of Honey's head, knowing the scalp would be warm, hot even. Hot Head. Jake had nicknamed her when she was just an infant. And Curtis had revived it of late, preferring it to Khufu, the name his wife was known by at the Center, to Vera, the name on the birth certificate, and to Honey, the name she'd given her daughter to offset the effects of "Hot Head." Honey, a name she gave to give her daughter options.

"Starved? Say no more," Honey said, walking off and yanking Clara along at the other end of the hamper. "Aunt Ludie swears she's going to put her extramean gumbo together tonight. Needless to say, I told her to put our names in the pot."

"We're not staying for the fireworks?" Clara pulled on the handle to make Honey slow up. "I thought we'd eat around here and then see the fireworks. I thought that was the whole point of parking in the lot instead of on the street, so we'd have access to the dunes and . . ." She felt panic welling up, time running away from her. "Five damn dollars to park just so we'd have a pass to the dunes, Honey."

"Whatchu care about five damn dollars, Mama? You a

rich lady," Honey said over her shoulder with a smile Clara knew was not a smile at all. If Honey's lackadaisacal attitude at the Center was a hot issue, then the money was a scorcher. Her daughter had married into a family on Striver's Row, had in-laws with little patience for "community," "the people," "development," and even less tolerance for how their son's mother-in-law, Clara, dispersed her funds and spent her time and tried to influence their son's wife.

"Not yet, I'm not rich. Not yet." Clara stumbled along in the sand and wondered if she'd live long enough to see the money, at least to sign it over to the Center and its works. The suit the former GIs had brought against the Army had dragged on for years. And though the medical reports had grown sharper from "radiation exposure a high-probability factor in the development of malignancies," to "disabilities a direct result of the veterans' involvement with the nuclear test program"—and though the lawyers for the National Association of Atomic Vets were optimistic despite the sorry box score of twenty recognized suits out of hundreds of claims, and though the Board of Veterans' Appeals had overturned earlier VA rulings, the Army was still appealing, denying, holding out.

"It's easier walking along the beach," Honey was saying, shifting direction sharply and wrenching Clara's arm, her thoughts. "And maybe we can find some sandblasted bottles for Daddy's collection."

Nineteen eighty, deadline for probable-future choice imminent, people collecting shells, beer cans, stamps, rally buttons, posters, statistics, snapshots. Middle-aged woman in loose flesh and tight overalls pulled past old men sissy-fishing along sandbar in rolled-up pants. Tips of rods quivering like thin silver needles the Chinese doctor placed along meridian, electricity turned on, mother prayers turned up drowning Muzak out. Line pulled in, fish flopping its last, hook through gills, tail fin lashing at fisherman who's wrecked its life. Life already ruined. Woman on leave from Department of Wildlife recites fish kills typed up daily. Agriculture—insecticides, pesticides; industrial mining, paper, food, metallurgy, petroleum, chemical plants, municipal sewerage system, refuse disposal, swimming pool agents.

"Remember the church fish fries here when I was little? You'd leave me with Aunt Ludie to go visit the tearoom. Remember, Mama?"

Dog River, Alabama; Santa Barbara Harbor, California; Anacostia River, D.C.; Mulatto Bayou, Florida; Salt Bayou, Louisiana.

"Mama, you look beat. Wanna rest?"

Slocum Creek, North Carolina; Radar Creek, Ohio; San Jacinto River, Texas; Snake River, Washington.

"Why don't you sit down on the rocks while I put this stuff in the car."

"Girl, don't you know my sitting days are over? And there's work to do and we need to talk." But she let Honey take the whole of the hamper onto her shoulder and march off with it. So there was nothing for Clara to do but find a dry rock not too far out on the breakwater wall and sit down, be still, be available, wait. She slumped. The weight of the day, of unhealth, relationships, trying to organize for the end, pressed her down onto the rocks, her body yearning to return to the earth—disoriented, detached and unobliged. And then the picture flashed. The bush. A maze of overgrown hedges and thickets, prickly to the eye. She, looking for a path and it suddenly there, bones at the mouth of the passage. On her knees inching through briars. Inching forward to the edge. And nothing there at the drop. No matter which way she turned, the view the same. The world an egg blown clean.

IV

"They say, Honey, that cancer is the disease of new beginnings, the result of a few cells trying to start things up again."

"Your point being?" Honey was picking her teeth, weaving in and out of boardwalk traffic, deliberately allowing, it seemed to Clara, cyclists, skaters, parents pushing baby strollers, to come between them.

"That it's characteristic of these times, Honey. It signals the beginning of the new age. There'll be epidemics. And folks, you know it, are not prepared."

"And so?"

They were side by side now, veering around a "sidewalk" artist down on his knees, pushing a plate of colored chalks along the boards, drawing rapidly fantastic figures that stumped those strollers who paused to look, dripping the ice cream or sweaty cups of beer on the artwork. Together, they walked briskly past the restaurants and bars, the kiddie park, the wax museum, the horror house, finally talking. But Clara was still dissatisfied, had still not gotten said what she'd come to the beach to say to her only child. And she still did not altogether know what it was. When my time comes, Honey, release me 'cause I've work to do yet? Watch yourself and try not be pulled off of the path by your in-laws? Develop the gifts, girl, and try to push at least one life in the direction of resurrection?

"You do understand about the money?" Clara was hugging close as marines, couples, teenagers walking four and five abreast, threatened to shove between them. She felt Honey's arm stiffen as though she meant to pull away.

"Money, money, money. I'm sick of the subject. Curtis, his mother . . . And his father, you know, has his eye on a liquor store and keeps asking me if . . ."

An elderly couple clumping along in rubber-tipped walkers separated them. Then an Asian-American family Clara dimly recalled from the old neighborhood streamed between them, the mother spitting watermelon seeds expertly through the cracks in the boardwalk, the father popping kernels from what was evidently a very hot cob of corn, one youngster cracking into a sugar-glazed apple, the other absentmindedly plucking tufts of cotton candy from a paper cone as though it were a petaled daisy.

Liquor store. Clara frowned, her face contorted from the effort to salute her old neighbors, answer Honey, and continue the dialogue on the inside all at the same time. And so she almost missed it, not the Fotomat Honey was pointing toward where summers before they'd horsed around, meeting up with odd characters they never told Jake and, later, Curtis about; posing as sisters or actresses fresh back from madcap adventures on the Orient Express, they would give each other fanciful names and outlandish histories to flirt with. She almost missed the tearoom. Jammed between the tattoo parlor and the bingo hall, looking tinier and tackier than she remembered it, was the tearoom where Clara had watched, under the steady gaze of Great Ma Drew, her work emerge clear and sharp from the dense fog of the crystal ball that good sense had taught her to scoff at till something more powerful than skepticism and something more potent than the markings on her calendar forced Clara's eyes to acknowledge two events: motherhood, and soon (despite all the doctors had had to say about Jake's sluggish sperm and her tilted uterus), and a gift unfolding right now, a gift that would enable Clara to train the child.

Clara linked arms with Honey and steered her toward the tearoom with her hips. The woman, though, lounging against the Madame Lazar Tearoom sign was neither the seer Drew, nor any of the gypsified Gypsies or non-Gypsies that had taken over the business during Honey's growing-up days. She was a young, mariny woman in a Donna Summer do—a weave job, Clara's expert eye noted—wearing exactly the kind of jewelry and flouncy dress, vèvè-encrusted hem and metallic smocking in the bodice, that Clara always associated with the Ioa Urzulie Frieda. Clara felt Honey resisting, her hard bone pushing through flesh against her.

"Sistuh, are you gifted?" Honey challenged, before

Clara could speak, could get her balance, Honey still steeling herself against her.

The woman's eyes slid insolently over them. Clara was about to give in and let Honey steer along to the dunes, but the woman flashed, and Clara felt a reaching-out come in her direction, and then a mind probe, bold, prickly, and not at all gentle.

"She's telepathic," Clara whispered, pulling Honey up short. "But can she see, I wonder. Can she see around the bend and probe the future?" Honey sucked her teeth and stood her ground between the two women. And now the woman smiled and Clara dropped Honey's arm and dropped, too, her shield. At this point in time, Clara mused, I can afford to be open to anything and everything.

"How far can you see?" Clara asked, setting up a chain reaction of questions on the inside for the woman to touch upon. She waited. In an open-bodied position, Clara invited the woman to move in.

"Mama, come on, damnit."

And then Clara felt the woman withdraw. And it was Honey's turn to smile. She was gifted, this new Madame Lazar. She was simpatico. But business is business, no freebies here. The woman slid her eyes over Honey in dismissal, and to Clara she jerked her chin in the direction of the incense-fragrant interior and passed, sashaying in her noisy crinolines and taffetas, through the curtain.

"Oh no, you don't," Honey said, linking arms and shoving her hip hard against Clara's, almost knocking her out of her clogs. "She has a gift alright, Mama, but no principles. Liable to put a hex on you," she grinned, "plus take all your money. Let's go."

"Now wait a minute." Clara tried to disengage her arm and back up for a moment to get her thoughts lined up, but Honey was pulling her along like an irritated parent with an aggravating child. Hex, Clara thought, trying to get it organized. UF_6, the gaseous form of uranium, was called hex and that was something to talk about. Gifts and principles—exactly the topic to get to an appraisal of the Center's work. Money perfect. But Honey would not give her a moment. Who was the mother here anyway? Clara squinched up her toes, trying for traction, trying to dig in. She yanked hard on her daughter.

"Whatcha so mad about, Mama?"

"Well, damnit, what are you so angry about, and all week long too?" They were falling over the chalk artist, causing a pileup in front of the tattoo parlor. "You're mad because I'm leaving you?" She was clutching the lapels of her daughter's shirt, breathing hot breath into her face, her body shuddering. "Oh, girl, don't you know it's the way of things for children to bury their elders?" She barely had the strength to hold on as Honey dropped her face into her shoulders, pressing her beaded braids into Clara's skin. They stood in the throng, getting bumped and jostled by sailors coming out of the parlor displaying their arms and banging each other on the back in congratulations.

"Please, Honey, you say the words over me, hear? No high-falutin eulogies, OK? Don't let them lie me into the past tense and try to palm me off on God as somebody I'm not, OK? And don't let anybody insult my work by grieving and carrying on, OK? Cause I'm not at all unhappy, and Jake's come to terms with it. I've still my work to do, whatever shape I'm in. I mean whatever form I'm in, you know? So OK, Honey? And don't mess up, damnit."

"You and your precious work," Honey hissed, catching Clara off-balance. And then a smile broke up her frown, the sun coming out, and Clara could bear the pain of the beads' imprint. "Fess up, Mama," grinning mischievously, "you're mostly pissed about the five dollars for parking, aincha?"

Someone on the dunes was singing, the music muted at first by the dark and the ocean breeze. Clara leaned back against Honey's knees and issued progress reports on the boat. Decked out in banners and streamers for the occasion, flying its colors on the mast overhead, it was easing its cargo of fireworks out to the raft where T-shirted lifeguards and parkees in orange safety harnesses and bright helmets waited, eager to begin.

She could feel Honey behind her—her knees softening at intervals, then jerking awake as the singer modulated—going to sleep.

"Take care, Honey, that you keep your eyes sharp and spirit alert," she instructed, her voice sounding to her already flat, lifeless, as if it traveled from a great distance and through a veil, vibrancy gone, her self removed to the very outskirts of her being, suspended over her flesh, over the sand, on the high note now sounding while the slap of the waves, a baby's ball buffeted by the waters, was being sucked under the rocks of the breakwater wall, and bits of conversation from blankets around them and from the boardwalk overhead, and then even the high notes, churned below her.

She was hanging in the music, in the swoop of the notes across the humps of the dunes so like beings rising from the sand, dipping down in sound between the childrens' pail-castles and grown-ups' plumped pillows, buoyed up again toward the moon, full, red and heavy, till the wail of a child and Honey's jerking pulled her back again inside her skin. Being dragged past them by a mother determined to ignore her son's bedtime tactic, a young child in a Hank Aaron shirt was trickling sand across Clara's toes and bawling, his tiny hand digging up another fistful from a bulging pocket to trail sand across the tufts of dune grass and up the steps to the boardwalk gate, people shoving over as though they recognized this tribal wiseman spreading the time-running-fast message to the heedless, then making sand-paintings on the boards, chalkings, the ritual cure for sleepwalkers.

"It begins," Clara said. But still Honey did not sit up to appreciate the view. The fisherfolk had parked their poles and taken up their perch on the rocks, couples on blankets propped each other up, the boardwalk crowd bunched along the railing, the overflow packed on the top steps, leaning into the mesh of the gate—the vista was wide open for the first whoosh of yellow and pink that careened across the night sky. The ahhhhh from the crowd harmonizing with the singer climbing an octave and the bedtime boy still wailing and wheeling around in the chalk drawings, smearing and stamping. A rocket shot out across the waters and exploded into a shower of red, white and blue that fountained down at the far end of the breakwater wall.

"Don't miss this," she said, her voice hollow again, drawn into the music, into the next burst of colors, pulses of energy like the frenzy of atoms like the buzzing of bees like the comings and goings of innumerable souls immeasurably old and in infinite forms and numerous colors. She was floating up, her edges blurring, her flesh falling away, the high note reachable now coming at her from nine different directions, sailing out with her past the boat's flag, echoing through blue through time. And she was a point of light, a point of consciousness in the dark, looking down on her body accusingly—how could it let her go like that?—but ready to be gone and wanting too to go back and nestle inside her old self intimate and warm, skin holding her in, bone holding her up, blood flowing. Her body summoning not yet. Her daughter a magnet, drawing her back.

A cluster of pinwheels came spinning from the boat deck, and the bedtime boy seemed content to whimper between wails. But the singer held on, leaning into the music, pressing sound into the colors. A salvo of sparklers shot out, streaking across the pinwheel's paths, sizzling.

She'd put sparklers on Honey's birthday cake the year Alvin Ailey's company came into town. Had thought it a brilliant change from pastel candles, but the children were frightened, leapt from the table, overturned the benches, dragged half of the tablecloth away in tatters, knocked over the ruffled cups of raisins and nuts, and the punch bowl too. She tried, as they scooted away bursting balloons which only made it worse, tried to explain, as they tripped entangled in crepe paper streamers and string, taking off to the woods before she could assure them, those children of the old neighborhood who'd never seen Chinese New Year, who'd never celebrated the Fourth of July with anything louder than an elder's grunt "Independence for whom?" or "Freedom, my ass!" or anything noisier than a grease-popping what-the-hell barbecue, who'd never seen a comet or heard the planetarium's version of asteroid, the running children who'd never been ushered from bed to watch the street rebellions on TV or through the window and have explained why things were so—doing the hundred-yard dash to the woods fleeing sparklers, Honey right along with them, leaving her with frosting on her chin and hundreds of lessons still to teach.

"You chuckling, coughing, crying, or what?" Honey's voice was drowsy. And Clara didn't know the answer, but remembered the twenty-five dollars' worth of box-seat tickets to see the Ailey dancers, and the exhausted birthday sprinter falling asleep in the middle of *Revelations*, Jake shaking her by the shoulders to at least watch a few dollars' worth.

"That a human voice or what?" Honey sounded neither irritated nor curious, her way, Clara supposed, of letting her know she was still available for talk. The boy was still crying and the note was still holding as firecrackers went off, sounding powerful enough to launch a getaway spaceship. "Ain't it the way," Jake had said just that morning, huddled over the pale, "they mess up, then cut out to new frontiers to mess up again." The singer climbing over the thundering, holding out past the crowd's applause, past the crowd's demand for release, past endurance for even extraordinary lungs, the note drawn thin and taut now like a wire, a siren, the parkees, looking now like civil defense wardens sending up flares from the shoot machines, cannons. And still the singer persisted, piercing, an alarm, stepsitters twisting round in annoyance now, the first wave of anger shaking through the crowd at the railing, a big man shoving through to the gate and to hell with a dune pass, heroic, on the hunt for the irritant to silence it. Then a barrage of firecrackers heading straight across the water, caused many to duck before reminding themselves, embarrassed, that this was Sunday at the beach, holiday entertainment and all's well.

"A jug of wine, a crust of pizza and thou for Crissake," someone was saying. Then the note shuddered to a gasping halt and the bedtime boy's wail was cut short by a resounding slap heard on the dunes. After a faint ripple of applause, attention turned fully to the lifeguards prying open the last crate, the parkees spinning out the remaining pinwheels to hold the audience until the specialty works that would spell out a message, the final event, could be crammed into the cannons and fired off.

"Girl, wake up and watch my money."

Honey, knees wobbled against Clara's back, glanced round and smiled at her efforts to come awake and keep her mother company.

There was no way she could carry her child to the car anymore, lay her down gently in the back seat, cover her over with a dry towel, and depend on tomorrow for what went undone today. Clara turned toward the water and joined the people, attentive to the final event about to light up the sky.

MADAME BAI
AND THE TAKING
OF STONE MOUNTAIN

I

Headachy from the double feature, she tells Tram and Mustafa that she'll take a rain check on beer and carousing. The rest of the household, after all, expect her back by ten o'clock for an English conversation lesson.

"A coffee?" Mustafa suggests.

She frowns. Tram frowns. They stand there, jostled by the people coming out of the Rialto. She views it all as a tableau: three figures in the city landscape, winter gray, winter gray, reward posters on poles. Then as a bit of footage when they move along. That is what seeing her neighborhood, her city constantly on the news, has done to her perception.

Mustafa shrugs. "Home then." His coat, elegantly draped around his shoulders, falls in soft, straight folds, his sleeves swinging like regal robes as he saunters across the street to get a paper. From the back he could be her father. All he needs, she's thinking, is a horn case and his beret a little more ace-deuce.

She stands hipshot at the curb as her mother would, but she does not tap her foot. She can't chance it, the wind beating at her back and she still wobbly from that particular loss. It's a new way to be in the world, she's been discovering, unmothered.

"Rain check?" Tram gazes at the wintry sky, perplexed wrinkles scarring his broad-boned cheeks. She explains the figure of speech, the wind now at her throat, shoving the words back to her. Tram listens, his arms crossed in front, hands shoved up his quilted sleeves, an untippable figure, a pyramid. She shifts her weight to match his stance.

Two young bloods, in defiance of the curfew, shoot out of Luckie Street and race between cars bouncing over the parking lot braker. Mustafa, reading the headlines aloud, rejoins his companions. She zooms in on the newsprint type, then looks away, not correcting Mustafa's pronunciation. She widens the lens to incorporate a blind man tapping along the pavement toward them. There is, she decides, too lively a curiosity behind his shades. She watches warily as the man stops by the boys inspecting the kung fu posters outside the movie house. The boys move on and so does the man, his chin stuck out as if to sniff the wind, the aromas from the restaurant, the boys. She tenses. To her list of suspects—Klan, cops, clergy, little old ladies with cookies, young kids in distress used to lure older ones, adults in Boy Scout gear—she now adds blind people.

"Oh God," she mutters, stopping. The blind man, hooking his cane in the crook of his arm, picks up his pace, tailing after the boys. She opens her mouth again to call out a warning, clutching a fistful of Mustafa's mohair sleeve as if that will anchor her for the bellow. The boys race down a side street toward the bus stops by Central City Park. The blind man continues on straight ahead toward Marietta. She exhales.

"Yes?" Mustafa is studying her, his eyebrows arched so hard in query, his narrow forehead all but disappears under his beret. Tram, hunched up like all of Atlanta, shivery and intense, growls, "What?"

She flops her hands around, helpless. The two men exchange a look. Their landlady/friend/English instructor bears watching, the look says. Tram lifts an elbow for her to catch on to. Mustafa tucks the newspapers away, not bothering to pull his sweater cuffs down. She hesitates to take his arm. His wrists are deformed. He swings his coat open like a cape and invites her in. They move up Forsyth, heads ducked, bodies huddled. She's grateful, wedged between the two, for the warmth, support. And grateful too that Mustafa has not offered his latest theory on the missing and murdered children. He's not in the habit of talking freely in the streets. He reserves his passionate tirades against global fascism to the late-night talk fests in the kitchen, having learned a hard lesson.

They hung him from the ceiling by the wrists. The same Israelis whose parents had had them baptized in '36, then sent to the convent school in Mustafa's district to save them from the Nazis. The same school Coptic Christians of the district sent their children to, to save them from the backwardness of Jordanian society. The same district whose faithful evicted the French nuns to save Islam from the infidels. The same infidels who turned the city over to the invading Israelis, grown and in uniform, claiming God's real estate covenant, who converted the old convent into an Army base to save the city from terrorists. Mustafa, a brash young student then, had been relating this history to a companion when they grabbed him and dragged him off for interrogation on the ropes.

"Whatcha got up your sleeves, Chinaman?"

She cannot believe her ears. They heard that selfsame line delivered just moments before in badly dubbed stereophonic sound, followed by a whistling knife spun from a tobacco brown silk sleeve that pinned the speaker's shoulder blade to a beam in the rice shop. Courtesy of Hong Kong Eternal Flame Films, Ltd.

Four white punks in gray hooded sweatsuits have slipped up alongside, cutting them off. They carry what looks like a three-foot grappling hook, something you'd use to drag the river with. She freezes.

"Whatsa matter?" the leader leers, jiggling the pole. "No speaky de English?" The Confederate flag snaps down at the sharpened end.

Mustafa slides away and quickly rolls his paper into a bat. Tram gets into a crouch, staring hard at the belt buckle insignia of the big-bellied punk. In the East it would be the reassuring shorinji kempo symbol, but in the West, the interlocking Z's have been corrupted into the swastika. They're jabbing the pole straight at Tram's midsection, the flag snapping like a whip, like teeth. She fingers the pick comb in one pocket, her key ring in the other.

"Chinky Chinaman no speaka de English." The leader with hobnailed wristbands grins to his cohorts. "Speak gook then," he prods Tram, no grin.

Tram leaps back, then lunges suddenly into a high-kicking spin, pulling his fists out of his sleeves as he lands. Two of the punks slam hard against the doughnut-shop window. The others stumble between the newspaper boxes near the curb. The sound of the crash, of the hubbub as diners move from the counter of the shop to the window, the resounding clang as the pole hits cement, shuddering underfoot, propels her. Mustafa gets off a few good whacks before his weapon buckles. She's leaning hard on the punk against the window, her pick in his gut, her keys grating against the bridge of his nose. Tram pulls her away to make room. She drags the punk with her.

"The cruel and lively Thai boxer legs," Mustafa announces to the crowd joining them, bouncing the big-bellied one off the *Wall Street Journal* box and letting him fall hard against the *Atlanta Journal/Constitution*'s. She hears glass shatter and expects to see the doughnut shop window in a slow-motion breakaway. She brings her knees up into the punk's groin, then rams both elbows down hard in a V between his collarbones. He goes down.

Tram's final spin ends with one foot catching the leader on the side of the head, the other foot shoving Big Belly into the street. The other two are scrambling backward in a spatter of glass. She's kicking at them while Mustafa, his coat blown to the ground, backs them into the gutter. Brakes screech, tires squeal, as the hooded ones race across toward the construction site, leaping hurdles of haystacks and sandbags.

"Well alright, alright." A brother in seaman's cap and sweater, jelly on his front teeth, dusty sugar down his front, slaps Tram on the back in appreciation, pokes Mustafa in the shoulder and helps him on with his coat. He bends and retrieves her keys, his body moving in sportscaster reply.

"That was something," he says, raising his hand high to give five, hesitating as though not sure who to give it to. She extends her hand, family. He sizes her up, considering— twentyish, Red Bone, krinkly riney fringe ridging the edges of her hat. She knows that look. It's a stingy five he gives as though she, skin-privileged, doesn't need it. And then his hand slides away, leaving the keys and leaving her with a bad feeling.

"Really something," he says over his shoulder, the Hawk spurring him and the crowd back inside.

Mustafa brushes off his coat. Tram stands back hard

on his heels, squinting toward the construction site awaiting a sneak attack of rocks and rubble. His calves strain against denim in back, thighs bulging in front, wind plastering his sweater against his chest so that eight separate segments of abdominal muscles lift like bas relief. He looks like sculpture, she's thinking, though the sculptor in the household has long since made that observation. The raised scar on his rib cage like a length of packing twine, the quilted jacket a packing mat—statuary ready for shipping. They hook arms again and move to the bus stop, saluted by raised coffee mugs and banging soup spoons as they pass the shop.

She hopes the bus will be overheated. Though her companions shelter her from the wind, she is chilled through, brittle, on the brink of cracking. They talk across her, warm breath smoke signals. They speak to each other across a colonial bridge, in French, Mustafa reliving the battle so much more graphic than the kitchen demonstrations Tram gives at the house, Tram complaining that breaking bones is not why he studies the arts, not why he's come all the way to Atlanta to await the arrival of the celebrated Madame Bai.

"Clearly, my friend"—Mustafa switches to her colonial tongue—"the first to make the phrase 'What is up the sleeve, Chinaman?' did not meet a warrior before." He invites her to join him in a chuckle. She can't risk it. She's clamping down hard, jaws tight, stomach clenched.

"I'm Vietnamese," Tram says flatly, ignoring the compliment and peering for the bus.

"The scoundrels cannot know this," Mustafa says. "Chinese, Laotian, from Korea or Japan—all as same the things," he says, drawing two tapered fingers close together and mumbling "*Même chose,*" having bungled the idiom in English.

She does not offer instruction. Tram has shoved two blunt-nailed fingers in her face, offering them up for examination. These fingers, he has explained at length at the house, he will return home with and help heal the wounds of war.

"Two fingers," he says, shoving them toward Mustafa, "and I can work. Go in"—probing Mustafa's lapel—"find disease, snatch it too quick for scar tissue to wake." He snips off a button and drops it into Mustafa's palm.

"Fine hands," Mustafa mumbles, pocketing it.

"For health, not breaking bones." Tram adjusts his clothes, fingering the ridge through his sweater. He fastens the toggles of his jacket and shoves his hands hard up his sleeves.

A healer from the Montagnard hills sealed Tram's gash with a mud-and-dung pack, then bound the ribs with vines, and brewed a tea for the fever. Tram, a young schoolboy, had been dragged from the schoolhouse by Diem's secret police and tortured in order to break the schoolmaster down. His tormenters would gain international notoriety that same year as the designers of the infamous, crippling tiger cages.

"You are offended to be called Chinese?" Mustafa grins, trying to fit a cigarette into his ivory holder. His hands are shaking, she notices. She looks away. "You are jealous maybe of the great Chinese?"

"What Chinese have?" Tram growls, taking the bait.

"Fried noodles and Bruce Lee." It's not the usual taunt Mustafa offers that plunges the whole household into heated debate as to whether Mao makes it a gang of five.

"Chao Gio restaurant on Peachtree have fried noodles," says Tram. "And Bruce Lee, the myope and luster after things Western, is dead. "

Mustafa shrugs, but his coat refuses to drape in its usual regal manner. His fingers, clumsy, shred tobacco down his coat, ruining what might have been an elegant portrait: Jordanian poet, ivory tusk smoldering, cape blown against body, high collar misterioso. He tosses the broken cigarette away and pockets the holder. She winces. He looks like something out of Madame Tussaud's. She thinks of her mother, waxy and spent.

"There will be news on the television," Mustafa says quietly, fishing out his bus pass. "Another child found murdered."

Tram catches her from behind under the armpits. Mustafa leads her to the curb, rummaging in his pockets for a hanky. She dumps lunch into the gutter.

II

Madame Bai arrives on a drizmal day the week of the inauguration. There are two kung fu movies playing at the Rialto. There are always two kung fu movies playing at the Rialto. The bill is not in honor of the warrior-healer celebrated in shaolins and ashrams around the globe, revered by every master of the arts, quoted in all the texts. The Tai Chi

Association near Lenox Plaza silk-screens new T-shirts. But the yin-yang figure is not bordered by the ideograms that hallmark the flag of Madame's nation, Korea. Her presence in the city is not the occasion for the new apparel. Not a line of copy is devoted to her coming to Atlanta, magnet now for every amateur sleuth, bounty hunter, right-wing provocateur, left-wing adventurer, do-gooder, soothsayer, porno filmmaker, scoop journalist, crack shot, or cool-out "leader" not born from the fire of struggle.

The Reagans, Carters, and the hostages home from Iran hog the news. The best of medical and psychological attention is mobilized for the hostages. Less than little is available for the Vietnam vets suffering from shell shock, stress, and Agent Orange genetic tampering. Gifts of things, of cash, of promising jobs, await the returnees. But a minister in Cleveland gets on TV to tell people not to send a dime to the parents in Atlanta. "They were getting along alright without us before their children got killed. They can get along alright without our help now." And the media ferret out still one more "leader" to say "The mothers are cashing in," or "Not racially motivated," or "No connection with violence against Blacks in other places." And the FBI with poison pen leaks "The parents are not above suspicion." And as solidarity groups form and a movement seems to mount—"The parents did it."

In the northeast section of the city, yellow ribbons snap from flag poles, trees, door knockers, wrists. In the southwest green ribbons and black armbands are worn solemnly. The red, white and blue waves merrily over articles in *Thun-*

derbolt and *Soldier of Fortune* that urge good Christians to prepare for race war now that niggers, gooks, and commie jews and other mongrels are rising to take over God's country.

Tram runs a vacuum over the dining room floor, lifting the skirt of the tablecloth pointedly to route the household from its roundtable discussion over the latest National States Rights party rag which features faces of Blacks, Asians, Hispanics, and presumable Jews superimposed on apes' bodies. Mustafa, an elaborate headdress of pillow-cases protecting his hair, goes to tack the Korean flag on the door and hang a sign of welcome for Madame Bai. Panos, at the top of his lungs, sings anti-junta songs and restrings his oud. Jean-Claude takes up his position at the ironing board, composing aloud angry op-eds on the refugee situation. Maaza, the Ethiopian filmmaker, and Madas, the Chilean novelist, snap out the sheets and fold, eager to collaborate on a project showcasing the celebrated visitor, English narration to be supplied by their landlady/English instructor/ friend.

She's in the kitchen inching out saffron into the rice, explaining to the couple from Bahia mincing peppers that democratic action can be taken too far. A collective vote was made to postpone English lessons—and with it, her salary—until Madame is settled in her studio school. Tram drowns out her complaints, calling over the vacuum and the singing, to review once more the self-defense system Madame Bai has designed especially for women, a sleight-of-hand place-ment on critical organs while maintaining an ingratiating mien that psyches out the aggressor. So quick a placement, it bypasses the eye. So deft a grip on a critical organ, the mind is discouraged.

"Days to follow," Mustafa, on cue, calls out from the doorway, "the rogue is coughing up blood and urinates rust. Kidney punctured."

"But illusion of tough intact," croons Panos.

"And not a clue as to who, what, when, why or how," drawls Maaza, bored.

"Yeh," she hollers from the kitchen. "And all you need to apply is seven years of anatomy and fifteen degrees in one or more of the martial arts."

She is prepared for a light-filled imminence to grace them in the parlor, for an amazon to perform strike rock fist on the door, for Madame to pole-vault dragon fire through the window, pigtail flying, or to materialize ninja-style in the shadows of the fireplace. They assemble in the living room to wait like schoolchildren, the house aromatic with rosemary, curry, ouzu, and stinking with nuoc mam that could not be voted down, though close, five to three. Madame Bai arrives like an ordinary person, steps in behind Tram on soft cloth shoes, bows, sits, eats, pins and unpins the iron gray topknot held together by golden, carved fibulae. With Tram as translator, Madame jokes, converses and proves herself to be the sagelike wonder he'd promised all along. By 9 P.M. Madame has stolen away all of her students. A collective decision is made to redistribute the usual thirty dollars a week for room, board and English lessons into fifteen dollars for her and fifteen dollars for Madame.

"There is such a thing as taking democratic action too far," she complains for months at Madame's studio.

They begin with a roster of forty—adepts from the Oracle of Maat, the uraeus cobra logo on all of their practice suits, instructors from the Tai Chi Association, two medicine men from the Creek lodge, a clan grandmother from Seminole County, herbalists from Lagos, shiatsu therapists and Rolfers from the Atlanta School of Massage, Fruit of Islam from the Bankhead mosque, two ex-bodyguards from Mayor Jackson's corps, and her erstwhile students of English grammar and conversation. By Easter she is experiencing a body-mind-spirit connection she'd imagined possible only for disciples in the nether regions of snowbound Nepal. Attendance drops off as the weather turns warm, her boarders long since returned to the fold, restoring the good health of her budget. She stays on, spending most of her nights plowing through *Gray's Anatomy* and sticking pins in the red dots of her pressure-point chart. She's made a marshal of the citizen search team because of her calm and logical way in the woods.

Wholesale defection begins in June when the headlines around the country announce the monster's been nabbed. One man charged with two counts of murder, the defense hanging literally by a thread, carpet fiber that keeps changing color from yellow in May to purplish green by June. One man, two counts, leaving twenty-six "official" deaths still on the books and an additional thirty-eight not even being investigated. The circus tents are taken down. Eight hundred cops are withdrawn from the neighborhoods. One hundred state highway patrolmen are returned to the rural districts. Roadblocks banish. Armed helicopters disappear. Neighborhood security patrols disperse. Safety posters are taken down. One man, two counts, and amnesia drifts in like fog to blanket the city. "Let the Community Heal Itself" are the sermons. Back to normal. She grunts. Medfly in California, a tsetse plague in Atlanta, she masters butterfly metamorphosis and needs only five hours of sleep to keep working.

One by one, they leave Madame's studio, complaining. Silent sitting too hard. No mats, no hot sweat rooms. No ka-li charts or picture books to study. No striking bags or apparatus for stretching the legs. No shurikens, iron fans, nunchaku sticks. Not even an emblem to patch on a sweater, transfer to a T-shirt, solder on a key ring. No name for the school even. Too hard, too quiet, no good. Madame smiles and wishes them well on life's journey, then intensifies training for those that remain—the Oracle of Maat folks, the brothers from the mosque, Tram and her. She is learning to be still as her mother used to counsel, to silence the relentless chatter inside in favor of that small-voiced guide she is experiencing as a warm hand steering at the base of her spine. She appoints herself town crier, alarm clock at least for the cadres of the neighborhood who continue to monitor the Klan, organize, analyze, agitate, and keep watch over the children.

III

They are sitting in a sana she cannot even pronounce. Nerves frayed and searing, muscles screaming for release, she sits beyond endurance until she becomes the sana and is calm, pointed, focused, and sure. Madame dismounts from the only cushion in the room and glides to the center of the circle sitters and lowers herself to the floor, facing the window. She, looking at Madame's back, traces the carver's line along each of the golden fibulae to the points. She senses a summoning, as though her mother had set down a space heater before her, then dragged it slowly away by its cord for her to follow. Madame sending out her power, she figures, rising to walk around into the light. She sits back on her heels before Madame, palms on her thighs, ready. Madame's face turns from skin to old parchment, an ancient text she's been invited to read.

"One question, daughter." Madame says it in English. She listens, waits, as if all her life this question's been forming. Not a favor to tax her friendship, or a task to test commitment, but a question coming together and just for her. Daughter. It drives deep within to jimmy open a door long closed, padlocked and boarded over. It swings wide to a brilliant and breezy place she's not visited since the days she was held dear and cherished simply because she was she and not a pot to mend or dress to hem or chair leg to join. She smiles at Madame by way of signaling, Let the exam begin. Then panic grips the door to shove it to. She gathers the weight of the years into a doorstop. Test. She's heard of disciples who roam the earth unkempt and crazed by some koan a master has posed for solution: Why does the arrow never hit the mark despite the illusion of the bowman? Where does the dark go when the light is turned on? The door pushes against her back. She heaves against it, listing. The warm hand at the power base rights her. The door swings wide again.

"Stone Mountain," Madame says finally, as though she'd waited for the wrassling to cease.

Stone Mountain. A rock to prop a door with. A rock dropped into the pool of the mind. For a moment, she's in a muddle as rocks rear up out of the ocean, and she scrambles across reading the fossils sketched into the face. Then tumble down and she stumbles across rubble in a quarry, searching out particular stones. Stone Mountain. She leaps from rock ledge to mountain peak following goats who leave a trail of fleece on bushes. Or is it a Red Army libretto in the Peking Opera repertoire?

She exhales and lets it come to her. Of course. A mere thirty-minute ride out by U.S. 78. Stone monster carve tribute to the Confederacy mountain. Tourist trap entrapment of visiting schoolchildren lured under the spell of the enslavers of Africans and killers of Amerinds, lewdly exposed mammoth granite rock of ages the good ole boys think they can hide in from history. 865 feet high, the guide books say. 583 acres. The sacred grove of the wizard and greater and lesser demons who crank out crank notes in the name of Robert E. Lee, Jefferson Davis and Stonewall Jackson riding across the monument on horseback. She smirks.

Madame lifts her brows. Everything above her eyes slides up and back, taking her hairline out of view as though someone standing behind Madame, tugging at the mask and wig, is about to reveal the woman as a person she has known always, who has been there since the beginning just out of reach of peripheral vision, guiding her through her various rites of passage.

"What is it for?" Madame asks with her face in place.

"What is it for?" To rally the good ole boys, to dispirit the young, to celebrate the. She clutches the ropes as the scaffolding clanks against the side of the mountain. Madame, you could have called the Chamber of Commerce, the Tourist Bureau, asked any schoolboy at the Peachtree Academy. What is it for? Balanced, she leans out and runs her hands over the hind parts, the boots, then up into the uniforms. For this, I've been studying all these years and now all these months? Any almanac, encyclopedia, atlas could have answered your. Wind and rain have eroded a nose here, a ripple of hair there. Digging out an ice pocket just below Stoney's hand. What kind of shit is this? What is Stone Mountain for? A chink just deep enough to fit the point of the chisel in. Eighth Wonder of the World, they call. The hammering has enlarged a hairline fissure running from the brim of Stonewall's hat to the. Why ask me when a simple phone. Five sticks of dynamite shoved in just so he can bring the whole sucker tumbling down around. They say that staunch materialists rely on the sym. A people's army could.

"Teacher." The word bowls in the breeze of her chest

cavity, a resonating chamber. The words to be spoken already reverberating around the room. She hears the slap of flesh against wood as those around her, released from the sana by an imperceptible nod from Madame, sit readied awaiting instruction.

"Stone Mountain is for taking," she says.

BABY'S BREATH

And the women? Did he still see any of them, his mother wanted to know, sliding red rose into the dried bouquet. Louis shrugged. What was there to say? He'd believed himself deeply in love each time, been convinced they'd loved him. They said they did. But they kept killing his babies.

"And Norma?" His mother had been conducting their conversation with the rose he'd bought at the airport, now she used a sprig of pale tiny beads to draw his eyes toward the jug that held the arrangement. It bore her signature—a slab and coil terra cotta jug, amethyst encrusted sides, bowl-shaped at bottom, completely thrown open at the top. Louis acknowledged her handiwork with a quick, dim smile. He preferred to keep his eyes on her. He liked watching his mother feel her way through his business.

"She seemed very devoted to you, Louis." She was brushing her cheek against her shoulder girly-girly. He resisted the urge to pluck buds and bits of leaves from her cheek, her lashes. "She was special, yes?"

He shrugged again and turned toward the window. And she, satisfied for the moment with her floral arrangement and his answer, drank her coffee. Louis carefully slid two fingers into the venetian blinds and open-scissored himself a view of the block. There were plaster dwarves standing guard over garden hoses in his mother's yard and in the next. He'd pointed it out to Norma as a thing he might one day film—trolls from Vienna Woods in the Black yards, grinning black-faced jockeys in the White.

Norma had seemed special to his mother, Louis was thinking, staring out over the sewer grating that had been home plate, simply because Norma was the only one he'd ever brought home. She was more real then than the others—photos in his wallet merely, long-distance descriptions, hearsay from his brother Bobby. But special? Norma just happened to be on the scene at a time when he'd had money enough to come home on holidays. His shrug had been designed to say all that. His mother's muttering into her coffee mug was her way of saying she wasn't buying it but what the hell.

Louis frowned. "Seemed," "just happened to be"—a careless way to put it, careless and dishonest. He'd loved Norma, maybe loved her still. Sitting now at his mother's kitchen table, a hundred miles from Delaware, three years gone from the New York apartment Bobby had taken off his hands, he still felt for the them they'd been. And felt protective and alert, now that his mother was eyeing him over the rim of her mug, for any signal of a sneak attack. Norma had been "that skinny one" and "her" for the whole of a year.

He peered between the crack in the blinds. It was dark but for the spill of moonlight on the lawns. A mere five years ago, the silhouette of the bridge, sharp between the brick high school and the domed courthouse, would have been visible. Looking up from his homework then, he would count the lights strung round the marina, would listen intently to the brush and slap of the water against the boats docked there and dream himself aboard a yacht with one of the girls he tried to talk to, but Bobby always turned the dances out too soon and ruined what might have been a good thing. There was little he could see now, for a sodium streetlight had been installed just in front of the house. Too close and too bright, it bleached out the view. The only clear image in the dark of the glass was the reflection of the spray of baby's breath in the stoneware jug.

"You wanted to marry her, yes?"

He withdrew his fingers and let the blinds snap to. "I thought I did." He'd definitely wanted the baby, he knew that. Knew that the moment it had been conceived, and knew the moment and the rightness of it like he'd never known anything else. The knowing had come all of a rush like light, the certainty shimmering up his spine where Norma's heels were locked against his back. Something opened up to him and he was new all through and knew what he wanted to do, to be. For two years, fooling around with film courses at NYU and trying to be Miles Davis after hours, he'd been making up things to do, to be, and fashioning elaborate point systems to give some value to how he spent his life. But holding on to Norma, his body shuddering, his toes no longer trying for traction against the sheets, he knew.

And Norma had said she wanted the baby, was glad—scared, but glad. Her enthusiasm waned, though, in less than four weeks, and he found himself alone in the talking, the planning—wedding arrangements, natural birth classes, setting up housekeeping for real and not just playing at it. By the second month, she'd grown unreachably sullen. He would come to her with the light on and see her open, glistening, wet. But inside she was dry and no longer closed lovingly around him. Would clench her muscles too soon, too tight, and push him out.

He'd cut his last class one Tuesday and, rather than go to rehearsal, borrowed brother Bobby's car to pick her up at the clinic. His mother had taught him that attentiveness was the thing, so he spent the telephone money for yellow roses. She wasn't there, hadn't been in weeks. Lied to him later, said she had so gone and been told she might not be able to hold on to the fetus. She was so delicate, so frail. She was her parents talking at him. Her mother: Norma is small-boned, refined. Meaning that he was crude and not what they'd had in mind. Her father: We had misgivings about her going off to grad school; she's never been hardy. Meaning that they hadn't sacrificed for the likes of him. Who were his people anyway? And what, no undergraduate degree even? So alike in look and sound her parents were, like a pair of cymbals on either side of him that Sunday dinner in Delaware, it was just a matter of time before the tympani rumbled, and they crashed together to wipe him out.

Not waiting for spring break, he went on the road to make money. Her letter caught him in New Orleans, said she'd had a miscarriage. But she couldn't look him in the eye and say it when he blew the gig to fly back. She told the hairbrush it had been very scary, all that blood, all that pain. Told the eyebrow pencil that at least it was over. He felt the lights dim but kept his vigil in the mirror anyway, waiting for her eyes to meet him there. When she did look up, stand up, it was only to turn profile and pat her emptied-out belly. The Easter outfit her parents had sent would fit now, she said. He still waited for her in the glass, praying "Look at me." She didn't. When the semester ended, she took her degree and her trim daughter self home to Delaware. And he lay around in the dark a lot not answering the phone or the door, not picking up his books or his horn, his life bottomed out.

"Yeh, Norma was special," he said, feeling his mother's hand on his arm.

"But she broke your heart," she whispered. And he could feel his arm bulge in her grip. He didn't know whether it was the rose, the verbena or his mother's perfume, but some fragrance gave him ease. He'd comforted himself after Norma with the certainty that raising a child with in-laws like that would have been a disaster. "A Miscarriage of Justice," he called the tune when outrage and mourning was still the music of his days and nights. His buddies thought "She Gave Me Good Memories" a more suitable title if they got to record it. And then he comforted himself with blond hair: Carole of the long legs and the rabbit-in-residence, the test-tube device she'd gotten from her health collective. No guise, no lies, no delicacy, Carole bluntly told him she was going back to her husband and the baby was out of the question. Next morning he awoke from a nightmare warm and wet beside her, blood clots in the bed.

"Broke your heart, Louis. Broke your heart."

But then some woman would always be breaking his heart, to hear his mother tell it. He left himself wide open, just like her. Louis was like his mother; Bobby like his father. She would work that in if he let her. He drew away from her mothering hands, searching for something to say about her new drying technique or the new jug, anything to steer her away from her theme song: Bobby had been unwanted, Louis unexpected, but it had been their father who was the mistake. He didn't like what happened to her face when she spoke of his father. And didn't like what happened to him, had been happening for so long he and his father still stuttered at talking, met only in the old dog, the Irish setter they cared for together, touched through.

"And the other one, Louis? The one you took to Puerto Rico. Think you might get back together again? This new one seems kind of . . . rough." She was running her hand over the beadwork in her caftan just as he was fingering the embroidery on his shirt, wondering where he'd adopted that particular habit of the self-caress. "What was her name? The one last winter?"

Toxemia. The doctor had told them, addressing Louis exclusively though, which made Wynona mad, that a diet of junk food was dangerous to mother and child, especially since mother was no spring chicken and drank too much. And that had made Wynona sputter. And so did the jars of vitamins, the blender, the juicer, his experiments with stir-fry and tofu. He found bags of potato chips squashed down in the hamper, sticky candy wrappers and greasy doughnut bags stuffed in the corners of her linen closet, soda cans in the shoe bag, bottles everywhere. She was devoted to junk, addicted. "I never had a problem a gooey eclair couldn't solve," she liked to joke. His nagging and then the pregnancy itself was the problem. Chocolate cake and brandy was her solution for a time. "I've had all the babies I can afford," she said, barring his way to the bedroom. And it did no good explaining that he was reliable, loved her, was not like the others, he cared—for she'd already set his bag and horn case in the hall. And it did no good swearing he would stick by her, wanted the responsibility and "afford" had nothing to do with it—for she'd demanded her key back. And it did no good writing her how he could adequately, lovingly care for her, the boys, the baby—she sent the letters back. And in a week's time, it had done no good clocking her moon, counting the tampons in her linen closet, or contemplating a pinhole or two in her diaphragm—a D & C and it was all over.

"Wynona just couldn't get into the baby thing all over again," he said.

"I can understand that. Now what about this latest one?" When he didn't answer, she grabbed up the mugs and dumped cold coffee into the sink. "You ought to try getting married first, Louis, then starting a family. That's how it's usually done, you know?"

He raised the blind, trying to figure it. Such a sudden change in weather. So cold, so angry, so bristly. Had he missed a beat somewhere? How different it had all been on his last visit. They'd walked along the wharf arm in arm and visited her studio. And she'd said, "She must be crazy, Louis, not wanting your baby." And her warmth and the waters had surrounded him, protecting him against the bumps and jolts of the world. Now each time she went by his chair, setting up the ceramic coffeepot for another go, the breeze was chilly. Louis pulled the newspaper he'd brought in from the airport toward him. Maybe he could wait her out. They'd have another cup of coffee and then stroll down to the studio and he'd touch the still-damp bowls and jugs and tell her they were beautiful, she was beautiful.

"Women you run with lately are too damn old for you anyway. Who's this new one? Older than me, I bet."

"Oh, I don't know." He wanted to say more, to shift the tone back to the familiar, but she was looking at him over her shoulder in that heating-up way. He felt self-conscious folding the paper lengthwise then up in back as if he were on the subway standing up. She had told him often, more a warning than an observation, that he handled a newspaper just like his father, and used it the same way too—to block her out. He knew he should put it down, get rid of it. But instead he leaned over and smacked her across the behind. "Oh, I don't know, I kind of like old ladies," he said playfully, trying to smooth over whatever had put the edge in her voice. She swatted him with the potholder and beads broke from her caftan and rolled toward his feet.

"You need to be serious, my friend," she said in a tone she usually reserved for Bobby. "What the hell have you to offer any woman with anything at all on the ball? No degree, no place of your own, no bank account, no prospects even of a good job. And the only time you had anything to offer was that trip to Puerto Rico and that you won in a contest." She set the coffee jug down hard on the table and more beads scattered to the floor. "And if you keep futzing around with your music, bub, you won't have doodly squat."

He was grateful for the "bub." But something hot and sour spread across his back when he bent to retrieve the beads, something like fear. Things weren't going right. He didn't know this tune. He'd missed a beat somewhere. "I can tell you've been dealing with white girls." Khadeja's voice rang in his ear. "Your rhythm's off, your rap is lame, your music's weak." He tried to concentrate on what his mother was saying, but he couldn't catch the swing of it. "Damnit, Louis, you're twenty-four years old. Too damned old to be a child prodigy, you know." She dumped clean spoons on the table, and the clang resounded long after she'd gone back to the stove to get the water.

Louis was stunned. This was the sort of line she might run out to Bobby, but never to him. She'd always assured him he was special, was better than the, was above the, didn't have to bother to. Nothing to offer? He looked at his mother, but she was a blur. Her anger was sudden and total and disfiguring. This was the woman his father had drawn for him on summer visits—a brimming-over woman growing indistinct with rage. This was the woman he'd defended to his father, to his brother, to his ladies who always let slip some Freudian innuendo about what she'd done to him. But what had she ever done to him but love him, lift him, cheer him when he couldn't even hold the strings of the violin down? What had she ever done but fume and storm when reports were unkind, or when someone snitched that they didn't live in the district, wrassle the principals to the mat? And when he performed, there she was in front row perfect poise, applauding just him. Sold her washer and dryer to buy a guitar and amp when he'd thought that was his ax. And recently offered to sell her kiln when he and Khadeja worked up a movie script.

He wondered if he was as much a blur, a distortion to her. He squinted at his mother and at himself as through a frame, as though he stood in the yard with his father, his brother, the women and a camera. And it was all there in the glass: a candle-lit kitchen, the enormous spray of dried flowers and the one wet rose, himself hugging a newspaper as if to ward off a blow, his mother coming toward him with a pot of steaming water, her jaws puffed out with more words to slug him with.

"I work like a slave to get you off to college, and what do you do? You drop out of school because you don't feel like taking exams. Don't feel like taking exams." It was the sort of sneer that used to punctuate her harangues about their father, he and Bobby holding their breath, afraid to look at each other and find their father there.

"Have that kiln running around the clock and take in clumsy students without an ounce of sensitivity in their whole bodies. Why? So there'll always be fare for you to come home. And what do you do? You hit town looking like you just jumped out of one of those hippy freak thrift shops, and not even straight out, just to give these bastards something to gloat over." She looked up suddenly as though the neighbors had gathered in the yard and any minute she might raise the window and spit in somebody's eye. "And they always hated us, ohhhh, cause I was nobody's easy woman and my boys weren't nodding their lives away on the corner. Damnit, Louis, I have done my job. I have raised my boys. I have stuck to my craft. But what the hell are you ever doing but knocking up some woman right and left and draping it over with some romantic crap. You know, damnit, you know? I mean, shit, Louis." She poured hot water in the coffee jug and the hairs on his arms cringed.

He waited, pressed the newspaper flat against the table and waited, stared into the yard and saw only the streetlamp and the moon spill and the eyes that were merely his own reflecting in the glass. He waited. When she blew this particular riff on Bobby, there was always the refrain "just like your father," followed by a chorus or two of "thank God for Louis." Louis didn't steal bikes, didn't break windows, didn't bring the police to the house at all hours of the night. Louis always remembered flowers. He waited for a hand on the back of his chair, on the back of his neck. But she had moved away from him, had left the kitchen, had left him among the ashtrays and the beads rolling among the leaves and buds shed from the spray of dried flowers.

She was in her bedroom. He could hear the mattress sigh, and he knew she had not flung herself down to cry, but had crawled across the width of the bed and eased her body down, weary. He supposed he should go in to her, massage her back, tell her he would do better. It used to make everything alright when Bobby messed up or his father called up, three sheets to the wind, to say he was tired of busting his balls and she and her boys could go to hell.

Louis examined his hands, half expecting printer's ink to have tattooed on his palms. He had wonderful hands, Khadeja had recently told him, but she grew quickly indifferent to them when he put down his horn. But then they all had said that and done that. Only his mother had said year in and year out, "Thank God for Louis and his wonderful hands." He eased them into the loop of the cord and lowered the blinds inch by inch, keeping the moon and the light and eyes from coming in.

THE WAR
OF THE WALL

Me and Lou had no time for courtesies. We were late
for school. So just flat out told the painter lady to quit
messing with the wall. It was our wall, and she wasn't even
from the neighborhood. Stirring in the bucket, she mumbled
something about she had permission to paint on it from the
owner of the barbershop. That had nothing to do with it as
far as we were concerned. It was our wall. We'd been pitch-
ing pennies against the barbershop wall since we were very
little kids. We'd played handball and pop fly against that
wall since so-called integration when the crazies cross town

shut the park down and poured cement in the swimming pool so we couldn't use it. I'd sprained my neck boosting cousin Lou up on that wall so he could chisel Jimmy Lyon's name on it when we found out he wasn't ever coming home from Vietnam and teach us how to fish.

"If you lean close," Lou said to the painter lady, "you'll get a whiff of bubblegum and kids' sweat and that'll fix you. This wall belongs to us kids of Talbro Street." Lou was standing hipshot next to her beat-up ole piece of car, with out of town plates, jabbing the air as he spoke and sounding very convincing. But she paid us no mind at all. She snapped the brim of her straw hat down and hauled her bucket up the ladder.

"If anybody has a right to do anything to this wall," Lou shouted up to her, "it's Mrs. Morris."

Mrs. Morris ought to take the wall to court as evidence, I was thinking. Last month in the night, some cops got rough with the Morris boy cause he was out late and didn't answer their questions fast enough to suit them. They rammed his shoulder against the wall and might have done worse if Mr. Eubanks hadn't happened along. He told the cops that the Morris boy was a fine person, just a little slow. So they let him go.

"You're destroying evidence," I said to the painter lady when she started making big sweeps with her brush. "You're going to go to jail."

She went right on about her business, which made me mad. Lou had to drag me away I was shaking her ladder so bad.

"You don't even live around here," I hollered over my shoulder. I thought of a lot more to say, but we were passing my folks' restaurant. And that's all my mama would need to hear, me sassing a grown-up.

When we came from school, the wall was slick with white. The painter lady was running string across the wall and taping it fast here and there. Me and Lou leaned against the gumball machine outside the pool hall and watched. Then she started chalking the strings with a chunk of blue chalk. Across the way, Mrs. Morris and her boy were leaning out their kitchen window watching. When the painter lady snapped the strings, the blue chalk dust measured off halves and quarters up and down and sideways too. Lou muttered something about how hip that was. But I dropped my book satchel on his toes to remind him we were at war.

Then the Morris twins crossed over the projects and hung back at the curb to watch. The twin with the red ribbons was hugging a jug of cloudy lemonade. The one in yellow ribbons was holding a plate of dinner away from her dress. Some good aromas were drifting out from under the tent of tinfoil, and pale green juice from the greens was leaking on the twin's socks. The painter lady paid no more attention to them and the gift of supper than she did to me and Lou or the fire hydrant. When she wanted to deepen a line, she just reached around behind her for the blue chalk. When she wanted the scissors to cut the string or lay the blade flat to pry the tape loose, she just fumbled behind her amongst the stuff she had laid out on a sawhorse table. I figured the woman for a rude, no-nose fool. Next to my mother,

Mrs. Morris cooks up the tastiest-smelling food in the neighborhood.

Side Pocket came strolling out of the pool hall to see what me and Lou were studying so hard. He gave the painter lady the once-over, checking out her paint-spattered jeans, her chalky T-shirt, her floppy brim hat. He hitched up his pants even though he had on a belt and suspenders and kind of glided over toward the table.

"Whatcha got there, Sweetheart?" he asked the twin with the plate.

"Suppah," she said all soft like and country, which is the Morris way.

"For her," the one in yellow said, jutting her chin toward the painter lady's back.

Still she didn't turn around. She was rearing back on her heels, her hands jammed into her back jeans pockets, her face squinched up like the masterpiece was taking shape on the wall by magic. We could have been gophers crawled up a rotten hollow for all she cared. Lou was saying something about how great her concentration was. I gave him a butt with my hip, and his elbow slid off the gumball machine and he stumbled.

"Good evening," Side Pocket said in his best ain't-I-fine voice.

But the painter lady was acting like a mental case. She was up on the milk crate, over to the step stool, up and down the ladder hanging off it to reach a far spot. She was scribbling all over the wall like a definite crazy person and not even looking where she was stepping. It was like those old music movies where the dancer taps all over the furniture, kicking chairs over but not skipping a beat, leaping over radios and all. Lou looked like he wanted to applaud, but I had my foot on his feet and an elbow in his ribs. It was quite a show, but it wasn't right. The twins standing there were being ignored. Mrs. Morris and her boy were nearly hanging out the window trying to signal the twins to step up and be bold.

"Ahh," Side Pocket cleared his throat. The painter lady paused, one foot on the milk crate, one foot on the top of the step stool. "Errr ahhh, these young ladies here . . ." Side Pocket was running out of words, so I jumped in.

"Your dinner's getting cold, Lady. And least you could say, 'Good evening.'"

Then she kind of turned. You could tell she didn't recognize anybody. I mean, we could have been penguins or bags of laundry she was resting her eyes on for a second till she swung her head back to work.

"Ma'am?" At last the twins stepped forward and not a moment too soon. Side Pocket was sputtering, not used to women ignoring him like that. And Mrs. Morris and her boy were practically out on the window ledge trying to coax the girls forward. "Mama said to bring you some suppah."

I was kind of off somewhere from hearing Frieda Morris say "suppah" like that, all soft like a wad of cotton, so I didn't hear whether the painter lady said anything or not. But she did walk over, her eyes "full of sky," as my grandmother would say, meaning in a daze, a trance, another place. She wiped her hands on her jeans, rolled back a bit of tinfoil, then wagged her head as though it was a horse's head instead of ham, greens, yams and cornbread.

"Thank your mother very much," she said with her mouth full of sky too, sounded like. "I've brought dinner along actually." And then, without even excusing herself or anything, she was back on the ladder drawing in a wild way. It was too much for Side Pocket, so he went back into the poolroom with the sides of his mouth pulled down. It was too much for me too, so I dragged Lou away to go meet my Daddy at work.

From the telephone company to the restaurant, me and Lou were waiting for a pause to get our two cents in. We wanted to tell my Daddy about the painter lady and ask if he had any good ideas for running her back to wherever she came from. But Daddy was for talking about the trip to the country, how Lou could come with us because the old folks always appreciated another pair of hands on the farm. We forgot about the war for a while and went on in the back of the restaurant to do our chores.

Later that night, come to find the painter lady was a liar. She came into the restaurant and leaned against the glass of the steam table 'lowing as how she was a very starved person. Me and Lou peeked over the service ledge and listened. We'd never really heard her speak more than a sentence or two. She was really running off at the mouth: Was that a ham hock in the greens? Was that a neck bone in the pole beans? Did my mother have any vegetables cooked without meat and especially pork?

"I don't care who your spiritual leader is," Mama said

in that way of hers. "Eat in the community, Sistuh, you eat pig by and by, one way or t'other."

We were in the back cracking up. Lou was tearing up lettuce for the salad pot. I was scrubbing out the muffin tins. We were waiting for my mama to fix her wagon cause my mama don't take no stuff off nobody in her place. Plus, she can't abide people who don't speak to elders when they walk into a place, and the painter lady hadn't said boo to a soul, young or old. So mama waited on everybody else first.

But the painter lady kept right on with the questions, even after she took a stool at the counter. Was there cheese in the baked macaroni, she wanted to know. Were there eggs in the potato salad? Was the iced tea already sweetened with sugar? Mama was fixing Pop Jacobs's plate at the time, piling on another spoonful of rice each time another stupid question came up. Me and Lou wondered where in the world the painter lady was from that they make potato salad without hard-boiled eggs.

"Do you have any bread made with unbleached flour?"

Me and Lou cracked up, me bending low over the suds, Lou chopping onions, laughing and crying at the same time. I could hear my mama doing that whistle sigh through the gap in her front teeth, but I could also hear Pop Jacobs cackling. He was happy with the whole deal, his plate was heaped high.

Mama finally ran out of customers to wait on first, so she started taking the painter lady's order. She couldn't make up her mind whether she wanted broiled fish and a salad or a vegetable or vegetable plate. She finally settled on pan trout once mama assured her that, yeh, she knew how to pan-cook a trout without a lot of oil. But just when Mama reached for a plate to put the salad on, the painter lady leaned over the counter.

"Excuse me. One more thing." She had a chalky blue finger in the air.

Everybody in the restaurant was holding their breath to hear what the painter lady would say next and whether Mama would fling the plate. I boosted up on the sink. Mama was blowing a wisp of hair out of her eye, tapping one foot and holding that plate like a Frisbee.

"Yeh?" Mama said. "What is it?"

"Can I get cucumbers and beets in that tossed salad?"

Mama leaned her hot face right close to the painter lady's and the customers kind of leaned forward too. "You will get," Mama said, "whatever Lou tossed. Now sit down. And be quiet." And the painter lady sat down and shut right up.

All the way to the country, we tried to get Mama to open fire on the painter lady. But Mama said she was probably from up north and didn't know any better. Then Mama said that she was sorry she got on her like that cause she was a decent person, just very picky about her diet.

"As we all should be," Mama sighed, cutting her eye at the bag of potato chips I'd just finished.

Me and Lou did not want to hear that. Who did she think she was coming into our neighborhood and messing with our wall?

"Wellllllll," Mama said, pulling into the gas station so Daddy could take his turn at the wheel, "she's some kind of artistic person. It ain't easy to get folks to look at your work if you stuck away somewhere. So she's painting in public. I guess that's alright."

Me and Lou definitely did not want to hear that. We wanted to hear something better than that, especially after we told Mama how she igged the twins and turned Mrs. Morris's hospitality down. Mama got quiet for a long while, the muscle in her jaw jumping. I expected to hear her call the painter lady a "barbarian." That's one of my grandma's words for people who forget to honor the ways. But when me and Lou kept on about it, Mama said to hush cause she was tired. She climbed into the back seat and dropped down into the warm hollow Daddy had made in the pillow.

All weekend we tried to scheme up ways to take our wall back. Daddy said we were getting sickening about it. Mama said to sit down and be quiet. My grandparents said to quit dropping cake crumbs between the sofa cushions. Me and Lou were miserable until a movie came on about New York. In one scene a train pulled into the station covered from top to bottom, side to side, windows too, with drawings and writings done with spray paint. Granddaddy said the ones who did it should have to scrub it clean with toothbrushes. Grandma said it was a shame kids in New York didn't have something better to do . . . like chores. Mama said, "Hrmph." And Daddy was asleep. So he didn't see me and Lou slap five. We couldn't wait to get back to the block.

We couldn't find a can of black spray anywhere. But in a junky little hardware store downtown, we put our allowance together and bought a can of white epoxy, the kind you touch up old refrigerators with when you're trying to sell them. We'd spent our carfare, and it was too late to use our schoolbus passes. We had to walk home lugging our books, our gym shoes and shorts, and the bag with the can of spray paint.

When we got to the corner, it looked like a block party. The only things missing were the food stalls. The whole neighborhood had turned out, gathered on the sidewalk. Side Pocket and his buddies were standing leaning on their cue sticks, hunching each other. Daddy was there with one of the linemen he catches a lift with sometimes. Mrs. Morris had her arms stretched wide, resting on the shoulders of her children on either side of her. Mama was talking with her cooking spoon, looking like a drum majorette leading a parade. Customers were standing with her, napkins silly at the throat. Mr. Eubanks came out, followed by a man in a striped poncho, half his face shaved, the other half full of foam.

"She really did it, didn't she?" Mr. Eubanks huffed out his chest like he'd just performed major surgery and the patient lived. "Didn't she though?" He started pressing people around him. Lots of people answered quick when they saw the razor in his hand, but you could tell he didn't know he had it, which made it all the funnier to me.

Mama called us over. And then we saw it—the wall.

ICE

None of the grown-ups can look us kids in the face
because of the puppies. They must have been squeal-
ing in the cold, and Lady, the mama dog, probably raced
from door to door scratching and howling trying to get
somebody's attention. It must have been awful for her. The
grown-ups can't say they weren't around and didn't know
the pups were freezing, because every single one of them was
at home all day long. Folks who work at the post office
work nights. Folks who work at the hospital are still out on
strike. Folks who work at the bottling plant were laid off till

further notice. And folks who work in the city were excused
from their jobs because the highways aren't clear yet.

Seems to me the old men who live on the corner with
the meanest dog in the world could have taken the puppies
in, put them in a box with an old sock or two, and set them
in the basement away from Mean Dog. And the crazy old
lady who lives at the other end of the block could have
called them in. They would have come. Puppies don't have
any better sense than to come to a crazy old calling lady.
Somebody should have helped Lady, for there's just so much
a mama can do. At least that's what my mama is always saying when she throws down the dish towel and stomps off to
her studio back of the house.

We kids left for school this morning muffled to our
eyes in pulled-up collars and yanked-down caps and scarves
wrapped round and round like bandits. We stumbled along
to the bus in layers and layers of clothing, shouting to Lady
to get her pups out of the street. Little Marcy was shooing
them away from Mean Dog's yard because Mean Dog is
likely to break his chain and attack anything and everything
in sight. Last month, for example, when Lady's litter was
barely walking, he broke loose and got hold of three pups.
Our parents kept calling us in. The weatherman had said a
storm was coming up fast. But we were busy beating Mean
Dog with our book satchels and lunch buckets to make him
let go of the puppies. It was like a shark movie when Mean
Dog got hold of the runt and that furry little head started
disappearing into that huge mouth. But then Tommy Jeeter
came by on his skate board, and that was the perfect thing

to go upside that mean dog's head with. He kept twisting around growling and snapping at us, but we kept shoving that skate board at him. Tommy Jeeter grabbed one of the pups and I grabbed the other. And for one wonderful moment, Mean Dog dropped the runt and backed off and Marcy almost got it. But then his huge white paw came down on the poor thing like a stone. And it got mashed so hard into the ground, you couldn't tell mud from pup from grass.

So Marcy was shooing the puppies away from Mean Dog's yard, and Marcy's mother kept hollering for her to get on the school bus with the rest of us stumbling aboard in our fat clothes like helpless astronauts. We were mumbling about the wonderful thank-you cards we would send the mayor for sending an emergency school bus and messing up our holiday. And then we were banging on the windows, trying to tell anybody who could hear us to get Lady and her puppies out of the cold.

Aunt Myrtle was in the driveway pouring steaming water on her car door, trying to get the lock to unfreeze. But when she saw that the key would still not turn, she just dropped the kettle right there in the driveway and scooted back into the house. It was that cold. My mama was waving the bus good-bye from the warm side of the storm door, wrapped in two quilts mummy-style with my old skating cap on her head, so I doubt she could hear. My stepfather and the two other men who led the strike at the hospital were on the curb, talking, beating their gloves together, jumping up and down in their boots and explaining ways to keep warm. At our house, we'd been burning the telephone books, the Christmas tree, gift boxes, even my old doll-house—anything that fits in the fireplace and will give heat.

Just as the school bus pulled off, it skidded on a skin of ice on the sewer grating that's home plate in nice weather. And right away all the parents huddled in doorways in bathrobes and coats and blankets started hollering directions to the driver to cut his wheels this way and pump the pedal that way. They were making so much noise, they didn't hear us, didn't notice Lady shivering for all her fat and fur. And the puppies, scrambling out of the street finally to take shelter in Miss Norma's carport, got no attention whatsoever.

My stepdaddy built a doghouse for Lady and the pups. But they wouldn't stay put. The day after Lady had her puppies in the carport, Miss Norma packed them in a milk crate and set them out on the sidewalk like it was a case of pickup and delivery. Me and Marcy and Tommy Jeeter went round with a coffee can I grabbed before my mama could stuff her paintbrushes in it, and we collected enough for a sack of dog meal but not enough to buy a doghouse. So we asked my stepdaddy to build one. While he sawed wood and sang work songs, we cut pictures out of *Ebony* and *Sepia*. And while he nailed the house together and sang about rivers rising and floods flooding, we went through my mama's sketchbook. And while he sanded the whole thing down, he let Tommy Jeeter hold the huge basketball of tinfoil he's been building since a long-ago war, a time when the government paid people to save bacon grease and newspapers and rubber bands and things. Tommy Jeeter kept rolling the crinkly thing around on the rug, saying, "And you never once sold it." He said that about five times. You could tell that he would have sold it; Jeeter would not have spent his life strip-mining gum and candy wrappers. It was a fine doghouse when my stepdaddy finished, but the dogs hardly ever used it. Lady was always begging up and down the block at kitchen doors, and the pups were always right behind her, "doggin her steps," as my mother would say when she means for us kids to get out of her face so she can paint in peace.

When the school bus passed Bowker Street on the way home, we knew something bad had happened, because we didn't see Kwame on his bike throwing newspapers. It is the thing to do when you get to the corner of Bowker and Third—watch Kwame straining up the hill, standing on the pedals, his head thrown back and his hood slipping off. You think that any minute his clothes will pop loose with all that effort and fly up the hill like the kites we write wishes on and release on the first day of carnival. The bus turned into our block and we saw Kwame's bike sprawled in the middle of the street. We got off that bus so fast, we didn't even fool around with last tag and "See you later, alligator." We flew. Kwame was in Miss Norma's yard cracking the ground with the heel of his boot, trying to make the ice give the puppies up.

There were two of them, gray and stiff and dead. Their mouths were puckered as though somebody had come along with a sewing machine and stitched their faces. It was more like they had snarled at the end, had growled and taken their anger into death with them and would come back in the next life meaner than Mean Dog to get us for not taking care. We found the other three all piled on top of each other by the mailbox, as though they'd been waiting for the mailman with the overdue packages to take them aboard or mail them to Florida so they could live. Tommy Jeeter, his hands shoved up his armsleeves, kept jiggling from one foot to the other, saying, "Oh wow, oh wow." He'd said, back when Lady's belly was dragging the ground and she could barely sneak up on the squirrels, that he wanted to train one of the litter as a hunting dog to present to his uncle. Sweet Pea and Brenda buried their faces in each other's furry shoulders and hugged each other's coat sleeves. Joanne just stood there watching Kwame with his pick-'n'-axe boot, cracking that same gum our teacher had tried to get her to throw away all day. Me and Marcy tried to make a fence with our legs to keep Lady away who was moaning and whining and running around in circles, trying to get to her dead puppies.

"You stupid old fool dog. Where were you when your puppies were freezing to death? Get out of here."

"Quit yelling at her, Joanne, wasn't her fault," Marcy tried to say. But as soon as she could get a few words out, the wind shoved them right back down her throat.

Brenda picked her face up from Sweet Pea's fur collar long enough to say, "Suppose that was you, Joanne? You wouldn't want your mother to just walk away and leave you there."

Joanne sucked her teeth. "Forget you, crybaby."

"Who you calling 'crybaby'?" Sweet Pea and Brenda were ready to fight.

"Oh shut up," Kwame said, looking around for something to put the puppies in. Marcy dumped her books right out on the ground and held her satchel open and Kwame plopped them in. I reached for a strap to help, but Marcy swung the load onto her shoulder and walked off. She looked just like the women in my mama's sketch pad, women with that same look carrying things on their back or on their heads, looking like they've just done something wonderful like dump their schoolbooks on the ground and offered their brand new book bag for toting. We all followed her to the hide-'n'-seek woods, Joanne stretching her gum in and out like she was having a very boring time.

"Hooo-hooooo."

We were standing by the home-free-all tree watching Kwame dig a hole and none of us wanted to turn around. We knew it was the crazy old lady calling us from her house on the hill at the corner. But she kept calling, so we did turn, and right away we were sorry. There she was in her window looking like some Halloween thing, her teeth not in her mouth, her old-timey shawl looking like a huge spider web, some weird thing on her head like a bowl cover you use for keeping the onion smells out of the Jell-O. Any other time, Joanne would have said, "I dare you to go up on her porch and tip over her rocker." But she didn't, went right on pulling at her gum. Any other time, Brenda and Sweet Pea would have taken off like Olympic runners, afraid the old lady might tell their grandfather she'd seen them lollygag-

ging in the woods instead of going straight home from
school. They didn't run. They kept handing Kwame sticks to
dig with that kept crumbling. The ice storm had made everything brittle. Any other time I would have held my breath
and prayed she wasn't calling me to pick up the pans and
plates. My Aunt Myrtle always takes food to Mrs. Blue because she's from "down home," and because she knew Aunt
Myrtle "when," and because she has a "gift," and just because. I was too cold to think of anything but how weird she
looked tapping on her window with a spoon.

"Maybe she wants to give us a shovel so we can bury
them," Tommy Jeeter said. Then he grabbed Lady by the
collar and took her off into the woods to find beer cans to
sell to his uncle who collects them.

"Let her bring it, then," Joanne said.

"It's cold and she's old. Why don't you go get it?"

Joanne gave Marcy a hot look. "Forget you, Marcy."
Then she strolled off in her sheepskin coat like she was in a
fashion show and we were buying.

"We gotta go," the twins said, shivering and shaking
and walking off.

"Guess God decided to take them," Kwame said,
meaning the puppies he had just buried. And it was too cold
to open my mouth and say that I'd always heard that God
receives, not takes. Besides, what would God want with
puppies? God is not running a pound. But someone has to
say some sort of words when dead bodies are put into the
ground, so I shut up. After a while, Kwame nodded to
Marcy and me and trotted up the block to deliver his papers.

Me and Marcy stood there looking at the mound of dirt and twigs and pebbles as though a certain amount of time had to be spent standing there in silence and mourning.

"Mrs. Blue is probably thinking the same thing could happen to her," Marcy said. "She could starve to death or freeze right there in the window and nobody would go and see about her."

I didn't say a word. I was numb. I tried to think of something hot to warm me up while we stood at the grave. All I could think of was the fire my mama used to draw. When she was a little girl in Holly Springs, Mississippi, some do-wrong people set a torch to her daddy's farm. And there was no firehouse in the Black community then. The fire was so bad, birds fell down dead from the sky. There's a drawing in red ink and charcoal of grandma trying to beat flames from the mattress, its insides jumping all over the yard like popcorn, and the emptied-out houses and sheds and barns for miles around glowing like coals in a grate. My mama drew the trees like giants with their hair on fire racing through the fields holding their heads, then crashing down and rolling around in the cornfields burning everything up. None of this made me warm. It made my teeth chatter all the more. My bones felt like they would shatter any minute.

"Maybe we should stop by on the way home," Marcy said. "Poor Mrs. Blue. I bet her house is like the cold box."

And I remembered the first time I ever saw Marcy with her spatter-paint-freckled self. She was in the butcher's with her parents, reading out loud all the signs. But when the butcher opened the cold room where the meat hangs, Marcy started whimpering. There was a rabbit hanging on a hook by its tail. "Ohhhhhhh, what have they done to the Easter bunny?"

We called her "Cotton Tail" for a long time, until we realized she was going to ignore us until we learned to say "Marcy." I was going to remind her of that time, but it didn't seem right to talk about it with the puppies there under the dirt.

"I'm going to see what she wants," Marcy finally said, and waited to see if I was going to move. I didn't. Mrs. Blue is a very spooky person and her house is dark and I don't like going in there. So Marcy went off by herself.

By the time I made the rounds of the houses, reporting what had happened to the puppies, the streetlights were coming on and the moon was chasing me. For a whole hour I fussed about the puppies dying right there under everybody's noses, and Aunt Myrtle didn't tell me to hush. And my stepdaddy rubbed his forehead a lot like he had a headache. And neither of them could look me in the eye. They just said soft things, short things, like the other grown-ups on the block. "A shame," or "Winter's mean," or "Poor Lady." When I went into my mama's studio to talk some more about how it wasn't fair, five puppies freezing to death with so many grown-up people right there at home, my mama squeezed some purple paint out on her paint plate real slowlike. "Bury them?" was all she said, and she wouldn't look me in the eye either.

I sat on my bed a long time putting together the story of the storm, how the berry bushes looked lovely at first, all silver and frosty, till the branches split and the bushes fell away. How Mrs. Robinson took a spill on the ice and the ambulance driver wouldn't take her until Marcy and me ran around with that same coffee can and collected thirty-two dollars. How the second wave of snow came and piled up banks of hard ice on the curbs and against porches and steps and cars. How my doll house got tossed into the fire; even though I was asked and did give permission, it hurt. And how the puppies died like that. It'll be a story for my children, I was thinking, sitting on my bed, just as my stepdaddy sings about the time the river rose and his town was flooded but people rebuilt the town and everything was alright. And just as my mama draws about that fire but people rebuilt the farm and she grew up to tell us about it. But what if my kids notice there's a hole in my story, I asked myself, a hole I will fall right through in the telling. Suppose they ask, "But, Mommy, didn't you go and see about the old lady?" So then I'll tell them how I put my boots back on and put them silly pot-holder mittens on too to carry one of Aunt Myrtle's casseroles down to Mrs. Blue. And with the moon pushing at my back, I'm thinking that maybe I'll sit with Mrs. Blue a while even though she is a spooky sort of person.

LUTHER ON
SWEET AUBURN

Luther is confused. Thinks I'm still a youth worker.
Thinks he's still a youth. Thinks this is Warren Street,
Brooklyn. That is, 1962. Stops me in the middle of Auburn
Street to ask for help. I'm coming out of Big Bethel Church:
joint meeting of Black and foreign students, a call for a rally,
press releases, position papers on the Cuban influx, Miami,
the Iranian situation there and here, one lit. student insist-
ing on reading Jerry Ward's poem into my camera eye:
". . . don't be surprised when Africans and Volcanoes disrupt in harmony . . . belch ash in your eye." I'm heading up

the block to the Peacock Lounge: my new play in rehearsal,
theme of hostage-keeping in U.S.—slavery, reservations,
ghettos, prisons, internment camps for Japanese, GIs in
stockades for organizing, cities hostages of Big Business, the
whole country kidnapped by thugs. Station manager not interested. Fine. The camera crew drive off. I'm preoccupied.

Luther is not Luther yet. Just a man coming out a barbershop saying something to me. I answer as I always do
men coming out a barbershop saying something to me. Not
like I answer sisters or elders or a man coming out of
Jameel's Natural Connection Restaurant, the Neighborhood
Art Center, the Institute of the Black World. My answer
pitched somewhere between a man coming out a bar and a
man coming out a building unknown. The man says something more; "Miz Nap" is in the man. The man becomes
someone from the old days in Brooklyn. I focus. The man
becomes Luther Owens, war counselor of the Sovian Lords.
(Sovian?! You illiterate motherfuckers better get in here to
my program least long enough to learn to spell "sovereign,"
shit. You must be the same lames that write "pussey" all
over the door with an *e*. Who's the nappy-head bitch hollering out the window? The new youth counselor for the center. She don't talk like a social worker. And somebody need
to tell her to pull a hot comb through her hair.)

War counselors are remembered. A deep thing with me
that goes back to growing up a girl with two older brothers
who didn't know how to throw down. Definition/function
of an older brother: he who protects, who punches open
space for sister to move through, who beats back trouble so

sister can explore and breathe leisurely. Brothers with no heart and no rep for rumbling were as much use to me as my mama's fox piece with the glass eyes.

We'd move to a new neighborhood when Mama could stand the old one no longer. First thing Mama would do is put gates on the windows and police locks on the door. Second thing she'd do is find a community center. Made more woven looped pot holders, lanyard key chains, and punch-'n'-lace leather purses in those days. First thing Charlie'd do is get his can of Royal Crown pomade and a stocking cap. Second, visit the girls in the building. First for Harry is to find a park. Second, sit down and bite his fingernails off. First off, I'd check the graffiti and find out whose turf we're on. Then I'd check out the war counselor and see if he ran to type.

The main thing I'd do was find the girlfriend and drop her. Easy enough, being new, with no she-said-that-you-said-that-I history. Element of surprise. Out of the blue, hands in her face, fists ripping out hair, nails tearing off clothes, a knee in her chest, her back on the sidewalk. Then I'm the war counselor's lady, not girl, lady they always said. (That ain't no miscellaneous bitch yawl, that chick got class. Did you see her mama? Lawdy. Whatcha doing hanging round them thugs, you got more class than that. Say, pretty lady, can I see you safely to the subway? These chumps round here liable not to know you Frenchie's class A spouse. Hey, Big Stockings! Cool it, Shorty. That ain't no way to talk to that one.)

War counselors were public tough and secret tender.

Not at all like the boys mothers pick out from the choir, the grocer's son, nephew of some down-home chum. They'd sit on your mama's sofa and mimic respectability. Jump you on the stairs, mug you in the movies, wrassle with you all the way back home, wanna drag you in the bushes. War counselors took you to see their mama for coconut cake under a dish cloth on top of the refrigerator. Take you to their Uncle Leroy's for fish sammich and Kool Aid and to the watermelon man who's got lockets and ankle chains and ID bracelet to put both your names on. Take you to the back of the barbershop to play whist with men with mustaches who say 'scuse me when they curse. Take you to the roof to feed the pigeons and lean you against the chimney talking about their plans in life, if drugs don't get'm or the cops or the next rumble. Take you to their godmother who tells you he writes poetry and use to play the piano 'fore he started running wild in the streets with hoodlums. Take you up and down the block parting the waters so everybody'll know—whatever age, color, sex, species—that you are officially not to be messed with cause you are the lady of the turrible war counselor of the turrible Bishops Chapmans Imperial Skulls Jolly Stompers Regal Gents.

Mothers' picks don't go on the block; they sit on that sofa and talk scary. Talk about working in the post office and becoming a cop and marrying you and living in St. Albans with kids to take to Macy's Thanksgiving Day Parade. War counselors give you jewelry and perfume and say how fine it is you're on the honor roll, bring you fried chicken, a jar of lightning bugs, dance on a dime with you and sweat up your hair and make you swear not to forget the folks on the block.

I came back but to a block called Warren Street. Came with memories, with basketballs and leotards, Du Bois and Malcolm posters, equivalency diplomas and my hair au naturel. Hired Luther sight unseen. Saw his name in the school yard, on the police station wall, the Center's bathrooms, scratched into the piano on the second floor. Saw women reach into their bags at the mention of his name, saw them clutch their tear-gas fountain pens and curse. Saw grown men clench their fists at the sound of "Sovian." And at "Luther," get rocks all in their jaws. (Who's this Luther person? What's his name doing on payroll and I haven't even interviewed him yet? We don't do things that way in this settlement house. Which one is he? He's an artist. We should hire him when he shows. Artist. Artist. What kind of artist on Warren Street? Artist-type artist. Plus a security artist. When he shows when he shows when he. Goddamn.)

The director of the neighborhood settlement house was Irish and suffering from amnesia, assuming his people ever knew the art of conjuring people up. I doodled, duplicating the extensively embellished signature Luther left all over the neighborhood while the director ranted and raved about policies and procedures and the budget and me keeping my place. A tall, lanky scatter-teeth dude come up to my window asking if I'm the Miz Nap he's heard about. He ignores the director and challenges me to a game of handball. Not the soft, pink Spauldeen. The mean little hard black ball. Grabbed my gloves from the radiator rung and left the director standing there pondering my "file cabinet"—folders, address cards, program sheets, time sheets, paperback books, plays-in-progress notes, conjuring doodles stuck in the rungs of the radiator. Luther Owens.

"Look here, Miz Nap, I'm trying to get a job at the Butler Street Y. Come talk to the people for me, you always could talk people into things. I was coaching a drill team over on Gordon, but that was temp work for summer. I'm thinking about hooking up with the Shrine of the Black Madonna people, they look after their own, but first I've got to find a place to stay."

We cross the street to the service station for soda. Luther treats me to a pack of peanut butter crackers. Tells me all about reform school, knife wound in leg, 36D Catherine's babies and the warrant, Brooklyn College SEEK, drugs, jail, Dean Street Doris's babies and a warrant, some woman dragging him off to Atlanta then dumping him when his car broke down. All the things you tell a social worker friend. I don't say I am a TV producer now, write plays, wanna make films. Then I'd get his saga all over again packaged for stage and cameras.

"You still painting, Luther?"

The bottle stopping, his lips out like a fish, Luther stock still, staring out beyond the gas pumps to the pigeons fluttering in Big Bethel's bell tower, remembering the time we took off a hobby store to get him supplies—me, him, Buzzy, 36D Catherine and Spyboy the Strong Eater of Just One. (Ain't this a bitch, a social worker on a heist. You sure you ain't setting us all up for a bust for a promotion? Awww c'm on, Nap's alright. I don't think it's right. You supposed to set an example for us. I will maybe, tomorrow. Meanwhile, grab that paint set, get them brushes and let's get out of here.)

"Naaw." Then takes a drink, holds it in his cheeks for a long time before he swallows. No gasping or sucking for air like I do. And what am I doing here drinking soda, eating white flour crackers out of a machine, being with Luther who's all about need and you gotta and help me while folks up the block are waiting on me, waiting to make their/our contribution to the acclamation of Auburn, sweet Auburn, that spawned many a musical genius before it fell apart. "Naaw, Miz Nap, I don't paint anymore."

"Well I don't social work anymore. "

"Is that right?" He frowns, blinks, gets a squinting fix on the pigeons through the green of the Sprite bottle. "That's a shame," he says, dropping his shoulders. In much the way the old gent pumping up the tire to our left does when the air seeps out. A metaphor for what has happened to this once vibrant neighborhood.

"But hey, Miz Nap, maybe you could get a job at the Y."

"I've got a job, Luther."

Stun. Frown. Say what? Big sister. Little mama. Always there. Never off the clock. Not a social worker. What can this mean? Luther thinking with his hands, sloshing soda, licking his knuckles making huhh? sounds.

"How old are you, Luther? And how did the sixties

manage to pass you by, you who were in hailing distance of Brooklyn CORE?"

"Thirty-three."

"I'm thirty-eight. Can you get to that, Youngblood?"

Cars roll over the hose and set off the bell. The old gent's assistant gets up slowly, gas wanted or just a U-turn? Slumps down again to stare, weary, still waiting for the promised transformation of Auburn. Across the way, the students are streaming out of the church, exchanging numbers, shaking hands, looking pleased with their work. I wish I'd kept the camera crew. Long shot of stairs cluster—an in-the-flesh refutation of the apathetic myth, the movement-is-over propaganda.

"Thirty-eight? No shit?"

"No shit, Luther."

"I heard that," he says, turning slowly the way he used to set up for a hook-shot. "I heard that," his shoulders in a slump, ramming his empty bottle in the rack.

ESSAYS AND
CONVERSATIONS

READING THE SIGNS, EMPOWERING THE EYE

*Daughters of the Dust and
the Black Independent
Cinema Movement*

CULTURAL WORK
AIN'T ALL ARTS AND LEISURE

In 1971, Melvin Van Peebles dropped a bomb. *Sweet Sweetback's Baadassss Song* was not polite. It raged, it screamed, it provoked. Its reverberations were felt throughout the country. In the Black community it was both hailed and denounced for its sexual rawness, its macho hero, and its depiction of the community as down-pressed and in need of rescue. Film buffs vigorously invented language to distinguish the film's avant-garde techniques and thematics from the retrograde ideology espoused. Was *Sweetback* a case of Stagolee Meets Fanon or Watermelon Man Plays Bigger Thomas?

Hollywood noted that Van Peebles's *Sweetback* was making millions and that the low-budget detective flick *Shaft* by Gordon Parks, Sr., also released that year, was cleaning up too. By 1972, headlines in the trade papers were echoing those from the twenties—"H'wood Promises the Negro a Better Break." I could wallpaper the bathroom with *Variety* headlines from the days of *Hallelujah,* through the forties accord between Du Bois/NAACP and Hollywood, through the "Blaxplo" era, to this summer's edition covering Cannes and the release of works by Lee, Rich, Vasquez, Duke, and Singleton and still ask the question: Never mind occasional trends, when is the policy going to change? Some fine works got produced despite the "Blaxplo" formula: revolution equals criminality, militants sell dope and women, the only triumph possible is in a throw-down with Mafia second-stringers and bad-apple cops on the take, the system is eternal.

Nowhere would the debate over *Sweetback* prove more fruitful to the development of the Black independent sphere than at the UCLA film school. By 1971, a decentering of Hollywood had already taken place there, courtesy of a group of Black students who recognized cinema as a site of struggle. A declaration of independence had been written in the overturning of the film school curriculum and in the formation of student-generated alternatives, such as the Ethnocommunications Program and off-campus study groups. The significance of the LA rebellion to the development of the multicultural film phenomena of recent years has been the subject of articles, lectures, interviews, program notes, and informal talks by Sylvia Morales, Renee Tajima, Charlie Burnett, Julie Dash, Moctesuma Esparza, and most especially, most consistently, and most pointedly in connection with the development of Black independent film, by Clyde Taylor. Some of *Sweetback*'s techniques and procedures were acceptable to the insurgents, but its politics were not. The film, nonetheless, continued to exert an influence as late as 1983, as is observable in Gerima's *Ashes and Embers,* in which an embittered and haunted 'Nam vet is continually running, finding respite for a time with folks in the community. The film closes not with "The End," but "Second Coming," as in *Sweetback.*

The Black insurgents at UCLA had a perspective on film very much informed by the movements of the sixties (1954–1972) both in this country and on the Continent. Their views differed markedly with the school's orientation:

> • accountability to the community takes precedence over training for an industry that maligns and exploits, trivializes and invisibilizes Black people;
> • the community, not the classroom, is the appropriate training grounds for producing relevant work;

• it is the destiny of our people(s) that concerns us, not self-indulgent assignments about neurotic preoccupations;

• our task is to reconstruct cultural memory, not slavishly imitate white models; our task leads us to our own suppressed bodies of literature, lore, and history, not to the "classics" promoted by Eurocentric academia;

• students should have access to world film culture—African, Asian, and Latin America cinema—in addition to Hitchcock, Ford, and Renoir.

The off-campus study groups, which included cadres from two periods—Charles Burnett, Haile Gerima, Ben Caldwell, Alile Sharon Larkin, and Julie Dash—engaged in interrogating conventions of dominant cinema, screening films of socially conscious cinema, and discussing ways to alter previous significations as they relate to Black people. In short, they were committed to developing a film language to respectfully express cultural particularity and Black thought. The "Watts Films," as their output was called in the circles I moved in then, began with Gerima's 1972 *Child of Resistance,* in homage to Angela Davis, an instructor at UCLA before the state sent her on the run, and his 1974 feature *Bush Mama.* Both starred Barbara O (then Barbara O. Jones), an actress who hooked up with insurgents early on and has been with the independents since, working as performer, technician, and now as filmmaker (*Sweatin' a Dream*).

In 1977, the insurgents' thematic foci became discernible: family, women, history, and folklore. Larry Clark's *Passing Through*, Charles Burnett's *Killer of Sheep*, and two shorts by Julie Dash—*Diary of an African Nun*, based on a short story by Alice Walker, and *Four Women*, based on the musical composition of Nina Simone—made it a bumpercrop year. The edible metaphor is deliberate, and ironic. Proponents of "Third Cinema" around the world were working then, as now, to advance a cinema that would prove indigestible to the imperialist system that relentlessly promotes a consumerist ethic. And the works of the LA rebels reflected radical cultural/political theories of the day. The Black-community-as-colony theorem, for example, informs Burnett's portrayal of both the protagonist's family and Watts. The omnipresence of sirens, cruisers, and cops defines the neighborhood(s) as occupied territory. The family is portrayed as a potential liberation zone. In *Bush Mama*, the besieged Dorothy comes to consciousness through her daughter's questioning. While filming, Gerima's crew became the target of the LAPD, who equate Black men with expensive equipment with criminality; the attempted arrest was filmed, and the documented incident on screen in the fictional feature provides a compelling argument. This treatment of family and setting continued to inform the later films of Gerima, Burnett, and Billy Woodbury.

Alile Sharon Larkin's treatment of terrain in her 1982

film *A Different Image* is the same. She uses the landscape (billboards and other ads that commercialize women's images), though, to highlight the impact sexist representations have on behavior in general (passersby who regard the heroine as a sex object) and on intimate relationships in particular (the heroine's boyfriend fails to see the connection between racism and sexism). Larkin's film demonstrates the difficulty in and the necessity for smashing the code, transforming previous significations as they relate to Black women.

Three shorts by Julie Dash—*Diary of an African Nun, Four Women,* and the 1982 *Illusions*—are in line with this agenda. We note four things in them that will culminate in her more elaborate text of 1991, her feature *Daughters of the Dust:* women's perspective, women's validation of women, shared space rather than dominated space (Mignon Dupree in *Illusions* presses for the inclusion of Native Americans in the movie industry, and she stands in solidarity with Ester, the hidden "voice" of the Euro-American movie star), and glamour/attention to female iconography.

In *Daughters of the Dust,* the thematics of colonized terrain, family as liberated zone, women as source of value, and history as interpreted by Black people are central. The Peazant family gather for a picnic reunion at Ibo Landing, an area they call "the secret isle." It is "secret" for two reasons, for the land is both bloody and blessed. A port of entry for the European slaving ships, the Carolina Sea Islands (Port Royal County) were where captured Africans were "seasoned" for servitude. Even after the trade was outlawed, traffickers used the dense and marshy area to hide forbidden cargo. But the difficult terrain was also a haven for both self-emancipated Africans and indigenous peoples, just as the Florida Everglades and the Louisiana bayous were for Seminoles and Africans, and for the Filipinos conscripted by the French to fight proxy wars (French and Indian wars). Dash's Peazant family is imperiled by rape and lynch-mob murder (whites are ob-skene in *DD*), but during their reunion picnic they commandeer the space to create a danger-free zone. Music cues and resonating lines of dialogue in *DD* link the circumstances of the Peazants at the turn of the century to our circumstances today. Occupying the same geographical terrain are both the ghetto, where we are penned up in concentration-camp horror, and the community, wherein we enact daily rituals of group validation in a liberated zone—a global condition throughout the African diaspora, the view informs African cinema.

Daughters of the Dust capsulizes the stage of independent Black filmmaking ushered in by the LA rebellion in other ways as well. Spiritual and religious continuum, a particular theme of Ben Caldwell's, is central to the *DD* drama. Folklore too is key. Two further decisions Dash made highlight her strategy for grounding *DD* in the discourse of committed Black cinema. She drew her cast from films by her UCLA colleagues: Barbara O (as Yellow Mary) was in Gerima's *Child of Resistance* and *Bush Mama,* and in Dash's *Diary of an African Nun;* Adisa Anderson (as Eli) was in Alile Sharon Larkin's *A Different Image;* Cora Lee Day (as Nana) was in Gerima's *Bush Mama;* Kaycee Moore (as

Haagar) was in Burnett's *Killer of Sheep* and Woodbury's *Bless Their Little Hearts*.

She also cast from films by other independents: Trula Hoosier (as Yellow Mary's woman friend) was in Charles Lane's *Sidewalk Stories;* Geraldine Dunston (one of Nana's daughters) was in Iverson White's *Black Exodus;* Tommy Hicks (as Snead the photographer) was in Spike Lee's *She's Gotta Have It;* and Verta Mae Smart-Grosvenor (as one of Nana's daughters) was in Bill Gunn's video soap *Personal Problems.* She also drew from industry-backed films by Black filmmakers and from industry White-directed, Black-cast films: Alva Rodgers (as Eula) was in Spike Lee's *School Daze,* Tony King (as Eli's cousin) was in *Sparkle.* Note too that the presence of Barbara O links *DD* to other works by filmmakers, for she appears in Saundra Sharp's *Back Inside Herself* and Zeinabu Davis's in-progress *A Powerful Thang.*

The effects of intertextual echoes resulting from Dash's casting strategem are best discussed in screen demonstration, rather than in on-the-page discussions, but one example can perhaps illustrate the point. The presence of Dunston from Iverson White's lynching-migration film deepens the antilynching campaign theme in *DD* and underscores the difference between the White lynch mob's picnic (the dead man's sons find orange peels and other debris near the hanging tree) and the Black family reunion picnic. The existence of *DD* makes it easier than ever for someone to produce an anthology film on Black U.S. history on the order of Kwati Ni Owoo and Kwesi Owusu's anthology film on African cinema, *Ouaga,* which combines film clips, interviews, and footage from FESPACO, the Pan-African film festival in Burkina Faso, and uses ideogrammed panels of cloth (event turned to story turned to punch line turned to proverb turned to ideograms woven in kente cloth) to segment the film's "chapters."

Dash's *Daughters of the Dust* is a historical marker. It not only promotes a back glance, it demands an appraisal of ground covered in the past twenty years, and in doing so helps clarify what we mean by "independent Black cinema." In its formal practices and thematics, *DD* is the maturation of the LA rebellion agenda. By centralizing the voice, experience, and culture of women, most particularly, it fulfills the promise of Afrafemcentrists who choose film as their instrument for self-expression. *DD* inaugurates a new stage.

> *I'm trying to teach you how to track your own spirit. I'm trying to give you something to take north besides big dreams*
>
> NANA

We meet the Peazants in a defining moment—a family council. Democratic decision-making, a right ripped from them by slavery and regained through emancipation, hallmarks the moment. The Peazants and guests gather on the island at Ibo Landing for a picnic at a critical juncture in history—they are one generation away from the Garvey and the New Negro movements, a decade short of the Niagara/NAACP merger. They are in the midst of rapid changes; Black people are on the move North, West, and back to Africa (the Oklahoma project, for instance). Setting the story amid oak groves, salt marshes, and a glorious beach is not for the purpose of presenting a nostalgic community in a pastoral setting. They are an imperiled group. The high tide of bloodletting has ebbed for a time, thanks to the activism of Ida B. Wells, but there were racist riots in 1902; in New Orleans, for example, Black schools were the paramount target for torchings, maimings, and murder. Unknown hazards await the Peazants up North. The years ahead will require political, economic, social, and cultural lucidity. Nommo, from an older and more comprehensive belief system than meanings produced by the European traditions of rationalism and empiricism, may prove their salvation.

The Peazants, as the name suggests, are peasants. Their characterizations, however, are not built on a deficit model. It is the ethos of cultural resistance, not the ethos of rehabilitation, that informs their portraiture. They are not victims. Objectively, they are bound to the land as sharecroppers. Subjectively, they are bound to the land because it is an ancestral home. They tend the graves of relatives. Family memorabilia are the treasure they carry in their pockets and store in tins, not coins. They are accountable to the orishas, the ancestors, and each other, not to employers. *DD* is not, then, an economically determined drama in conventional terms, wherein spectators are encouraged to identify with feudal positions—the privileged overlord or the exploited victim, and then close the mind as though no alternative social modes exist or are possible. The Peazants are self-defining people. Unlike the static portraits of reactionary cinema—a Black woman is a maid and remains a maid even after becoming a "liberated woman" through the influence of a White feminist, and even after making a fortune with a pancake recipe (*Imitation of Life*), and a Black woman is a prostitute and remains a prostitute in the teeth of other options (*Mona Lisa*)—the Peazants have a belief in their own ability to change and in their ability to transform the social relations of status quo.

While *DD* adheres to the unities of time, place, and action—the reunion takes place in one day in one locale scripted on an arrival-departure grid—the narrative is not "classical" in the Western-specific sense. It is classic in the African sense. There are digressions and meanderings—as we may be familiar with from African, Persian, Indian, and other cinemas that employ features of the oral tradition. *DD* employs a folktale in content and schema.

Instead of a "pidgin" effect, what the eye and ear have been conditioned to expect from the unlettered, the Ibo Landing characters use an imaginative and varied language—poetic, signifying, rhetorical, personal—in keeping with the productive artistry we're accustomed to outside Eurocentral institutions. In addition to affirming the culture, *DD* advances the idea that African culture can subvert the imposed one. Nana, the family elder, binds up the Bible with her mojo in a reverse order of syncretism. Continuum is the theme. The first voice we hear on the sound track is chanting in Ibo; the one discernible word is "remember."

A striking image greets us in the opening—a pair of

hands, as in the laying on of hands, as in handed down. They're a working woman's hands. Grandma's hands. They seem to be working up soil, as in cultivation, or maybe it's sand, certainly apropos for any presentation of an African worldview. And there's water, as in rivers. Then two voice-overs introduce the story. One belongs to Nana, the elder of the family, we will discover later: first, we see and hear her in sync during the film's present; later we see her in a flashback memory of bondage days, her hands sculling the dark steamy water of the dye vats, then, together with other enslaved African women, wringing out yards of indigo-dyed cloth. The second voice is that of the Unborn Child; we will see her later on screen, too, as a visitor from that realm that supports the perceived world. The dual narration pulls together the past, present, and future—a fitting device for a film paying homage to African retention, to cultural continuum. The duet also prepares us for the film's multiple perspectives. Communalism is the major mode of the production. There's something else to notice about the dual voice-over narration. The storytelling mode is indabe my children and crik-crak, the African-derived communal, purposeful handing down of group lore and group values in a call-and-response circle.

The story opens with the arrival of two relatives, Yellow Mary and Viola, accompanied by Yellow Mary's woman friend from Nova Scotia and a photographer hired by Viola to document the reunion of the Geechee family, whose homestead is in Gullah country. The family already onshore is introduced by the thud-pound of mortar and pestle, as in the pounding of yam—an echo of the opening of Sembène's *Ceddo,* also a drama about cultural conversion and cultural resistance; in *Ceddo,* which portrays forced conversion, the daily routine of the village, as represented by the pounding of yam, will be disrupted, as signaled by the next shot, a cross mounted atop one of the buildings. The pounding and the drums in *DD* also evoke a Dash antecedent about imposed religious-cultural conflict. In *Diary of an African Nun* a convert to Christianity hears sounds from the village and can't see she cannot continue to teach her people to smother the drums, stifle the joy, and pray (she realizes) to an empty sky. Shrouded in white, she chants, "I am the wife of Christ—barren and . . . I am the wife of Christ," as snow melts on the mountain revealing the rich, black, ancient earth.

Nana Peazant has called a family council because values are shifting. There's talk of migration. The ancestral home is being rejected on the grounds of limited educational and job opportunities. Haagar, one of Nana's daughters-in-law, is particularly fed up with the old-timey, backward values of the "salt-water Negroes" of the island. Her daughter, on the other hand, longs to stay; Ione's lover, a Native American in the area, has sent her a love letter in the hopes that she'll remain. Viola, the Christianized granddaughter, views her family in much the way Haagar does; Viola avers that it is her Christian duty to take the young heathen children in hand, which she does the minute she steps ashore. Nana struggles to keep intact that African-derived institution that has been relentlessly under attack through kidnap, enslavement, Christianization, peonage, forced labor gangs, smear campaigns, and mob murder—the family.

Nana and one of the male relatives of this multigenerational community do persuade several to stay, but realizing that breakup is imminent, that the lure of new places is great, Nana offers a combination of things for folks to take with them as protection on their journey, so that relocation away from the ancestral place will not spell cultural dispossession. As relatives wash the elder's feet, she assembles an amulet made up of bits and scraps. "My mother cut this from her hair before they sold her away from me," she says, winding the charm and binding twine around a Bible. Each member has a character-informed reaction to her request to kiss the amulet, the gesture a vow to struggle against amnesia, to resist the lures and bribes up North that may cause them to betray their individual and collective integrity. The double ritual performed, some Peazants depart and others remain.

Like many independent works of the African diaspora that conceptualize critical remembrance—Med Hondo's *West Indies,* the Sankofa Collective's *Passion of Remembrance,* Rachel Gerber and Beatriz de Nasciamento's *Ori—* DD's drama hinges on rituals of loss and recovery. The film, in fact, invites the spectator to undergo a triple process of recollecting the dismembered past, recognizing and reappraising cultural icons and codes, and recentering and revalidating the self. One of the values of its complexity and its recognition of Black complexity is to prompt us, anew, to consider our positions and our power in the USA.

While presenting the who o' we to ourselves, Dash also critiques basic tenets of both domination ideology and liberation ideology. An exchange illustrating the former occurs in a scene between Nana, the elder, and Eli, a young man fraught with doubt that his pregnant wife, Eula, may be carrying some White man's child. Their lines of dialogue don't mesh at first because each is caught up in her and his own distress—Nana is anxious lest Eli not be up to holding the family together in the North; Eli is too obsessed with doubt about the unborn child to be reasoned with. But then their speeches mesh.

> *"Call on the ancestors, Eli. We need to be strong again."*
> *"It happened to my wife."*
> *"'My wife.' Eli, you don't own Eula. She married you."*

Yellow Mary relates two stories that illustrate the latter point. Strolling along the beach with her friend and Eula, Yellow Mary recalls a box she once saw on the mainland, a music box. It was a bad time for her then, and she wanted that box to lock up her sorrow in the song. In the briefest of anecdotes, the process from sensation to perception to self-understanding to decision is mapped. Self-possession is a trait in Yellow Mary's unfolding of character; cultural autonomy is a motif in the entire *DD* enterprise. The allusion to both the sorrow-song and blues traditions in Yellow Mary's art-of-living anecdote sets the stage for a mini-essay on desire. Yellow Mary's walk, posture, and demeanor are in stark contrast to that of the Christianized cousin Viola. The careers of women blues singers in the twenties and thirties showed that Black women need not repress sexuality to be acceptable to the community. Unlike Yellow Mary, who must continually claim her sexuality, Viola has buried hers in Christian duty—that is, until perhaps Snead the photographer, thrilled to be part of the family circle, in a moment of exuberance kisses her.

Yellow Mary's second story is about a time worse than bad, the death of her baby. Her arms were empty but her breasts were full. The White family she worked for used her to wet-nurse their children. "I wanted to come home, but they wouldn't let me. I tied up my breasts. They let me go." The allusion here is to Toni Morrison's 1987 novel *Beloved*. While Paul D is remembering the scourgings and humiliations of manhood, Sethe is caught up in the memory of gang rape in which the young White men of the plantation suckled her. "They took my milk," Sethe repeats throughout Paul D's cataloguing of atrocities. The yoking of Black women's sexuality and fertility to the capitalist system of exploitation was a theme in Dash's work prior to Morrison's *Beloved*, however. *Four Women*, based on the Simone text, relates the tragedy of three women in history—Saphronia, enslaved; Aunt Sarah, mammified; and Sweet Thing, lecherized. The fourth woman is Peaches, politicized: "I'm very bitter these days because my people were slaves—What do they call me? They call me Peee-Chezzz!"

The struggle for autonomy (or, how many forces do we

have to combat to reclaim our body/mind/spirits and get our perspective and agenda respected?) is the concern of numerous Black women filmmakers—Camille Billops, Zeinabu Davis, Cheryl Chisholm, Ayoka Chenzira, Michelle Parkerson, Barbara McCullough, numerous others, and of course, Dash. What the Yellow Mary stories point to is the limitations of radical discourse that dichotomizes culture and politics, that engenders oppression and resistance as male, and that defines resistance as a numbered, organized, leader-led (male) action that is sweeping in process and effect. In tying up her breasts, Yellow Mary is a factory worker on strike.

Any ordinary day offers an opportunity to practice freedom, to create revolution internally, to rehearse for governance, the film promotes. A deepening of the message is achieved by having both Barbara O and Verta Mae Smart-Grosvenor, author of *Thursdays and Every Other Sunday Off,* on-screen. O's personal act of resistance in *Bush Mama* carries over to *DD* through the actress playing Yellow Mary, a domestic and a prostitute. The perspective of domestics, who are in a better position than most workers to demystify White supremacy, as Smart-Grosvenor's book indicates, is a still-untapped resource for Black political theorists (including Afrafemcentrists). Likewise the prostitute's.

The thesis of daily resistance spreads from scene to scene. Eula's silence about the White rapist, for example, is a weapon; it shields Eli from highly probable violence. However, as a metaphor for cultural rape, silence must be overcome; the film *DD* is the voice. Speaking Gullah is also resistance; it combats assimilationist designs. Gullah is an

Afrish first created by Mandinkas, Yorubas, Ibos, and others to facilitate intercontinental trade long before the African Holocaust. The bridge language on this side of the waters was recreolized with English. The authenticity of languages spoken by the Peazants, by Bilal, a Muslim on the island, by the indigo dyers and the Wallahs (met in flashbacks to slavery times) is one of the ways the film compels belief. The film's respectful attention to language, codes of conduct, food preparation, crafts, chair caning, hair sculptures, quilt making, and mural painting constitutes a praise song to the will and imagination of a diasporized and besieged people to forge a culture that can be sustained.

In the anticolonial wars and since, language has been the subject of hot debate in both diplomatic and cultural arenas. It is key to the issue of cultural-political autonomy, as in, for example, the development of national literatures and national cinemas. Which language shall a newly independent country adopt—that of the largest ethnic group within its colonialist-created borders, that in which the oldest literature is written, that in which the most compelling oral literature is transmitted, that which has been taught in the schools, namely the colonialists'? Kenyan writer Ngugi wa Thiong'o, Senegalese novelist and filmmaker Ousmane Sembène and Palestinian writer and theorist Ghassan Kanafani are a few stalwarts who have kept vibrant the arguments of Fanon, Cabral, and others concerning the imperatives of national culture. During the resistance struggles of the sixties in the U.S., writers in the various communities of color took up the vernacular-vs.-vehicular debate and also opted in favor of languages in which their constituencies experience daily life; hence, literature written in Yorican, Black English, and Spanglais, for example, rather than "standard" or "literary" English. Ousmane Sembène's use of Wolof in *Ceddo*, Euzhan Palcy's use of Martinican creole in *Sugar Cane Alley*, Trevor Rhone's use of Jamaican creole in *Smile Orange*, and Felix de Roy's use of Papiamento, the creole in the Antilles, in *Eva* and *Gabriella* are examples of noncapitulation to strategies of containment by official and monied types who argue that vernacular is neither a dignified vehicle for presenting the culture nor a shrewd way to effect a crossover to cosmopolitan audiences who may enjoy your cuisine and appropriate your music but prefer that you speak in standard Europese.

It is not surprising to observe, further, that those filmmakers who argue for cultural authenticity also work to forge a diasporic hookup. Sembène, for example, frequently links the Continent and Black USA; for example, through gospel music in *Ceddo* and with the Black GI in *Camp de Thieroy*. Palcy, in her screen adaptation of the Zobel novel, invents the character Medouze (who tells Jose about Africa) for the purpose of linking the Caribbean to the Continent; and for her second project, the Martinican filmmaker chose a South African work, *A Dry White Season*. Kwah Ansah's *Heritage Africa* is one of a host of efforts to revitalize in this decade the Pan-African connection. Three works by Haile Gerima make clear his position in this global agenda of cultural defense: *Harvest: 3,000 Years*, set in Ethiopia, *The Wilmington Ten—U.S.A. 10,000*, about the Ben Chavis case in the USA, and *Nanu,* a work-in-progress set in the Caribbean. Two works by newcomer Zeinabu Davis demonstrate continuum. In an early short, *Crocodile Tears,* Davis makes a connection in content; the story is about an African-American woman of the U.S. who goes to Cuba with the Venceramos Brigade, much to the consternation of her children. By the time Davis began work on her third short, *Cycles,* she had begun to fashion a deliberate diasporic aesthetic. *Cycles* speaks a Pan-African esperanto via altars, vèvès, chants to the orishas, Haitian music, African music, and a speaking chorus whose individual accents blend U.S. Northern-Southern-Midwestern with African and Caribbean.

Dash's *DD* evolved over a ten-year period in which independent Black filmmakers committed to socially conscious cinema were exchanging viewpoints with like-minded filmmakers throughout the diaspora, most especially in Britain and on the Continent. The diasporic links promoted in the sixties by St. Clair Bourne on the East Coast (editor of *Chamba Notes,* an international film newsletter) and Haile Gerima on the West Coast (organizer of the first U.S. delegation to FESPACO in Burkina Faso) continued into the eighties through the efforts of numerous programmers (for instance, Louis "Bilaggi" Bailey, founder of the Atlanta Third World Film Festival, and Cheryl Chisholm, who vastly expanded it), historians, curators, critics, supporters, and practitioners (Pearl Bowser serves to illustrate all known categories). Videographer Philip Mallory Jones's current three-channel installation, *Crossroads,* at the Smithsonian is emblematic of the diasporic connection. Dash's decision to set her feature and locate her production in the Carolina Sea Islands where African persistence is still discernible, and, further, to set the story at the turn of the century when retention was strong, enables her to situate the film in the ongoing history of the Pan-African film culture movement.

When Yellow Mary says, "You have to have a place to go where people know your name," she underscores what some people would call the Du Bois double-consciousness theme, and what others would call the difference between true or primary consciousness and false or secondary consciousness. It is the Ibo tale which Dash employs in *DD* that keeps the question to the fore—Where is the soul's proper home? *DD*'s is an unabashedly Afrocentric thesis in the teeth of current-day criticisms of essentialism.

NOMMO

Loss and recovery is established as a theme and an operation early on in *DD*. The operation begins with Dash's retrieval of a figure; that operation then leads us to a folktale. The landscape in the opening shots is hot, green, and sluggish. A boat glides into view. Embedded in the Black spectator's mind is *that* boat, *those* ships. As this boat cuts through the green, thick waters, we see a woman standing near the prow. She wears a veiled hat and a long, white dress. Embedded in the memory of millions is the European schoolmarm-adventuress-mercenary-disguised-as-missionary woman who helps sell the conquest of Africa as a heroic adventure. But this woman is not that woman. She's standing hipshot, chin cocked, one arm akimbo. The ebonics send the message that this is not Brenda Joyce/Maureen O'Sullivan/Katharine Hepburn/Bo Derek/Jessica Lange/Meryl Streep/Sigourney Weaver or any other White star venturing into Tarzan's heart of darkness to have a sultry affair with a pith-helmeted matinee idol, or with a scruffy, cigar-smoking cult figure, or with a male gorilla, in order to sell us imperialism as entertainment.

In this film, that hipshot posture says, Africans will not be seen scrambling in the dust for Bogie's tossed-away stogie. Nor singing off-key as Hepburn plunks Anglican hymns on the piano. Nor fleeing a big, black, monstrous, white nightmare only to be crushed underfoot. Nor being upstaged by scenery in a travelogue cruise down the Congo, part of a cluster of images that invite but don't commit. Nor being a mute and static backdrop for White folks' actions in the foreground, helping to make that passive/active metaphor of the international race-relations industry indelible. Nor being absent as cast members, ghosts merely in back-projected ethnographic footage purchased from a documentarist trained to go to people of color to study but not to learn from. Nor being absent altogether so as to make Banana Republic colonial-nostalgia clothing for a price clean-kill innocent.

The figure is claimed for an emancipatory purpose. The boat steers us away from the narrows of Hollywood toward salt-marshy waters that only look like the shallows. Bobbing near shore is a carving, the head and torso of an African rendered in wood. From the shape of it, we surmise that it was a "victory," a figure that rode the prow of a slaving ship. (In a later scene, Eli, husband of Eula, will baptize the "victory" and push it out into the depths.) The boat docks in an area richer still in meaning. A title comes onto the screen: "Ibo Landing, 1902." The date is important. The people whose stories will be told are one generation out of bondage. The date lingers on the screen six beats longer than the date in the 1985 Hollywood/Spielberg version of Alice Walker's film *The Color Purple,* which is set in the same period.

In *Purple,* "Winter, 1909" flashes over Celie bolting upright in bed in the extreme foreground, screaming, in terror, in labor. The flash of the date fails to orient sufficiently. The spectator needs a moment to assemble the history: chains, branding irons, whips, rape, metal depressors on the tongue, bits in the mouth, iron gates on the face in the cane brakes that prevent one from eating the sweetness and prevent one from breathing in the sweltering blaze that scalds the mask that chars the flesh. The brutalized and brutalizing behaviors of *Purple*'s main characters have a source. That Spielberg did not appreciate the import of the date is our first clue that *Purple* will be hobbled in fundamental ways— the cartoon view of Africa, for example, which is in keeping with the little-bluebird journey of the flyer that covers the passage of years and announces that Shug Avery's hit town. *Purple,* nonetheless, was/is of critical importance to at least one sector of the community who draw strength from it— incest survivors who need permission to speak of intracommunity violation.

The place name in *DD*, Ibo Landing, conjures up a story still told both in the Carolina Sea Islands and in the Caribbean. In Toni Morrison's 1981 cautionary tale, the novel *Tar Baby*, set in the Caribbean, it becomes the story of the hundred blind Africans who ride the hills. On deck, barely surviving the soul-killing crossing from the Tropic of Capricorn to the Horse Latitudes, the Africans took one look at the abomination on shore and were struck blind. They flung themselves over the side, swam to shore, climbed the rocks, and can be heard to this day thundering in the hills on wild horses. Haunting hoofbeats are a reminder to cherish the ancient properties and resist amnesia/assimilation/fragmentation. Paule Marshall also uses the tale to warn us not to bargain away wisdom for goods and "acceptance." The functioning of the Ibo tale in Marshall's 1984 novel *Praisesong for the Widow* is more precisely parallel to its role in *DD*.

Praisesong invites the reader to undergo a grounding ritual via Avey Johnson. A middle-aged widow living in White Plains, New York, Avey has all the trappings of success—stocks and bonds, wall-to-wall carpet, car, house, matching luggage. She's planning a trip to the Caribbean. She suffers, though, from a severe sense of loss. It registers as more than the loss of her husband. Like Jardine in the Morrison novel, Avey and Jay have been in flight; the fear of poverty and humiliation drove them to jettison cultural "baggage" for a fleeter, unencumbered foot up the ladder. Avey receives visitations from her dead elder, Great Aunt Cuney, who directs her to *remember*. Avey's journey toward wholeness begins with remembering the story of the Ibos as handed down through generations in the Carolina Sea Islands where she spent her girlhood summers. In short, in order to move forward, Avey has to first go backward.

The Ibos, brought ashore from the ships in a boat, stepped out on the land, saw what the Europeans had in store for them, and turned right around and walked all the way home to the motherland. Once just a tale, fantastic in its account of people in irons walking thousands of miles on the water, the account of the Ibos' deep vision becomes an injunction to Avey. She must learn to see, to name, to reconnect. Great Aunt Cuney used to say of her grandmother, who handed down the tale, that her body might have been in Tatum, South Carolina, but her mind was long gone with the Ibos. Avey finds strength in the tale and continues her journey; its success rests on her ability to read the signs that speak to the persistence of the ancient world(s) in the so-called New World. This practice of reading and naming releases nommo—that harmonizing energy that connects body/mind/spirit/self/community with the universe. Avey "crosses over" to her center, her authentic self, her real name, and her true work. As Avatara, she assumes the task of warning others away from *eccentricity*. She stands watch in luxury high-rises for buppie types with a deracinated look. She collars them and tells her story.

In *DD*, the Ibo tale is both rejected and accepted by various characters. But the film's point of view is that it has protective power. In his nonlinear narrative *Ashes and Embers,* Gerima argued that folktales have healing power. The story of a 'Nam vet who has to come to grips with his positionalities as a Black man in the imperialistic U.S., *Ashes and Embers* moves back and forth between the past and present, and between the city and the countryside. Nate Charles Garnett (named for Nat C. Turner) is still haunted by the war eight years later. Wired ("like a ticking time bomb," a Korean vet he meets says of them both) and belligerent, he intentionally repels and attracts those who love him—his Gran, his lover Liza (played by Kathy Flewellan, a dark-skinned "actress who plays a featured role, rare; a woman with independent radical politics, rarer; which she studies within a group and acts on in the community, most rare on screen. She's also the featured actress in Davis's *Cycles*) and her son, and a neighborhood elder who runs a TV repair shop.

The drama gathers momentum when the elder tells Nate what his options are: "Keep running, go hide in the movies, lobotomize yourself with that escapist stuff or draw strength from the strong men. They're your models—Du Bois—Robeson." The elder's speech on the strong men (as in the poem by Sterling Brown, subject of a 1985 film by Gerima and his students) propels Nate back to the ancestral place by train. Cross-cutting between Nate on the train and Gran by the fire with Liza, Gerima heightens the drama. Remembering the handed-down tale Gran used to tell him, Nate experiences from it the clarity and coherence necessary to "cross over." Gran is relating the very same tale to Liza, a tale passed down through the family since the Denmark Vesey uprising. "Listen to what I'm telling you and don't forget. Pass it on. Pass it on." It is a compelling account, passionately rendered, expertly paced.

"Crossing over," a term steeped in religion, as in crossing over into Jordan (Baptist and other), crossing over into sainthood (Sanctified, Pentecostal), crossing to or coming through religion (Country Baptist and AME Zion) crops up frequently in the speech of those on Ibo Island. Used by Haagar, the daughter-in-law eager to get her family off the island to more sophisticated environs, it suggests that she may fall victim to the worship of Mammon. Used by one of the men trying to persuade Eli, the distraught husband of Eula, to stay and be an antilynching activist, it equates responsibility with sacred work. The phrase "making the crossing," spoken by several characters, carries two meanings: being double-crossed, as in being rounded up for the Middle Passage; and being Ibo-like by sending the soul home to the original ancestral place, Africa.

"Crossing over" also calls to mind the contemporary phrase "crossover" as in "Whitening" a Black film project, or yoking a Black box office star to a White one in order to attract a wider, or Whiter, audience. *DD* is not a crossover project.

EMPOWERING SIGNS

The TV experiment *All in the Family* proved that commercial success was/is in the offing for those who would pitch to a polarized national audience. White and other bigots were affirmed by the prime-time Archie Bunker show. White and other liberals read the comedy as an exposé and applauded its creators for their wit. Black and other down-pressed folks, eager for any sign of American Bunkerism being defanged, tuned in to crack.

There is no evidence in *DD* of trying to position a range of spectators, as many filmmakers find it expedient to do. *DD* demands some work on the part of the spectator whose ear and eye have been conditioned by habits of viewing industry fare that masks history and addicts us to voyeurism, fetishism, mystified notions of social relations, and freakish notions of intimate relations. Most spectators are used to performing work in the dark. But usually, after fixing inconsistencies in plot and character and rescripting to make incoherent texts work out, our reward is a mugging. *DD* asks that the spectator honor multiple perspectives rather than depend on the "official" story offered by a hero; it asks too that we note what particular compositions and framing mean in terms of human values. The reward is an empowered eye.

In *DD*, the theme of cultural resiliency determines composition, framing, music, and narrative. In conventional cinema, symbol, style, and thematics are subordinated to narrative drive; except, of course, that an ideological imperative overrides it all: to construct, reinforce, and "normalize" the domination discourse of status quo that posits people of color as less than ("minority," as they say).

Snead the photographer is a reminder of how ritualized a form of behavior taking pictures is, and that it need not be aggressive. His character changes in the course of the film. Initially bemused, curious about the backwoods folk Viola regards as heathens, he becomes the anthropologist who learns from "his photographic subjects." After interviewing people on the island, Snead discovers a more profound sense of his own self. The photographer character, the camera, the stereopticon, and kaleidoscope function in *DD* as cameras and video monitors do in *The Passion of Remembrance* by the Black British collective Sankofa. The film-within-a-film device, as Maggie Baptiste works in front of the monitor, accomplishes in the independent Black Brit film what shifting sight lines and the behavior of Snead do in *DD*—to call attention to the fact that in conventional films we're seduced by technique and fail to ask what's being filmed and in whose interest, and by failing to remain critical, become implicated in the reconstruction/reinforcement of a hierarchical ideology.

Dash not only expresses solidarity with international cadres whose interrogations have been throwing all codified certainties about film into crisis for the past twenty years; she also contracted as director of cinematography a filmmaker who questions even the 24-frames-per-second convention. In the early forties, when Dizzy Gillespie announced that 3/4 and 4/4 time signatures were not adequate for rendering the Black experience, bebop was ushered in. It didn't arrive in a tux. It came to overhaul the tenets of Black improvisational music-making and music-listening. Arthur Jafa Fiedler, as his film shorts such as *P.F.* indicate, is announcing no less.

Frame rates, the speed at which the sprocket-driven

gears push film stock through the chamber of a camera, include, among others, 16 frames per second, 18, 24, 25, and so on. Of these technological possibilities—and even these are fairly arbitrary—24 has been the standard since the "talkies," not, apparently, because the synchronization of sound and visuals requires it, but because findings in the fields of kinesics and psychophysiology suggest that the 24-frame rate gives a pleasurable illusion of reality. In *P.F.*, by orchestrating frame rates, Fiedler gives us something else; he multiplies the possibilities for multiple-channeled perception on the part of the spectator. For a project, namely *DD*, that asks the spectator to do as Avey did, read the signs, Fiedler is the perfect practitioner.

By the by: a number of Black psychologists and forensic lawyers are working in the combined field of kinesics and psychophysiology to explore the virulent and criminal impact of racist stressors (a sense of entitlement, belief in Black inferiority, a predisposition to hog space, to break through a line, presume, engage in demonic-oriented Black/White discourse, complain about the music, set the pace) on Black individual and communal health.

One of the "signs" is signing, which the children do in games, and which Eli and several men do to talk across distances. The film poses the question asked of inventor Lewis Lattimore by Pan-African-minded folks at the turn of the century: How shall a diasporized people communicate? Answer: independent films. Trula Hoosier (Yellow Mary's woman friend) from Charles Lane's independent silent film *Sidewalk Stories* (mother of the little girl) has very few lines in *DD* but is in a great many scenes. Her silence is initially disconcerting but then seems functional, drawing attention to both the Gullah language and signing. In the woods where Eli (played by Adisa Anderson, the boyfriend from *A Different Image*) and his cousin (played by Tony King who, in *Sparkle,* beat up on Lonette McKee, who later starred in Dash's *Illusions*) silently perform an African martial art known in Afribrasilia as capoeira (the subject of a film by Warrington Hudlin, founder of the Black Filmmaker's Foundation, which distributes, among other films, *A Different Image* and *Illusions*), cousin Peazant's reading of the signs of the time is what prompts him to speak, in order to persuade Eli to stay and be an activist. "They're opening up Seminole land," Cuz says, "for White settlers and Northern industrialists, not for we": a sure sign that there'll be an escalation of White-on-Black and White-on-Red crimes. Geraldine Dunston, who plays the mother of the Christianized Viola, is an actress who appeared in Iverson White's independent film about lynching, resistance, and migration, *Black Exodus.* Her presence adds weight to the antilynching campaign argument of Eli's cousin. The presence of a Native American in the cast, lover of one of the Peazant's granddaughters, drives home the multicultural solidarity theme, earlier sounded in Dash's *Illusions.*

There's a particularly breathtaking moment that occurs on the beach shortly after Nana has stressed the necessity of honoring the ancestors. It's a deep-focus shot. Close in the foreground are the grown-ups. They are facing our way. The men are in swallowtail coats. Some have on homburgs as well. Some are sitting, others standing. Two or three move across the picture plane, coattails buffeted by the breeze. They are talking about the importance of making right choices. Someone says that for the sake of the children they must. We see, across a stretch of sand glinting in the sun in mid-ground, the children playing along the shore. Several of the grown-ups turn to look over their shoulders and in turning, form an open "door." The camera moves through, maintaining crisp focus, and approaches the children, except that the frame rate has slowed, just enough for us to register that the children are the future. For a split second, we seem to go beyond time to a realm where children are eternally valid, are eternally *the* reason for right action. The camera then pulls back, still maintaining crisp focus, as we backtrack across the sand, entering present time again as the grown-ups' conversation claims our attention again. Not virtuosity for virtuosity's sake, the past-present-future confluence is in keeping with film's motive impulse to celebrate continuum.

There are two things remarkable about the take. One, the camera is not stalking the children. I do not know how that usual predatory menace was avoided, but one contributing factor is that the camera is not looking down on them. Two, no blur occurs as is usual in conventional cinema. Throughout *DD*, no one is background scenery for foregrounded egos. The camera work stresses the communal. Space is shared, and the space (capaciousness) is gorgeous. In conventional cinema, camera work stresses hierarchy. Space is dominated by the hero, and shifts in the picture plane are most often occasioned by a blur, directing the spectator's eye, controlling what we may and may not see, a practice that reinscribes the relationships of domination ideology.

When last we were on this Carolina Sea Island terrain in the movies, it was the 1974 Hollywood/Martin Ritt adaptation of *The Water Is Wide*, a nonfiction account by European-American Pat Conroy. In the film a blond, blue-eyed charmer (Jon Voight), come to rehabilitate Black youngsters, is pitted against a stern Black principal (Madge Sinclair) who won't let the children have any fun. The camera is in league with the ingenuous rascal who "teaches" the nine- and ten-year-olds how to brush their teeth. The camera joins the White man in the trees swinging his feet; in foreshortened perspective, it looks like he's penetrating their skulls. When the shots don't look like a mauling, they look like an auction-block frisking as teacher, made to look eight feet tall, looks down into the molars of the upturned, worshiping faces. With Voight as educational missionary in this colonial treatise, the history of forcible removal of children of color from their homes by agents of the European settler regimes in the U.S. (Navajo most especially), Australia (Aborigine), and Africa, eager to indoctrinate them in White-run boarding schools, White foster homes, and White-run mission schools, respectively, is masked. My movie guide books refer to *Conrack* as "a gentle and moving story about a white teacher who goes to help culturally deprived youngsters on a South Carolina island."

There are wonderful moments of the children in Dash's

DD that call to mind the children in Burnett's films. In *Killer of Sheep*, their ubiquity and vitality help keep the "bad luck" incidents, the cracking of the car engine, from being the flat tire on the family outing. The children try to coax Stan out of his job-benumbed state. His wife (Kaycee Moore, who plays Haagar in *DD*) tries to coax him into recognizing her needs. Dinah Washington sings "This Bitter Earth" as they dance. It's hopeless; actress Moore moves out of the frame, frustrated.

At the end of *DD*, Haagar (Kaycee Moore) is also frustrated. Her daughter hops from the boat to ride off into the sunset with her Cherokee lover. What a totally corny and thoroughly wonderful and historic moment it is (shades of Osceola). Though children in Burnett's more recent film *To Sleep with Anger* are not directed as well as previously (why couldn't the camera swivel and pivot rather than have the adult performers continually lift the children as though they were disabled?), there is that great moment on the roof when the young boy throws the pigeon into the air and coaxes it to fly, and the pigeon soars, circles, never leaving the shot, and comes right back. An operative metaphor for home; the home that in fact houses a tension, for the householders thought they had resolved the Southern culture–Northern culture contradiction, only to have Harry (the Danny Glover character) track in all the "hoodoo mess" Haagar of *DD* is eager to flee.

DD has a look of its own. I recall hearing that it was shot in 35mm and reduced to 16mm to reduce graininess. I don't think so. It feels in scope like 70mm or higher, encouraging the spectator's belief in limitless peripheral vision, for indeed a world is being presented. For all the long shots, neither a picture-book nor an unduly distanced feel results. The spaciousness in *DD* is closer to African cinema than to European and Euro-American cinema. People's circumstances are the focus in African cinema, rather than individual psychology. The emphasis placed on individual psychology in dominating cinema deflects our attention away from circumstance. Social inequities, systemic injustices, doctrines and policies of supremacy, are reduced to personal antagonisms. Conflict, then, can be resolved by a shrink, a lawyer, a cop, or a bullet. Not, for example, by revolution.

By the time the unborn Peazant child will come of age in the twenties, the subversive potential of cinema will be in the process of being tapped in this country, by African-Americans in Philadelphia, Kansas, New York, and Texas, and by European-Americans in New York, Philadelphia, and California. By the time U.S., cinema becomes industrialized in California, that potential will have been tamed, will have been brought into line with structures of domination and oppression. But the camera in the hands of Snead, a character who undergoes a transformation from estranged scientist to engaged humanist, and the other two pre-kinescope props, the stereopticon and the kaleidoscope, in the hands of the Peazant women, prompt us to envision what popular narrative, for example, might be like were dread, sin, and evil not consistently and perniciously signified in dominating cinema within a matrix of darkness, blackness, and femaleness. The props and their attachment to particular characters in *DD* keep central the distinctiveness of conscious Black cinéastes in opposition to commercial filmmakers, and in relation to independent Black filmmakers who regard the contemporary independent sphere as a training ground or stepping-stone to the industry, rather than as a space for contestation, a liberated zone in which to build a cinema for social change.

Two Spike Lee performers in key roles—Alva Rodgers as Eula, Tommy Hicks as Snead—are a reminder that Lee, who'd been a member of the Black Filmmakers Foundation alliance in the early eighties, opted for a route not taken by members of the conscious wing of the movement. In harnessing independent strategies with commercial strategies, Lee's been able to situate a range of spectators, often polarized spectators, thereby meeting the demand for social relevance, that is, the illustration of issues and the representation of Black people (without interrogations), and at the same time not letting go of a basically reactionary sensibility (homophobic/misogynistic/patriarchal) that audiences have been trained by the industry and its support institutions to accept as norm, as pleasurable, inevitable.

There's a promo still from *DD* that shows an expanse of beach and sky. A solitary figure in a long dress strolls along the tidemark carrying a tattered parasol. A moist, romantic scene, it's reminiscent of a promo still from *Diva*, the 1982 Beineix film. African-American opera star Wilhelmina Wiggins, in a long dress, holds an umbrella in the dawn drizzle. There's an expanse of gray sidewalk grounded in fog. The solitary figure is surrounded by misty sky and air. End of comparison. *Diva* masks a theft-of-the-Third-World shadow text with a mystery-thriller format cover. Although the young, White, French guy steals her voice and her concert gown, the Diva responds with warmth. Their inexplicable friendship is straight out of the international race-relations files that say we are flattered by rip-off (or, "Everything I Have Is Yours" in the key of F sharp). The happy-go-lucky, roller-skating Vietnamese girl who lives with the romantic White hero in the far-out loft is a character designed to mask French colonialism in Indochina in the past and the more recent terrors of the Vietnam War and Operation Babylift. At war's end, Saigon was like a burning building from which Vietnamese parents lowered their children to safety, never dreaming that those below would equate catching with owning, with having the right to fly them away, give them away, sell them away. "Like puppies," say those who are still petitioning the U.S. government for the return of the stolen children. Many of the 1975–1977 petitioners wound up in the concentration camp at Fort Chaffee, Arkansas.

Larry Clark's 1977 *Passing Through* addresses the issue of rip-off. He uses conventions of the action flick to protest cultural banditry. The kidnap-pursuit-shootout plot is driven by a communal sense of urgency: Black improvisational music must be rescued from the mob-controlled recording industry. *Passing* indicts status quo; *Passing* proposes a solution. An emancipatory impetus informs the ideology the independent film espouses.

The precinematic artifacts in the hands of Snead and

the Peazant women, then, are like the mojo-bound Bible in the hands of the ancestral figure Nana. They speak to the power in our hands. As actress Smart-Grosvenor from the Bill Gunn work bends to kiss the amulet, we are reminded of Gunn's relationship to the independent sphere. Twice in the seventies Bill Gunn, contracted to produce Hollywood formulaic work, slipped the yoke and created instead two works of conscious cinema. His 1973 *Ganja and Hess,* which was supposed to outdo *Blacula,* a 1972 stylish horror film starring William Marshall, did explore the blood myth, and in the bargain fingered capitalism, Christianity, and colonialist Egypto-anthro-archaeo tamperings as the triple-hell horrors.

Gunn's 1975 *Stop!* was supposed to present a modernized Tarzan plot wherein foregrounded Whites undergo rites of passage against the backdrop of "Third World natives." The prototypic films—the Tarzan, Trader Horn, King Solomon's Mines adventures—did not acknowledge the circumstances of the indigenous peoples at all. Their literary sources, the empire literature of the Victorian period, did, but whether apologist (Kipling) or critical (Conrad), no revolutionary alternative was ever envisioned in the Eurocentric approach. In this era, when a revolutionary alternative cannot be denied, the turmoil is used to make dangerous the playing arena in which the White heroes find themselves—as in *In the Year of Living Dangerously,* for example. In *Under Fire,* Russell Price (Nick Nolte) pays no price for breaking an agreement and taking pictures of Sandinistas in the camp, nor for failing to guard the pictures from the murderous mercenary Oates (Ed Harris). Price's "innocence" feeds Oates; and hundreds of Nicaraguans are murdered so that Price can come to consciousness. In *Stop!* Gunn reverses the colonial-oriented relationship of empire dramas. Actual Puerto Rican independistas are foregrounded as the heroes of the text they determine. The White actors' characters and plot premises of the genre supply the motivations for moving around the island. Predictably, both films were placed under arrest, that is, shelved in the studio vaults. Fortunately, Gunn kept the work print of *Ganja and Hess,* and its screening over the years created a sufficient groundswell to buttress his suit against the studio. Shortly before his death, Gunn won full rights to *Ganja and Hess.* Shortly after his death, *Stop!* was released in time for a Whitney show.

As a performer, Gunn appeared in *Ganja and Hess,* and in Kathleen Collins's 1982 independent film *Losing Ground.* The film has two settings: Manhattan, where the main character, a philosophy professor, teaches; Nyack (where Gunn and Collins were neighbors, and where much of *Ganja and Hess* had been shot), where she lives with her husband, a painter (Gunn). A self-controlled woman who has cultivated a resolute rectilinearity in response to both her earthy mother and her Dionysian husband, the professor is looking for change, longs to get loose, find her ecstasy. She finds it when a student filmmaker persuades her to take on the role of a vamp in his version of *Frankie and Johnny.* The artist husband, meanwhile, is dancing it up with a Latina neighbor. There's a wonderful moment when the dancing couple hold still for an excruciating, suspenseful second before dropping into the downbeat of a doo-wop ten-watt blue-bulb yo-mama-ain't-home basement-party memory of a git-down grind-'em-up: the kind of sho-nuff dancing Stan's wife (Kaycee Moore) was looking for in *Killer of Sheep*.

The late pioneer black woman filmmaker Kathy Collins Prettyman was a liberating sign. And the fact that a number of sisters have found their voices in film augurs well for community mental health. The task now is to crash through the cultural embargo that separates those practitioners from both their immediate authenticating audiences and worldwide audiences.

ARE EE ES PEE EE CEE TEE

ARETHA

One of the highpoints in *DD* is a women's validation ceremony. Several characters in the drama need it. Two expressly seek it—Eula, "ruined," and Yellow Mary, despised. From the start, Nana and Eula welcome Yellow Mary into the circle. The other women relatives roll their eyes and mutter at the approach of Yellow Mary and her companion. Actress Verta Mae Smart-Grosvenor (author of the classic cookbook *Kitchen Vibrations: or, The Travel Notes of a Geechee Girl* and librettist of *Nyam: A Food Opera;* the presence of the culinary anthropologist gives authenticity to the Geechee Girl Productions project, not to mention the merciless preparation and presentation of food) delivers the line, "All that yalla wasted," which the others take up to shut their relative out. There are beautiful interactions between Nana and Yellow Mary, in the way they look at each other and touch. The two actresses appeared together fifteen years ago in Gerima's *Bush Mama*. Dorothy, played by Barbara O, rattled by the noise of sirens, neighbors, social workers, and the police, found little comfort in the niggers-ain't-shit-talking neighbor played by Cora Lee Day. And there's a great moment between Yellow Mary and Haagar that comes straight out of Gerima's *Harvest: 3,000 Years*. One of the many memorable scenes in *Harvest* is the long-take walk of the peasant summoned from the fields by the landlord. The camera is at the top of a hill, to the right and slightly behind the murder-mouthing landlord. Without a cut, the peasant tramps across the fields, trudges over to the hill, scrambles up, grabbing at scrub brush, boosting himself on the rocks, and reaches the top, where he's tongue-lashed by the landlord. In *DD*, Haagar stands arms akimbo at the top of a sand dune, giving Yellow Mary what-for. The take is not a long one, but the camera placement is the same as Gerima's. Yellow Mary comes up the dune while the older, married mother of two, who outranks her in this age-respect society, mouths off. Just as Yellow Mary reaches the top, a hundred possibilities registering in her face (will she knock Haagar down, spit in her face, or what?), she gives Haagar a look and keeps on stepping. Hmph.

Eula initiates the validation ritual by chiding the relatives who were ready enough to seek Yellow Mary's help when a cousin needed bailing out of jail, but now slander her. "Say what you got to say," Eli interrupts, impatient. "We couldn't think of ourselves as pure women," Eula recounts, "knowing how our mothers were ruined. And maybe we think we don't deserve better, but we've got to change our way of thinking." Nana contributes wisdom about the scars of the past, then Eula continues, "We all good women." She presents Yellow Mary to the family circle and continues her appeal. "If you love yourself, then love Yellow Mary." Both women are embraced by the family. Then the wind comes up, rippling the water in the basin the elder's feet are being washed in, rippling the waters where the boat awaits for the departing Peazants.

Dash's sisters-seeing-eye-to-eye ritual has its antecedents in *Illusions*. Mignon Dupree (Lonette McKee) is a production executive in a Hollywood studio during the forties. Because of the draft and because she's mistaken for White, the Black woman has an opportunity to advance a self-interested career. That is not her agenda. She proposes that the studio, cranking out movies to boost the war being fought "to make the world safe for democracy," make movies about the Native American warrior clans in the U.S. armed services. The studio heads got no eyes for such a project. All attention is on a problem—the White, blond bombshell star can't sing. A Black woman, Ester Jeeter (Roseanne Katon), is brought in as "the voice." Ester sees Mignon and recognizes who she is. Mignon sees Ester and does not disacknowledge her. Ester is placed behind a screen, in the dark, in a booth, to become the singing voice of the larger-than-life, illuminated starlet on the silver screen. Mignon stands in solidarity with Ester. Unlike the other executives who see the Black woman as an instrument, a machine, a solution to a problem, Mignon openly acknowledges her personhood and their sisterhood.

The genre that Dash subverts in her indictment of an industry that rejects false images (democracy, U.S. fighting troops, the starlet) is the Hollywood story musical, specifically *Singin' in the Rain,* a comic treatment of the Hollywood careers ruined by the "talkies." In *Singin'* there is the obligatory ritual that informs the history of commercial cinema—the humiliation of a (White) woman. While the non-singing star, played by Jean Hagen, is "singing" at a show biz benefit, the stage hands, who resent her fame and fortune, raise the curtain to reveal the singer, played by Debbie Reynolds. Does the Reynolds character stand in solidarity with the humiliated woman? Hell no, it's her big career break. *Singin'* provides Dash with a cinematic trope. Victoria Spivey, Blue Lu Barker, Lena Horne, and other musicians contracted by Hollywood for on-screen and off-screen work provide the actual historical trope, for the Reynolds character image is false too. Behind that image, in the dark, behind a screen, in a booth, was a Black woman. Dash's indictment, as well as her thesis about what cinema could be, carries over from *Illusions* to *DD.* The validation of Black women is a major factor in the emancipatory project of independent cinema.

As Zeinabu Davis often points out, a characteristic of African-American women filmmakers is tribute paid to womanish mentors and other women artists. Ayoka Chenzira, formerly a dancer, produced two shorts based on her training—the 1989 animation *Zajota and the Boogie Spirit,* which chronicles the history of struggle and ends with an image, the drum disguised as a boom box, and the 1979 documentary *Syvilla: They Dance to Her Drum,* a tribute to her dance teacher Syvilla Fort. In 1975, Monica J. Freeman produced a documentary on sculptor Valerie Maynard. In 1976, Cheryl Fabio (of the Black Filmmakers Hall of Fame in Oakland) produced a documentary on her mother, the poet Sarah Fabio. In 1977, Dash based two films on texts by Black women, Alice Walker and Nina Simone. In 1979, Carroll Parrot Blue produced a documentary on artist Varnette Honeywood. In 1981, Kathe Sandler produced a documentary on dance instructor Thelma Hill. In 1985, Michelle Parkerson produced documentaries on singer Betty Carter and on the Sweet Honey in the Rock music troupe. In 1986, Debbie Robinson produced a documentary on four comediennes. In 1987, Davis produced a documentary on trumpeter Clora Bryant. In 1991, Dash collaborated with Jawole Willa Jo Zollar of the dancing/singing/acting performance art group Urban Bush Women to produce *Praise House,* in which the feminine principle is advanced as divine; one of several breathtaking moments involve dance lifts of sisters by sisters. All of these answer the question posed by Abbey Lincoln in the September 1966 issue of *Negro Digest:* "Who Will Revere the Black Woman?"

Roll Call:
Julie Dash, Ayoka Chenzira, Camille Billops, Carole Munday Lawrence, Jackie Shearer, Alile

Sharon Larkin, the late Kathy Collins, Michelle Parkerson, Carroll Parrot Blue, Kathe Sandler, Jesse Maple, Pamela Jones, Yvonne Smith, Elena Featherstone, Zeinabu Davis, Barbara McCullough, Debbie Robinson, Ellen Sumter, Pearl Bowser, Nadine Patterson, Carmen Coustaut, Teresa Jackson, Omomola Iyabunmi, Cheryl Chisholm, Daresha Kyi, Funmilayo Makarah, Ada Mae Griffin, Sandra Sharp, Fronza Woods, Portia Marshall, Carmen Ashurst, Denise Oliver, Gay Abel-Bey, Monica Freeman, Cheryl Fabio, Helene Head, Malaika Adero, Jean Facey, Aarin Burche, Mary Ester, Pat Hilliard, Imam Hameen, Mary Naema Barnette, Shirikana Amia Gerima, Louise Fleming, Ileen Sands, Edie Lynch, Lisa Jones, Barbara O, Madeline Anderson, Yvette Mattern, Darnell Martin, Millicent Shelton, Denise Bird, Desiree Ortiz, Michelle Patton, Stephanie Minder, Claire Andrade Watkins, Annette Lawrence, Linda Gibson, Joy Shannon, Jacqueline Frazier, Sheila Malloy, Sharon Khadijah Williams, Dawn Suggs, Monona Wali, Demetria Royals, Gia'na Garel, Muriel Jackson, Nandi Bowe.

Julie Dash's *Daughters of the Dust* is a historical marker. It's suggestive of what will hallmark the next stage of development—a more pronounced diasporic and Aframcentric orientation. Another marker occurred in the period when *DD* was in the first stage of production—the September 1989 gathering of independents of the Native American, Latina/o-American, African-American, Asian-American, Pacific Islander–American, Middle Eastern–American, and European-American communities. "Show the Right Thing: A National Multicultural Conference on Film and Video Exhibition" was convened by a committee, predominantly women of color, for and about people of color in the independent sphere. Held at New York University, current base of filmmaker Chris Choy, the two-day series of panels on theoretical and practical concerns were presented by people of color practitioners, critics, and programmers from the U.S. the U.K., Canada, and Mexico. In addition to panels and caucuses, hundreds of tapes of film and video were available for screening. The short subject has advanced greatly since the days of the "chasers," when theater managers used them to clear the house after the vaudeville show. Interactions among the all-American assembly at "Show" made clear that the conference title was a double injunction: internally, for responsible practice; externally, for a democratized media.

The "Show" conference, the first gathering of its size on record, was in contradistinction of state policy from the days of Cortez through the days of COINTELPRO to current-day cultural brokers manufacturing hype for the upcoming Quincentenary—keep these people separate and under White tutelage. Coming so soon on the heels of the Flaherty Seminar held in upstate New York that August—a predictably mad proceeding in which colonialist anthroethno types collided with "subject people" who've already reclaimed their image, history, and culture for culturally specific documentaries, animations, features, experimental videos, and critical theory (the program of lectures and screenings of works primarily drawn from the African diaspora was curated by Pearl Bowser; an unprecedented commandeering of the guest curator's program time was used to screen post-glasnost works from Eastern Europe, and the highlight of the usurping agenda was a screening of the spare-no-expense-to-restore Flaherty/Korda colonist work *Elephant Boy*)—"Show the Right Thing" was an opportunity for people of color and their supporters to recognize in each other the power to supplant "mainstream" with "multicultural" in the national consciousness, even as two dozen conglomerates escalate the purchase of the U.S. mind by buying up television stations, radio stations, newspapers, textbook companies, magazines, publishing houses, and film studios that control major production funding, distribution, exhibition, at home and abroad, particularly in neo-colonialist-controlled areas, and continue to exert a profound influence in universities where most filmmakers and critics are trained.

The next stage of development of new U.S. cinema will most certainly be characterized by an increased pluralistic, transcultural, and international sense and by an amplified and indelible presence of women.

BRIEF NOTES

Re: Programming with Daughters of the Dust

PROGRESSIVE REPRESENTATIONS OF THE BLACK WOMAN IN FEATURES
  Haile Gerima's 1974 *Bush Mama* (Ethiopia/U.S.)
  Sharon Alile Larkin's 1982 *A Different Image* (U.S.)
  Menelik Shabazz's 1981 *Burning an Illusion* (U.K.)
  Sankofa Collective's 1987 *The Passion of Remembrance*
    (U.K.)
  (EuraAm) Lizzie Borden's 1983 *Born in Flames* (U.S.)
  Julie Dash's 1991 *DD* (U.S.)

MAPPING HISTORY FROM THE CONTINENT TO WATTS
  Ousmane Sembène's 1977 *Ceddo* (Senegal)
  Sergio Giral's 1976 *The Other Francisco* (Cuba)
  Med Hondo's 1982 *West Indies* (Mauretania/France)
  Raquel Gerber's 1989 *Ori* (Brazil)
  Ayoka Chenzira's 1989 *Zajota and the Boogie Spirit* (U.S.)
  Julie Dash's 1991 *DD* (U.S.)
  Charles Burnett's 1990 *To Sleep With Anger* (U.S.)

ANCESTRAL FIGURES: "AN ELDER DYING IS A LIBRARY
BURNING DOWN"—FYE
  Safi Fye's 1979 *Fad Jal* (Senegal)
  Med Hondo's 1982 *West Indies* (Mauritania/France)
  Euzhan Palcy's 1986 *Sugar Cane Alley* (Martinique/France)
  Larry Clark's 1977 *Passing Through* (U.S.)
  Haile Gerima's 1983 *Ashes and Embers* (Ethiopia/U.S.)
  Julie Dash's 1991 *DD* (U.S.)

WOMAN TO WOMAN: FIVE DOCUMENTARIES AND THREE FEATURES
Julie Dash's 1983 *Illusions* (U.S.)
Camille Billops's 1988 *Suzanne, Suzanne* (U.S.)
Cheryl Chisolm's/National Black Women's Health Project's
  1986 *On Becoming a Woman* (U.S.)
Ngozi Onwurah's 1989 *Body Beautiful* (U.K.)
Camille Billops's 1988 *Older Women Talking About Sex* (U.S.)
Michelle Parkerson's 1980 . . . *But Then, She's Betty Carter*
  (U.S.)
Julie Dash's 1991 *Daughters of the Dust*
Julie Dash's 1991 *Praise House*

ACKNOWLEDGMENTS

TEXTS REFERRED TO:
Toni Morrison's *Tar Baby*, New York: Knopf, 1981
Paule Marshall's *Praisesong for the Widow*, New York:
  Dutton, 1984
Toni Morrison's *Beloved*, New York: Knopf, 1987
Abbey Lincoln's "Who Will Revere the Black Woman," *Negro
  Digest*, September 1966; also in Toni Cade's *The Black
  Woman*, New York: New American Library/Signet, 1970

WRITTEN TEXTS THAT INFORM MY TEXT:
Zeinabu Davis's interview with Julie Dash in *Wide Angle*, Vol.
  13, Nos. 3 & 4 (1991)
Gregg Tate's interview with Julie Dash in the *Village Voice*,
  June, 1991 issue

Pat Collin's *Black Feminist Thought: Knowledge,
Consciousness, and the Politics of Empowerment*, Boston:
Unwin Hyman, Inc., 1990
bell hooks's *Yearning: Race, Gender, and Cultural Politics*,
Boston: South End Press, 1990
Betinna Aptheker's *Tapestries of Life: Women's Work,
Women's Consciousness, and the Meaning of Daily
Experience*, Amherst: University of Massachusetts Press,
1989

SPOKEN TEXTS BY AND GABFESTS WITH:
Cheryl Chisholm on the empowered eye and on colonialist
metaphors
Françoise Pfaff on Tarzan and ethno footage
Eleanor Traylor on the ancestral place motif in African-
American literature
Zeinabu Davis on women paying tribute to women artists
Clyde Taylor (talks, Whitney Museum Program Notes, articles
in *Black Film Review* and elsewhere) on the LA Rebellion.
A. J. Fiedler's lecture-demonstration/screening at the Scribe
Video Center's Producers Showcase program in
Philadelphia, 1991
Ayida Tengeman Mthembe, who will be doing forums on the
relationship between U.S. policy toward Africa and the
representation of Africa, Africans, and African diasporic
people on the commercial screen

LANGUAGE AND
THE WRITER

I want to talk about language, form, and changing the
world. The question that faces billions of people at
this moment, one decade shy of the twenty-first century, is:
Can the planet be rescued from the psychopaths? The per-
sistent concern of engaged artists, of cultural workers, in
this country and certainly within my community, is, What
role can, should, or must the film practitioner, for example,
play in producing a desirable vision of the future? And the
challenge that the cultural worker faces, myself for example,
as a writer and as a media activist, is that the tools of my

trade are colonized. The creative imagination has been colonized. The global screen has been colonized. And the audience—readers and viewers—is in bondage to an industry. It has the money, the will, the muscle, and the propaganda machine oiled up to keep us all locked up in a delusional system—as to even what America is. We are taught to believe, for example, that there is an American literature, that there is an American cinema, that there is an American reality.

There is no American literature; there are American literatures. There are those who have their roots in the most ancient civilizations—African, Asian, or Mexican—and there are those that have the most ancient roots in this place, that mouth-to-ear tradition of the indigenous peoples that were here thousands and thousands of years before it was called America, thousands of years before it was even called Turtle Island. And there is too the literature of the European settlement regime that calls itself American literature.

There is no American cinema; there are American cinemas. There is the conventional cinema that masks its ideological imperatives as entertainment and normalizes its hegemony with the term "convention," that is to say the cinematic practices—of editing, particular uses of narrative structure, the development of genres, the language of spatial relationships, particular performatory styles of acting—are called conventions because they are represented somehow to be transcendent or universal, when in fact these practices are based on a history of imperialism and violence—the violent suppression of any other production of cinematic practices. Eduardo Galeano, the Latin American writer and cultural critic, speaking to this issue of convention and imperialism, once remarked that if Hemingway had been born in Turkey the world would never have heard of Hemingway. That is to say, the greatness of a writer or the greatness of any cultural production is determined by the power of that writer's country.

So there is the commercial cinema; there is also in this country the independent cinema or new American cinema or the new alternative American cinema, and it's being advanced by practitioners, theoreticians, programmers, and supporters of various cultural communities: the African-American community, the Native American community, the American Latino community, the Pacific Rim and American Asian community, and the American European community. And they insist on, or rather by their very existence challenge, the notion that there is only one way to make a film: Hollywood style; that there are only two motives for making films: entertainment and profit; and that there is only one set of critical criteria for evaluating these products. Within that movement there is an alternative wing in this country that is devoted to the notion of socially responsible cinema, that is interested in exploring the potential of cinema for social transformation, and these practitioners continue to struggle to tell the American story. That involves assuming the enormous tasks of reconstructing cultural memory, of revitalizing usable traditions of cultural practices, and of resisting the wholesale and unacknowledged appropriation of cultural items—such as music, language style, posture—by the industry that then attempts to suppress the roots of it—where it came from—in order to sustain its ideological hegemony. And so, there is no single American reality. There are versions, perspectives, that are specific to the historical experiences and cultural heritages of various communities in this country.

Many contemporary independent filmmakers were provoked into picking up the camera and trying to devise filmic equivalents for our cultural and social and political discourse as a result of their encounters with the guardians of English language purity. That is to say, they were moved by the terrorism—systematic, random, institutional, and personal—of those thugs who would have youngsters going through their educational careers believing that they need remedial English, that the language they speak at home may be OK for home but in the real world they are going to have to learn standard English in order to participate in this society. Many of the independent filmmakers have been hearing all their lives that you can't speak Spanish on school grounds, what you're speaking is not standard, is not appropriate, or you Chinese people have got to learn how to speak up and stop squeaking.

Before we get to the issue of what idiom one should speak in, there is the prior struggle of who may speak. The normalization of the term "minority"—for people who are not white, male, bourgeois, and Christian—is a treacherous one. The term, which has an operational role in the whole politics of silence, invisibility, and amnesia, comes from the legal arena. It says that a minority or a minor may not give testimony in court without an advocate, without a go-between, without a mediating something or other, without a professional mouthpiece, without someone monitoring the speaking and the tongue—which is one of the many reasons I do not use the term "minority" for anybody, most especially not myself. The second question is what will be the nature of the tongue? The independent filmmaker, who may not have any particular political agenda, who may not even have coherent politics but simply wishes to tell a story, discovers all too soon that the very conventions—the very tools, practices—in which that filmmaker has been trained were not designed to accommodate her or his story, her or his people, her or his cultural heritage, her or his issues, and that filmmaker will then face a choice: either to devise a new film language in order to get that story told or to have the whole enterprise derailed by those conventions.

If time were to permit it, I would look at the career of Luis Valdez, looking at two films, *La Bamba* and *Zoot Suit,* the first made for so-called crossover audiences, while the second was made for his authenticating audience: the Chicano community. So we can see the difference in film language, the difference in film practices. But we'll jump over that.

The importance of Sembène, as a practitioner, is an occasion for twenty-five years of film talk throughout the African diaspora, indeed throughout world film culture. And Sembène as an exemplary model of persistence and insistence on cultural integrity is at the moment immeasurable. So I'll jump over that and simply call attention to the language of space in Sembène's work. In Hollywood, space is hidden as a rule. For a more cogent, comprehensive, and coherent version of what I'm getting ready to say, I would refer you to an interview conducted in Ouagadougou at the Pan-African film festival in 1989 with Sembène by Manthia Diawara, the African cinema theorist, but here is the short drift: In Hollywood space is hidden. Once you get an establishing shot—Chicago skyline, night, winter—most of the other shots are tight shots. We move up on the speaker, we then shift for a reaction shot, tight space, and the spectator is supposed to do the work and figure out what is happening outside of the frame. But for a people concerned with land, with turf, with real estate, with home, with the whole colonial experience, with the appropriation of space by the elite or by the outsider, the language of space becomes very crucial within the cinematic practice. In *Mandabi,* recall the women in their space: the shadows from the building, the sun, the legs stretched out, the calabashes. We don't have to work to invent or re-create contiguous reality; we are very aware of the space, so that when someone intrudes and messes it all up, a tremendous statement is getting made that resonates historically.

In *Ceddo,* in the re-creation of seventeenth-century Wolof society, we don't get any tight shots because we are very much concerned here with the whole history of the appropriation of space. The king and the spokesman have their space, the imam on the blanket has his space, his people around him have their space. The princess and the *ceddo* are in a particular space, and he even throws a rope on the ground and says, "You stay on that side of the space or I will cut your throat." The Christian missionary is in his space. And then there is the space of future time: the fast-forward space. Further, there's the space when people are being hemmed up, shaved, renamed, and are about to undergo this traumatic experience. Just in front of the hemmed-up folks is a space that Sembène leaves vacant. In a non-African film, that space would be taken up with pictures and actions, namely the affixing of shackles and chains, the building of fires, and the use of branding irons to explain what is going to happen. Sembène leaves that space vacant and moves to the soundtrack. And on the soundtrack we get African-American music; we get spirituals to tell that story that will take place in another space. It's not Wolof music; it's not African music—that's from that other space. Rather, it's African-American music—a moment of diasporic hookup.

DEEP SIGHT AND
RESCUE MISSIONS

I

It's one of those weird winter-weather days in Philly.
I'm leaning against the wall of a bus kiosk in Center
City brooding about this article that won't write itself. Shop-
pers unselfconsciously divest themselves of outer garments,
dumping woolly items into shopping bags. I'm scarfed to the
eyes à la Jesse James, having just been paroled from the dentist. And I'm eager to get back to the 'hood where I've been
conducting an informal survey on assimilation. The term

doesn't have the resonance it once had for me. I'm curious as to why that is.

At the moment, gums aching, I'm sure of only four things: ambivalence still hallmarks the integrationist-vs.-nationalist pull in Amero-African political life; social and art critics still disrespect, generally, actual differences in the pluralistic United States and tend to collapse constructed ones instead into a difference-with-preference sameness, with Whites as major and people of color (POCs) minor; media indoctrination and other strategies of coercive assimilation are endemic, ubiquitous, and relentless as ever; and the necessity of countering propaganda and deprogramming the indoctrinated as imperative as ever. I'm sure also that I am not as linguistically nimble as I used to be when interviewing various sectors/strata of the community, for I've just blown a gabfest on identity, belonging, and integration at the dentist's through an inability to bridge the gap between the receptionist, a working-class sister from the projects, who came of age in the sixties and speaks in nation-time argot, and the new dental assistant, a more privileged sister currently taking a break from Bryn Mawr, who speaks the lingo of postmodern theory.

Across from the bus stop is a new luxury high-rise, a colossus of steel and glass with signs announcing business suites for lease. I wonder who's got bank these days to occupy such digs. Philly is facing economic collapse. Paychecks for municipal workers are often weeks late. The hijacking of neighborhoods by developers, who in turn are being leaned on by the banks, which in turn are being scut-

tled by the robber barons, who in turn are being cornered by
IRS investigators working for the Federal Reserve, whose
covers have been pulled off by Black and Latino task forces,
who in turn are harassed by Hoover's heirs. And while many
citizens are angry about the S & L bailout being placed on
the backs of workers one paycheck away from poverty and
obscurity, they are even more distressed by cuts in social services that have pushed homelessness beyond the crisis point.
I roam my eyes over the building, wondering if the homeless
union would deem it media-worthy for a takeover.

In the lobby of the high-rise is a sister about my age,
early fifties, salt-'n'-pepper 'fro, African brass jewelry, a
woolly capelike coat of an Andean pattern. She's standing
by a potted fern, watchful. She seems to be casing the joint.
I get it in my head that she's a "checker," a member of a
community group that keeps an eye on HUD and other
properties suitable for housing the homeless. A brisk-
walking young sister emerges from the bank of elevators.
Briefcase tucked smartly under one elbow, coat draped over
the left Joan Crawford shoulder pad, hair straight out of a
Vidal Sassoon commercial, the sister strides past the visitors-
must-sign-in information counter, and the older woman approaches her. I search for a word, rejecting "accosts,"
"buttonholes," "pounces," and "confronts," but can't find
a suitable verb for the decisiveness and intensity of the older
woman's maneuver. Obviously strangers, they nonetheless
make short shrift of amenities and seem to hunker down to
a heavy discussion forthwith, the older sister doing most of
the talking. She's not panhandling. She's not dispensing lit-

erature of any kind. She doesn't reach over to pin a campaign button on the Armani lapel. But she's clearly on a mission. What kind of scam, then, could it be? And if not a scam, what?

I now get it in my head that the older sister is Avey Johnson, sprung from the pages of Paule Marshall's 1983 novel *Praisesong for the Widow.* Avey, having rejected her deracinated life of bleached-out respectability in White Plains, New York, fashions a new life's work, taking up a post in buildings such as the high-rise to warn bloods of the danger of eccentricity and to urge them to (re)center themselves and work for the liberation of the people. I'm so certain it's Avey, I move away from the wall to go get in it. My daughter's voice chimes in my ear: "Mother, mind your own business." I head for the curb, muttering my habitual retort: "Black people are my business, sugar." A youngblood on a skateboard zooms by. His bulky down jacket, tied around his hips by the sleeves, brushes against my coat and stops me. The No. 23 bus is approaching. So is rush hour. And who knows how swiftly and mean the weather will turn any second. I board.

From my seat, I watch the briefcase sister spin out the revolving doors onto the sidewalk. She seems preoccupied, unsure, but not about whether to put on her coat. She walks to the corner. Her gait is no longer brisk. Her suit has lost its crispness. She swivels around, though, like a runway model and looks through the glass of the lobby. The older woman has a brother backed up against the newspaper rack. She's taken a wide-legged stance, coat swept back from her hips, fists planted on the rise of the bones, neck working, mouth going. He holds his attaché case in front of him with both hands as though to fend her off. The light changes and the bus moves on.

In *Praisesong,* it's the power of a handed-down tale that rescues Avey from an inauthentic life, from the bad bargain she made early on, surrendering up cultural authenticity in exchange for separate-peace acceptability. Through the tale's laying-on-of-hands potency, Avey undergoes a process of reading the signs and codes, a refamiliarization with blackness that releases the power of nommo and grounds her, so that she can adopt a responsible life. The tale is still told today in the Georgia and Carolina Sea Islands. The self-same tale informs too Julie Dash's 1991 screen masterpiece *Daughters of the Dust.*

In the opening of the independent black feature film, a boat glides into view. The terrain looks tropical. Dragonflies hover over the green-thick water. At the prow of the boat stands a woman in a large, veiled, creamy white hat. She wears a long, heavy, creamy white dress. This image is straight out of a million colonialism-as-fun movies. But this woman is standing hipshot, one arm akimbo, cocked chin, all attitude. These ebonics signal the spectator that Sister Dash has appropriated the iconography from imperialist entertainment for an emancipatory purpose. The boat pulls into the shallows, where a carving of an African, a figure once attached to the prow of a slaver ship, bobs close to shore. The boat docks. A legend appears on screen: "Ibo

Landing, 1902." Thereafter, the handed-down tale of the Ibos unfolds as part of the film's complex narrative.

When the boat brought the Ibos from the slaver ship, the story goes, the Africans stepped out onto the sand in their chains, took one look around, and with deep-sight vision saw what the Europeans further had in store for them, whereupon they turned right around and walked all the way home on the water to the motherland. In *Daughters*, various members of the Peazant family, gathered on a Carolina island for a final reunion picnic before migration splits them up, react to the tale in different ways. Several characters, urged by Nana, the family head, to remember, to resist amnesia, to take with them on their journey away from the ancestral place the faculty for deep-sight vision, draw strength from the story, as does Avey Johnson in the novel. "My body may be here," Avey's great-great-grandmother had said, passing along the tale, "but my mind's long gone with the Ibos." *Daughters*, like *Praisesong*, invites the viewer, the reader, to undergo a process to liberate the imperialized eye.

The No. 23 bus, heading for Chinatown, first cuts through a district that community workers call the Zone of Diminishing Options. In the three-block area around Race and Ninth streets are pawnshops that also sell used clothes, labor-pool agencies advertising dishwashing jobs in the Atlantic City casinos, a very busy blood bank, a drop-in shelter, the Greyhound terminal, an army recruiting office, and a hospice center. While draft counseling in the Zone, I'd often think of opening a gun shop, if only to disrupt the perverse visual gag. And while in the Zone, I caught a third of a provocative independent black film called *Drop Squad*. A community worker, cassette in hand, persuaded a pawnshop owner to play it on a set in the window.

Written by David Taylor, produced by Butch Robinson, and directed by David Johnson, *Drop Squad* is a satire about hijacking the hijacked. A nationalist organization puts the snatch on an assimilated corporate blood, straps him down in a chair in a red-black-and-green-draped community center, and proceeds to try to deprogram him. "You need to reacquaint yourself with you, brother," they tell him, assigning him to read Toni Morrison's *The Bluest Eye*. They take turns chanting a roll-call reveille: Soul Train, Garvey, Eleanor Bumpurs, Revolutionary Action Movement, Biko, Fannie Lou Hamer, W. E. B. Du Bois, Sharpeville, Billie Holiday, Frantz Fanon. They argue, threaten, cajole, insist, are determined to wake the brother up. He counters with equal passion for the individual right to be whatever and whomsoever he pleases. Frequently his arguments are sound, momentarily stumping his captors. But they are relentless in their campaign to call the brother home, to reclaim him for the collective mission of race recovery. Privileged as he has become through people's struggles, they argue that he has a debt both to himself and to his community blasted by drugs, violence, joblessness, homelessness, lack of access, and the politics of despair.

I reach Germantown. The Hawk, out now and bold, blows me toward the greengrocer on Chelten. Worker Khan Nguyen has been discussing assimilation for me with her customers, especially Vietnamese and African and East Indian Caribbeans new to the U.S. She reports that assimilation is synonymous with citizenship training. It's her take that while folks know that the intent of the training is to "domesticate" them, the emphasis on democracy and rights makes them "wildly expectant." Khan winks. She has not been tamed by the process. "It may be naïve of me," she says, warming to the subject, but the fact that "new immigrants take democracy more seriously" than it is generally practiced in a society built on theft and bondage, riddled by a white-supremacist national ideology, motivated by profit and privilege, and informed by fascist relations between classes, races, sexes, and communities of various sexual orientations, cultural heritages, and political persuasions, "means that, in time, they will become unruly." She leans on the phrase "in time," because I am frowning. I ask about citizenship as a bribe contract: we'll grant you citizenship, and in return you drop your cultural baggage and become "American," meaning defend the status quo despite your collective and individual self-interest. She repeats the phrase "in time," putting her whole body into it to drown me out. I stumble out of there, hugging a bottle of Jamaican vanilla extract (excellent wash for cleaning/deodorizing the refrigerator, by the by), hopeful.

I run into a young friend, Anthony (Buffalo Boy) Jackson, graffiti artist and comic-book-maker. I ask for his help, easing into the topic by explaining "assimilation" as I first encountered it in Latin (the changing of letters to make them sound in accord with letters nearby, i.e., *adsimilare* in Latin becomes *assimilare, excentricus* in Medieval Latin or *ekken-tros* in Greek becomes *eccentric* in English) and bio (the process by which the body converts food into absorbable substances for the maintenance of the system). Before I can get to the sociopolitical meaning, Anthony is off and running with "system," recounting a middle-school field trip to a marsh in the New Jersey Pine Barrens to study ecosystems. He loses me, but I chime in when I hear usable things like "symbiosis" and "parasites," and finally the ability of the amoeba to give alternate responses to its environment because of its shape-shifting ability.

"Hold it, Anthony, are you saying amoebas can transform the system? I mean, err-rahh, are they capable of collective action or are they basically loners?"

My friend is dancing and laughing at me. "The amoeba shall overthrow, right?" Big joke.

I walk him toward Burger King 'cause now he has an idea—the amoeba as mantua, shape shifter, ninja—and the tables are big enough to spread out on. I bring him back to my needs, and he tells me the issue is rip-off, not assimilation.

"Everything we do," he says, meaning breaking, scratching, rapping, dressing, "gets snatched up and we get bumped off." Which is why, he explains, he admires Spike Lee, because of Lee's control over the films and especially over the spin-offs that come out of Forty Acres and a Mule—CDs, books, T-shirts, mugs, caps, jackets. He ducks inside and shakes his head about me. I'm old enough to know what the deal is, and the deal is rip-off.

Down the block, toward Wayne Avenue, is a produce truck where people frequently gather to talk over the news of the day. Trucker Mr. Teddy, a blood from Minnesota, tells me that only Europeans were invited to become truly assimilated. "And assimilation went out when *Roots* came in and busted up the whole melting-pot con game." According to him, nobody's been melted—not Norwegians, not Germans, not Japanese, and definitely not Africans. He talks about the Swedes in the Midwest who, in reclaiming their heritage, particularly their seventeenth-century socialist tradition, have rejected assimilation. "Hmm," sez I, and venture to ask if these unmelted Amero-Europeans he speaks of reject as well their race/skin privileges, the socio-eco-political and psychic profits derived from U.S. apartheid. "Now that would be un-Amurrican." He chuckles and slam-dunks a cabbage into my bag.

Across the avenue in front of the newsstand where folks are lined up to buy lottery tickets, the daily floor show is in progress. It features an old white guy who shuffles along the strip panhandling from the newsstand, past the wall bordering the Super Fresh, past the Woolworth, to the area near the bank where vendors line the curbs all the way down to Germantown Avenue, where I got off the No. 23. Some black people derive great pleasure from helping a down-and-out white person. The same pleasure, I suspect, that film-buff friends of mine enjoy watching a wrecked Chet Baker fall totally apart on screen in the docu *Let's Get Lost*. There are always folks about, fingering the videotapes on the tables—today *Highlights of the Clarence*

Thomas–Anita Hill Hearings is selling for eight dollars—who crack on the generous-minded who give money to panhandling whites. "Christian duty my ass! Let that ole cracker beg in his own neck of the woods." But the consensus notion is that Old Whiteguy is pretty much in his neck of the woods, that he lives, in fact, in posh quarters on Wissahickon Avenue. Should anyone voice that, they are charged with being proracist, at least stereotypic in thinking that all white people are well-off. "Well-off or not," someone is saying as I reach the performing arena, "he's getting fat off black people." That remark triggers a mention of Jim Crow, talking low, and slavery. So a few people make a point of jostling the old man. Should anyone object and call the behavior racist, as in reverse racism, that provokes still another discussion: that some in the race seem to live outside of history and don't appreciate the fact that a race war is going on and that it wasn't bloods who declared it; whereupon statistics are ticked off about infant mortality, life expectancy, illiteracy, unemployment, and other aspects of the war. Meanwhile, Old Whiteguy is steadily collecting loose change, wending his way toward a sister who vends around our way only occasionally.

I don't know her name yet, but I admire her titles: Sam Yette's *The Choice,* Chancellor Williams's *The Destruction of Black Civilization,* and everything that Angela Davis ever published. Should a youth bedecked in gold try to get past her, she'll beckon her/him over and give a mini-workshop on black miners in South Africa, apartheid, and the international gold trade. Should a youngblood stroll by in a Malcolm T-shirt ("By Any Means Necessary") she will get very generous with her wares. Old Whiteguy is another matter.

"You want a what—a quarter!?!" she says. "I'll give you a quarter." Images of Old Whiteguy tied to two horses being lashed in opposite directions flood my dentist-traumatized brain. She looks him up and down and says quite seriously, "Hey, you used to be a young peckerwood, so why ain't you president?" He grins his drooly grin, hand still stuck out. Book Sister turns to the incense seller in a crocheted cufi at the next table. "Come get this clown before I'm forced to hurt him."

Before dark, I reach home, a co-op whose comfy lobby I'd thought would ensure me neighbors enough for a round-table discussion on this article. But the lobby's empty. I drop in on my neighbor Vera Smith. She takes a hard line on both aggressive assimilationists and seemingly spaced denialists, folks quick to call behavior manifested by Book Sister and jostlers as racist, folks who swear that things are all right, or would be all right if Black people weren't so touchy, mean, and paranoid. I say something like "consciousness requires a backlog of certain experiences." Vera ain't going for it. From day one, she says, there's enough evidence around to peep the game and resist. "So it's a decision to be like that," she says. "And it takes a lot of energy to deny what's obvious." Denialists don't want to see, don't want to belong, don't want to struggle, says Vera, putting a pin in it.

We talk into the night about a lot of things. A first-generation U.S. Bajun, she shares with me her plan to have dual citizenship, from the U.S. which she automatically has, and from Barbados also. I'm profoundly pleased for her, and for us, for whenever a Br'er Rabbit slip-the-yoke operation can be achieved, it puts another plank underfoot at home *base*.

I ride the elevator, thinking about people I've known growing up (not that all these years aren't my formative years) who worked tirelessly to maintain a deep connection with the briar patch and its ways of being. No matter where they journeyed in the world or what kinds of bribes they were offered to become amnesiacs, they knew their real vocation was to build home base, sanctuaries, where black people can stand upright, exhale, and figure out what to do about the latest attack. And so they kept faith with the church of their childhood, or the UNIA or Father Divine movement (both alive and well in Philly, by the by), or the family farm in Alabama, or the homestead in the Islands, sending money, cement, clothing, books, lumber, weapons, certain that home base is not where you may work or go to school, but where the folks are who named you daughter, daddy, mama, doctor, son, brother, sister, partner, dahlin', chile.

I rinse my ravaged mouth out with warm salt water and hit the keyboard. As my young friend said, the issue is rip-off. Invisibility is not a readily graspable concept for a generation that grew up on MTV, Cosby, Oprah, Spike Lee, Colin Powell, and black folks on soaps, quiz shows, and the nightly news. Not only are black folks ostensibly participating—so what the hell does invisibility mean?—but what is generally recognized at home and abroad as "American" is usually black. A hundred movies come to mind, but not their titles, sorry. For instance, the one about two lost young Euro-Ams who find themselves in what they think is a time warp, the terrain woefully fiftyish, but discover that they've landed in a Soviet spy school, in an American village erected for the purpose of training infiltrators to pass as "American." The two are enlisted to update and authenticate the place and the curriculum. Everything they present as "American"—music, speech, gesture, style—is immediately identifiable, certainly to any black spectator, as black.

As for alienation, or as Dr. Du Bois limned it in numerous texts, double-consciousness and double vision, people coming of age in a period hallmarked by all-up-in-your-face hip-hop and an assertive pluralism/multiculturalism as well don't see barriers as a policy as old as Cortez, as deadly as COINTELPRO, as seductive as the Chris Columbus hype chugging down the pike, and more solid than the Berlin Wall, given the system's monstrous ability to absorb, co-opt, deny, marginalize, deflect, defuse, or silence.

I don't know what goes on in classrooms these days, but in informal settings the advice of the Invisible Man's granddaddy, "Undermine 'em with grins," is inexplicable Tomism. The paradoxical paradigm of the Liberty paint factory episode in Ellison's novel, the necessity of mixing in black to concoct pure white, is just a literary joke thought up by some old-timey guy on an equally old-timey typewriter. The three aspects of alienation as traditionally experienced and understood by my elders, my age group, and the generation that came of age in the sixties—alienation from the African past (and present—Was there ever an American airline with direct flights to the motherland?), alienation from U.S. economic and political power, alienation from the self as wholly participating in history—don't register as immediately relevant.

I spend a fitful night fashioning questions to raise with myself in the morning. What characterizes this moment? There's a drive on to supplant "mainstream" with "multicultural" in the national consciousness, and that drive has been sparked by the emancipatory impulse, blackness, which has been the enduring model for other down-pressed sectors in the U.S. and elsewhere. A repositioning of people of color (POCs) closer to the center of the national narrative results from, reflects, and effects a reframing of questions regarding identity, belonging, community. "Syncretism," "creolization," "hybridization" are crowding "assimilation," "alienation," "ambivalence" out of the forum of ideas. A revolution in thought is going on, I'm telling myself, drifting off. Modes of inquiry are being redevised, conceptual systems overturned, new knowledges emerging, while I thrash about in tangled sheets, too groggy to turn off the TV.

It drones on about Maxwell, the publishing baron who allegedly went over the side of his private yacht at two in the morning. All commentary reduced to the binary, as is typical of thought in the "West": suicide or homicide? I smirk in my sleep, sure that Maxwell used a proxy corpse and is alive and chortling in, say, Belo Horizonte, Brazil. Jim Jones, no doubt, is operating, courtesy of the CIA's answer to the Witness Relocation Program.

Still half-asleep, I rummage around in dualisms which

keep the country locked into delusional thinking. The Two-Worlds obsession, for example: Euro-Ams not the only book reviewers that run the caught-between-two-worlds number into the ground when discussing works by Maxine Hong Kingston, Leslie Marmon Silko, Rudolfo Anaya, and other POCs, or rather, when reducing complex narrative dramas by POCs to a formula that keeps White World as a prominent/given/eternal factor in the discussion. Two-Worlds functions in the cultural arena the way Two-Races or the Black-and-White routine functions in the sociopolitical arena. It's a bribe contract in which Amero-Africans assist in the invisibilization of Native Americans and Chicanos in return for the slot as *the* "indigenous," the former slaves who were there at the beginning of the great enterprise called America.

The limits of binary opposition were in evidence in a manuscript I'd been reading on the way to the dentist's office. Articles that called Black cinema "oppositional cinema" to Hollywood totally ignored practitioners operating in the independent circuit, and focused instead on Spike Lee, Matty Rich, John Singleton, Joe Vasquez, and Mario Van Peebles—filmmakers who take, rather than oppose, Hollywood as their model of filmmaking. The articles reminded me of the way the establishment press during the so-called Spanish-American War labeled the gung-ho, shoot-'em-up, Manifest-Destiny-without-limits proponents as imperialists, and the let's-move-in-in-the-name-of-hemispheric-hegemony proponents as anti-imperialists. Meanwhile, only the Black press was calling for a genuine help-liberate-then-cooperate-not-dominate anti-imperialism. All that is to say, there are at least three schools of Black filmmaking in the U.S.: that which produces within the existing protocol of the entertainment industry and may or may not include a critique (Fred Williamson, for example); that which uses enshrined genres and practices but disrupts them in order to release a suppressed voice (Spike Lee, for example, who freed up the B-boy voice in his presentations, not to be confused with interrogations, offering a critique of U.S. society but not rising above its retrograde mindset re women and homosexuals in order to produce a vision); and that which does not use H'wood as its point of departure, but is deliberate and self-conscious in its commitment to building a socially responsible cinema, fashioning cinematic equivalents for our sociopolitical/cultural specificity and offering transformation dramas (Julie Dash, Haile Gerima, Larry Clark, and other insurgents of "La Rébellion," who, in the late sixties, drafted a declaration of independence in the overturning of the UCLA film school curriculum).

The limits of binary thinking are spooky enough, I'm thinking, as the birds begin, but what are the prospects for sound sense in the immediate future now that conglomerates have escalated their purchase on the national mind? Since the 1989 publication of the Chomsky-Herman tome and the fall 1991 issues of *Media Fair*, which drew a scary enough picture of media control by white men of wealth, the noose has tightened. And today seventeen corporations own more than 50 percent of U.S. media—textbook companies, newspapers, magazines, TV stations, radio stations, publishing houses, film-production companies. And computerization makes it all the easier to expunge from available reference material those figures, movements, and lessons of the past that remind us that radicalism is also a part of the U.S. tradition. Without models, how does any citizen break out of the basic dualism that permeates social, educational, political, economic, cultural, and intimate life in this country? I refer to the demonic model abridged below:

We are ordained	You are damned
We make history	You make dinner
We speak	You listen
We are rational	You are superstitious, childlike (as in minor)
We are autonomous and evolved	You are shiftless, unhinged, underdeveloped, primitive, savage, dependent, criminal, a menace to public safety, are needy wards and clients but are not necessarily deserving
We live center stage, the true heroes (and sometimes heroines)	You belong in the wings or behind the scrim providing the background music

We are pure, noble, upright	You are backward, fallen, tainted, shady, crafty, wily, dark, enigmatic, sly, treacherous, polluted, deviant, dangerous, and pathological
We are truly human	You are grotesques, beasts, pets, raisins, Venus flytraps, dolls, vixens, gorillas, chicks, kittens, utensils
We were born to rule	You were born to serve
We own everything	Even you are merely on loan to yourself through our largess
We are the dicks	You are the pussies
We are entitled	You are obliged

I slap the alarm clock quiet and roll over, pondering my own journey out of the lockup. Pens crack under me, paper rustles. When in doubt, hew close to the autobiographical bone, I instruct myself. But my own breakout(s) from the lockup where Black/woman/cultural worker in the binary scheme is a shapeless drama with casts of thousands that won't adhere to any outline I devise. I opt instead for a faux family portrait to narrate what I can't essay.

II

SPLIT VISION AND
AMERICA THE BEAUTIFUL

José Feliciano is on the radio singing "Ohhh beautiful for spacious skies." Everyone holds still, alert to meaning in each stressed note, breath, and strum. Elbows on the table, Aunt Clara studies the pattern of kernels in her corn on the cob as Feliciano builds, reining in his passion then unleashing it. Cousin Claude, the barbecue fork his baton, stands on tiptoe to hit the high notes. "America, America" comes out in preposterous falsetto, but nobody laughs or complains. Fragments of the tune, raspy and off-key, snag in the throat of Granddaddy Daniels. He leaves off singing to say that nobody lets loose on "America" like Aretha or Ray Charles. It takes a blood to render the complex of longing, irony, and insistence that characterizes our angular relationship to this country.

The song over, Cousin Claude forgets he came indoors to take orders; he drifts around the living room while the burgers burn out back. Aunt Clara makes pulp of her corn on the cob; the attack has less to do with food, more with what a hunger the song has stirred up. Granddaddy Daniels clears his throat, spits phlegm into a hanky, then makes a big production out of folding the paper and backing it to the crossword puzzle. The youngsters on the floor doing homework lean in the old man's direction. Clearing the throat is usually a prelude to storytelling, but his pencil point keeps piercing the newsprint, a signal that he's not in a storying mood about, say, why he never rises when "The Star-Spangled Banner" is sung at the stadium, but will shush everybody and strain forward when a "cullid person" is doing the hell out of "America, the Beautiful." Eventually he bobs his head up and down and says that the Latino brother kicked much butt.

Cousin Claude waltzes into the kitchen and dances one of the Moten sisters away from the chopping board. He's humming the last few lines of the song, his lips tucked in and "brotherhood" growling in the throat, then ricocheting off the roof of his mouth, the final notes thin and trailing out to sea as, the dance over, he bows and heads through the door. The Moten twins, "healthy" women who cook in their black slips and stockinged feet, resume arguing about whether or not hard-boiled eggs are going into the potato salad this day, goddamnit.

Cousin Claude goes down the back steps one at a time like a child. He ponders aloud the mystery and history of Africans in the U.S. The elders, squinched together on the back-porch glider, call out, "Shut up," "Preach," or "Your food's on fire, Sugah," depending on how worked up they wish to get on the subject. When the call-and-response reaches a pitch, drowning out the DJ on the radio overhead in the kitchen window, Cousin Claude tries, without success, to lure the elders into a discussion of his childhood days when the household wars between the Danielses and the Motens threatened to split the family up and drive all the children crazy.

WAR ONE:

ASSIMILATION VS. TRANSFORMATION

It was Great-Aunt Zala, a Daniels, who would shake us awake when Mr. Paul came calling. We'd scramble up and brace ourselves against each other in order to reach our assigned-by-age positions on the horsehair couch that my daddy, a Moten, went and bought anyway during the 1930s Don't-Buy-Where-You-Can't-Work campaign in Harlem. Legs stuck out, heels hooked in the welting that edged the cushions, we'd manage not to yawn, suck our thumbs, or otherwise disgrace ourselves in front of a race man or race woman, who always seemed to come in the night to do their talking.

Some of the grown-ups didn't think children should be privy to conversations about the state of the race—our struggles, our prospects, our allies, our enemies. They kept us away from Speakers' Corner, union halls, poetry readings, outdoor rallies, tenant meetings, and even our own basement, where longshoremen—"Negroes," West Indians, Puerto Ricans, and Cubans—would meet to strategize against the bosses, landlords, merchants, union sellouts, cops, the FBI, the draft board, Immigration, Murder Incorporated, and other white forces in easy collusion when it came to keeping colored folks down.

The less the children know, the easier it'll be for them to fit in and make their way, seemed to be the thinking of half the household. They lobbied for lobotomy, in other words, convinced that ignorance was the prime prerequisite for assimilation, and assimilation the preferred path to progress. But Great-Aunt Zala went right on opening the door to Robeson, Du Bois, Claudia Jones, Rose Garner, J. A. Rogers, the Sleeping Car Porters and Maids, the dockworkers, and members of the Ida B. Wells clubs. The woman would just not let us sleep.

War Two:
Repatriation vs. Self-Determination

Cousin Claude entered high school the year of the World's Fair in New York. Grown, to hear him tell it, he had the right to join the Garveyites collecting signatures on a petition demanding reparations from the government and rematriation to the motherland. On April 24, 1939, the petition, signed by 2.5 million African souls, was introduced into Congress. Claude's mother, Aunt Billy, let it be known that she wasn't going no damn where on account of (a) she was part Narragansett on her father's side, (b) she was grandchild of many an enslaved African whose labor had further purchased her place in this land, (c) what was the point in going over there when the thing to do was to fight the good fight over here and change the government's policies that made life here and there and everywhere unbearable for colored people.

By freeing up this country from the robber barons and their brethren in sheets, the argument went, we'd free up half the world. So the first thing was to work hard and develop a firm base here from which to challenge the state. Forget this place, was Uncle Charlie's position; in Africa, we could build bigger armies with which to defeat colonialists and imperialists. Yeah, tell it to freedmen in Liberia slaving on Firestone's plantations, Aunt Billy would say right back. The children were drawn into the debates. Posters made from board-of-education oaktag filled the halls of the brownstone: "Back to Africa vs. Self-Determination in the Black Belt and the Rest of the Planet." Arguments waxed hot. Kinship loyalties frayed. Even after Congress tabled the bill and turned its attention to the war raging in Europe, there was no sleeping in that house.

WAR THREE:

SWING-VOTE POLITICS

VS. INDEPENDENT FORMATIONS

After what the black press called "Fighting the Two Hitlerisms" at home and abroad, the Cold War chill set in, which we, in Harlem, experienced as heat—HUAC ushering in a new Inquisition. Patriotism against Hitler made the blacks-as-inferior line too blatant, as Gerald Horne points out in his work on Du Bois, *Black and Red.* Blacks-as-subversives became the new line. We experienced a crackdown on thinkers, speakers, writers, organizers, and coalition builders. Independent thought was a threat to national security, the state mouthpieces said at the Smith Act trials.

The household split into ever-shifting factions over the 1948 presidential election. Play ward politics for local spoils and concessions and never mind the "big picture" vs. hitch our collective wagon to the NAACP and bloc vote vs. Up the Party! and Down with HUAC! vs. build the American Labor

169

Party and campaign for Henry Wallace vs. establish an independent black national party and to hell with all this switch-hitting that only keeps us locked into other people's tournaments.

An insomniac at twenty-two, Cousin Claude began reading everything he could get his hands on, haunting the Micheaux Liberation Memorial Bookstore on 125th street and Seventh Avenue and haunting us too, day and night. He took to quizzing his less-than-peers at the kitchen table: Did we know about Palmares, the sovereign nation self-emancipated Africans in Brazil created? Did we know about the maroon communities in the Sea Islands off the Georgia and Carolina coasts? Did we know that Oklahoma was going to come into the union as either an "Indian" state or a "Negro" state? Did we have any idea how stupid we were? If we weren't going to improve our minds, would we kindly change our names?

Cousin Claude was reading Du Bois as well, who in 1948 had just been bounced for the second time in fifteen years from the NAACP. Cousin Claude took to waking us up at night for our opinion of Dr.'s divided-self proposition: should we invest our time, energy, money, and African genius struggling to become first-class citizens in an insanely barbarous country whose majority despises both us and our efforts to humanize the place; or should we gather our genius together and create a society of our own, in this country or someplace else? Not an elder yet, Cousin Claude could be told to get lost and let us rest. But being a Daniels, he never did.

III

WHITE SIGHT AND THE BEE
IN THE HEXAGON

When I first ran across Dr. Du Bois's passage as a girl, I had a problem straightaway. It conflicted with what I'd learned early on through sight. Several, to prove their loyalty to America, enlisted and helped kill Japanese and other members of the Axis powers. I can't say for sure whether he said those volunteers manifested the gravest forms of White sight or not, because we mostly liked to talk about the Japanese-American battalions and African-American units that liberated the German concentration camps and how the State Department was determined to keep the participation of colored people secret. So in the newsreels we only saw White heroism. It was propaganda designed to promote White sight, we instructed each other.

Frenchy, a neighborhood friend whose bio homework I used to do in exchange for safe passage through the neighborhood, especially through Morningside Park, was a member of the Chapmans and used to refer to a moment in gang rumbling as white sight. Say you've been cold-cocked from behind. Your eyeballs commence to roll up in your head like they're seeking asylum in the mass of neuromelanin surrounding the pineal gland. You definitely need to get to Sydenham or Harlem Hospital. You could have brain damage. You could die.

According to Dear Diary, I'd been at camp shortly before reading the passage in *Souls of Black Folk*, and bees were very much on my mind. So while I was reading about the affliction of viewing the self from an outside and unloving vantage point, Dr.'s "veil" began to take on the look of one of those wood-frame screens beekeepers slide down into the apiary so as to collect the honey from the caged-up bees. Dr.'s seventh son sounded like he needed to see a healer, a seer, someone whose calling was to pierce that screen that somebody, who clearly does not wish the seventh son well, shoved down split the self, because they wanted his sweetness. And his eyes.

By the time I read the passage again, I had experienced enough to know that I needed my eyes, my sweetness, and my stingers. I did not know, though, that I'd already become addicted to the version of the world and my community as promoted by Hollywood movies. I merely noticed that race movies, like race records, were no longer on the scene. But I did not fully appreciate that my celluloid jones made me as up for grabs as a sleeping bee. I interpreted "twoness" as the split-vision struggle I thought I was valiantly waging to stay centered in the community's core-culture perspective and at the same time excel in the schools and various chump-change workplaces. I got poleaxed. I got sandbagged and *sanpakued*. I got stuck in the mask. I lost my eyes. I became unmoored.

But blessed, as many of us are, I never left the gaze of the community; that is, folks did not avert their eyes from me. And so I did not stay caged up long in secondary consciousness (Dr. says second sight) or false consciousness (as opposed to primary consciousness, or what Dr. calls true self-consciousness); at least not chronic not-consciousness-hood. For in the community, then as now, were at least four discernible responses to the way in which we are positioned in the U.S.: accommodation, opportunism, denial/flight, and resistance. Long before I learned to speak of these responses as "tendencies," I encountered the living examples, neighbors.

Accommodationists recommended that I read (not to be confused with analyze) White we-are-great books and Negro we-too-are-clean-so-please-White-folks-include-us-in works, and that I speak good English and stay off the streets. Opportunists taught me how to move through the streets and capitalize on the miserable and gullible, 'cause what the hell, the point was to beat Whitey at his own game, which was, don't you know?, taking off Black folks. The I-have-never-experienced-prejudice-in-the-all-White-school-and-church-I-attend types urged me not to regard as belligerent every racial encounter, for there were good White people if I looked hard enough and overlooked some of their ideas. All of which was helpful for "breaking the ice" at camps, integrating ballet schools, "proving" we were not what Dem said we were. Of course, many of us did not understand then how dangerous a proposition proving could be. James Baldwin put his mighty mouth on it a bit later, though talking to Dem: "If I'm not who you say I am, then you're not who you say you are. And the battle is on!"

While others saw in me an icebreaker, a lawbreaker, or a potential credit to the race, neighborhood combatants saw something else and spent a great deal of time, energy, and imagination encouraging and equipping me to practice freedom in preparation for collective self-governance (the very thing Hoover and the Red Squads called a danger to the national security—Black folks thinking they had the capacity to rule themselves). I became acquainted with Black books that challenged, rather than mimicked, White or Negro versions of reality. I became acquainted with folks who demonstrated that their real work was creating value in the neighborhoods—bookstores, communal gardens, think tanks, arts-and-crafts programs, community-organizer training, photography workshops. Many of them had what I call second sight—the ability to make reasoned calls to the community to create protective spaces wherein people could theorize and practice toward future sovereignty, while at the same time watching out for the sharks, the next wave of repression, or the next smear campaign, and preparing for it.

Insubordinates, dissidents, iconoclasts, oppositionists, change agents, radicals, and revolutionaries appealed to my temperament and my earliest training at home. They studied, they argued, they investigated. They had fire, they had analyses, they had standards. They had respect for children, the elders, and traditions of struggle. They imparted language for rendering the confusing intelligible, for naming the things that warped us, and for clarifying the complex and often contradictory nature of resistance.

Through involvement in tenants' actions, consumer groups, and other community-based activism, I began to learn how and why an enterprise prompted by an emanci-

patory impulse might proceed in the early stages as a trans-
form-as-we-move intervention but soon take on an assimilationist character. The original goal might be to oust the slum
landlord and turn the building into a co-op. But soon rank-
and-file men are complaining about the authority exercised
by the women officers. Founding members are opting for
historical privilege, arguing that their votes and opinions are
weightier than newcomers'. More solvent members begin
objecting to the equal-shares policy of the association and
start calling the less than solvent chiselers and freeloaders.
Finally, everybody's got it in for the elected chairperson.
And nobody trusts the treasurer. Then there's a purge, a
splintering, or the hardening of factions. And each falls back
on the surrogate lingo: "Same o, same o, niggers just can't
get it together."

The situation, in some respects, is worse in these days
of *Dallas* and *Lifestyles of the Rich and Famous*. Bigger-is-
better and grassroots-ain't-shit drive many a budding organization to grab any ole funding in order to enlarge. Say a
community organization comes together in response to a
crisis government agencies ignore. For a while folks operate
in the style of the neighborhood culture. But soon they begin
to duplicate the very inequities and pathologies that gave
rise to the original crisis: setting up hierarchal structures
that cut less aggressive members out of the decision-making
process. Underdeveloping the staff in favor of the stars. De-
ferring to "experts" whether they live on the turf, share the
hardships, and understand the conditions or not. Devaluing

the opinion of the experienced because they are less articulate than others. Smoothing over difference and silencing dissent in the name of unity.

Sometimes the virus in the machine is the funding, or a clique with a hidden agenda, or the presence of agents provocateurs, or media seduction. Most often the replication is the result of the failure to build a critical mechanism within the organization, the failure to recognize that close, critical monitoring of process is necessary in order to overcome the powerful pull domination and demonizing exert in this society. That is to say, we often underestimate the degree to which exploitative behavior has been normalized and the degree to which we've internalized these norms. It takes, then, a commitment to an acutely self-conscious practice to be able to think and behave better than we've been taught by the commercial media, which we, addicted, look to for the way we dress, speak, dance, shop, cook, eat, celebrate, couple, rear, think, solve problems, and bury each other.

Fortunately a noncommercial media exists. Independent-minded students, teachers, parents, fund-raisers, spectators, readers, theoreticians, programmers, curators, and practitioners are increasingly drawn to the independent media movement—the films and video, in particular, produced outside of the industry structure. The Independent Black Cinema Movement and now the Independent Multicultural Media Movement are generally made up of progressive-minded POCs who wage a battle against White sight, disconnectedness, indoctrination, assimilation.

POCs, for example, who have challenged White privilege over language have been producing in the last fifteen years books, films, videos, radio formats, poetry, performance art, sculpture, paintings, audio programs, criticism, theory, dramas, at a rate not previously recorded. It is more than a "heritage of insult," as Dr. often phrased it, that draws POCs together to organize neighborhoods, devise curricula, convene conferences, compare notes, collaborate on projects, or form coalitions. Frequently the moves are motivated by acknowledgment of multiple cultural heritage or biraciality. Sometimes they are compelled by a hunch that the answers to questions of identity lie in another's culture. Sometimes alliances are sparked by a determination to understand what is going on in this country that doesn't reach the nightly news or the campuses. As David Mura, Amero-Japanese writer in Minnesota, has frequently said, POCs find in the cultural work of other POCs what they can't find in the Saul Bellows and Updikes, or in Descartes and Plato.

Unfortunately it is not always easy to locate independent film programs mentioned in the quarterly *Black Film Review,* the Asian *Cinevision* newsletter, *Independent Film & Video* journal, or the publications put out by the Latino Film Collaborative and the Native American Broadcasting Consortium, or the National Black Programming Consortium's *Take One.* It's no simple task to locate the periodicals themselves, *Independent* being the only one that is found with any regularity in well-stocked book and magazine stores.

What's particular about this new crop of films and videos? For one, they don't flatten out cultural specificity in favor of "crossover." What is observable about them of late is the awareness that POCs are part of the authenticating audience. What might that mean in the future should artists of, say, the Chicano/Chicana community direct their work with Native American readers or spectators in mind? For one, it would probably mean the end of victim portraiture, the kind of characterization the down-pressed frequently engage in when addressing "the wider audience," as is said, based on the shaky premise that if only Dem knew the situation they would lighten up. Victim portraits are an insult to those struggles. Victim portraits send a dispiriting message to one's own constituency. What might happen if, say, Amero-Africans pitched our work toward Pacific Islander readers and spectators? We'd have to drop the Two-Race delusion, for one. What is and can be the effect of this swap meet, now that one out of every four persons in the U.S. is a POC? A reconceptualization of "America" and a shift in the power configuration of the USA.

SCHOOL DAZE

We heard four things about *School Daze* during the
spring of 1987 when Forty Acres and a Mule Filmworks was still on location in Atlanta: that it was a musical,
that it was tackling the subject of color caste in the Black
community, that it had an antiapartheid theme, and that it
was in trouble. The description was interesting: the bad
news, of serious concern. In cases of studio-backed independent projects in trouble, Hollywood executives usually
make the panicky decision to cut the elements that originally
made the work compelling. Examples of films gutted of

social relevance, formal innovations, or both are legion. That *School Daze* is not one of them is fortunate. Alert to the film's potential for countering the positive-images school's assertions that color bias played out decades ago and that "dirty laundry" is best kept in a lidded hamper anyway, community workers who use film in our practice were relieved by the late summer communiqué that *School Daze* was out of the woods. Programmers of independent film and video began planning how to use the new film to facilitate analyses of intracommunity dynamics.

One of the many valuable things shared in the multiple-voiced casebook *Uplift the Race: The Construction of School Daze* by Spike Lee, with Lisa Jones, is how to hang tough when beset by problems—the loss of critical location sites, the persistence of badmouthing rumors, severe plunges in morale, and competition with a production paying better rates for student extras. A Columbia Pictures executive dropped in for a mere minute, then went home satisfied. And the production team brought the film in for a February 12, 1988, release. To the screen came a good-looking, ambitiously mounted, imaginatively designed production characterized by a bold mix of both dance and musical idioms and performatory and acting styles.

Set at a southern Black college during homecoming weekend, *School Daze* takes a seriocomic look at caste, class, and gender contradictions among four rival groups of students: Da Naturals, the Gamma Rays, Da Fellas, and the frat members and pledgees of Gamma Phi Gamma. "*West*

Side Story with an apartheid twist," quipped a student DJ
on WCLK radio in Atlanta. Whether the remark was face-
tiously or reverentially intended, *School Daze* is a house-
divided pageant. It is a pageant in the sense that the
spectacle inherent in traditional ceremonies and rites of
homecoming (parades, floats, coronation balls, inductions
into secret orders) provides the rationale for the overall style
of the film.

It is a pageant too in the sense that confrontations between the groups are theatrically staged moments rather
than realistic debates about the issues. The disturbances are
broken up, either by an intervening character or by a scene
shift, leaving the parties unreconciled and the contradictions
unresolved. The function of the four groups of students is to
enact the divisive behaviors that impede unification of the
Black community. The film's agenda is to make a series of
wake-up calls that the punnish title suggests is necessary for
African folk asleep in the West.

The film begins as the Columbia Pictures logo is still
on-screen. On the sound track is the Middle Passage: the
wheeze and creak of the ship plowing through water, the dip
of the oars, the sounding of the ship's bell. As the prologue's
first visual appears, the familiar black-and-white graphic of
the slave ship, the old spiritual "I'm Building Me a Home"
begins. Using archival materials, Lee presents a chronicle of
a diasporized people's effort to make a home in the "new
world." Several things are accomplished during the historical unfolding. A faux history is created for Mission College,

the fictitious setting that functions as a microcosm. The viewer is reminded that much of our struggle in this land has been about the rights to literacy and autonomy and further that the educational institutions we have built are repositories for much of that history. The film also claims a position for itself in that history. Mission College becomes one of the "homes" alluded to in the spiritual "I'm Building Me a Home." The emancipatory enterprise, the Black nationalist quest for a collective "home," is presented from the time of Frederick Douglass to the era of the Black Panther Party. The prologue then segues to an antiapartheid rally, the movie's opening scene, in which a "Free Mandela" banner waves. As *School Daze* unfolds, its depiction of contemporary tribal rites is informed by the Fanonian observation that when we internalize the enemy doctrine of supremacy we jeopardize the liberation project.

Colorist, elitist, sexist, and heterosexist behaviors are presented—sometimes with a degree of hyperbole to signal satiric intent—through the four groups that constitute a hierarchy. The Gamma Phi Gamma forces command the most prestige and the most space on campus; also, they receive the most attention in the production (wardrobe, props, variety of settings, musical themes, spacious framing). Their agenda is to defend tradition at Mission and to perpetuate the prestige of their fraternity.

Committed to some degree to transforming tradition are members of the antiapartheid forces, Da Fellas. Their homes on campus are the shantytown construction, a dorm room, and a second-hand car. Members of this group open and close the film and are the subjects of the longest sequence in the film.

The prestige of the Gamma Rays is derived from two sources, their "preferred" looks (light complexions, weave jobs, tinted contact lenses) and their position as the sister order of G Phi G. Their agenda is the maintenance of the frat: the Rays clean the frat house, assist the pledgees in their initiation tasks, throw parties for the brothers, and make themselves available for sex. Although their labor is indispensable to the maintenance of the frat, they are not; they are replaceable by other female recruits. For the most part, the Rays speak an odd form of ventriloquy and are treated by the film as well as by the frat as groupies.

Called Da Naturals in the casebook, Jigaboos on screen, and "Rachel and them" in spectator parlance is the group we come to know the least. Unorganized and with no discernible agenda, these brown-skinned, working-class sisters frequently utter non sequiturs and a variation of the ventriloquy scripted for the Rays. Their "home" is the dorm. Their members loll on a bed, saying, "All men are dogs"; they shout from dorm windows, saying, "All men are dogs."

In the intervals between group confrontations are several sketchy stories that function as the narrative outline: the seduction and corruption of a fugitive Jigaboo, Half-Pint (Spike Lee); the punishment of an ambitious Wannabee, Jane (Tisha Campbell); and the blown opportunity of a campus organizer, Dap (Larry Fishburne), to develop political coherence. The stories make useful points about intracommunity contradictions. Unfortunately the film's agenda to make a wake-up call is undermined by the film's misogynistic and gay-hating sensibility.

Independent filmmaker Marlon Riggs responds to the homophobic bigotry in *School Daze* in his 1989 film *Tongues Untied*. A scripted performance-arts work about tribal rights and the tribal rights of Black gay men, *Untied* uses a clip from *Daze* in a section of the film that catalogues examples of heterosexist aggression by Black film- and video-makers. The clip is from the Greek show. Da Fellas launch into a call-and-response: "When I say Gamma, you say fag. Gamma (fag), Gamma (fag), Gamma, Gamma, Gamma, Gamma . . ." Da Fellas continue their disruption of the step contest by issuing threats to the fraternities they've labeled "fags"—"Get back or we'll kick your ass."

Lee's *School Daze,* Riggs's *Tongues Untied,* and Isaac Julien's *Looking for Langston* (a film frequently programmed with *Untied*)—each makes a claim on history while taking a position on the "dirty laundry" issue. *Daze* positions its statements on colorphobia and divisiveness as a counterpoise to the history of struggle chronicled in the prologue. *Untied,* through an innovative mix of idioms (autobiography, lyrical poetry, dramatic monologue, cinema verité–like scenarios, archival footage), challenges the attempt by the Black community to exclude its gay sector from Black radical history. Footage of gay rights marches is superimposed on footage of civil rights marches during the culmination of Riggs's assertive argument.

Looking is a meditation on Langston Hughes that uses

the Harlem Renaissance as a cultural reference point for Black gay artists in Britain. Julien sets up a wished-for call-and-response between Harlem of the 1920s and southeast London of the 1980s. He uses archival materials, clothing, literary utterances, and period music to script the yearned-for dialogue. The quest by contemporary Black gay poets for an ancestor, a forefather, a tradition, a past, has to override a double silence: Langston Hughes disclosed little about his sexual identity and the executors of the Hughes estate demanded, in addition to various cuts, that Hughes's voice be lowered on the sound track.

Tradition, Mission College's and the G Phi G fraternity's, is what Julian/Big Brother Almighty (Giancarlo Esposito) continually uses as his source of authority, especially in his war with Da Fellas. The radical tradition that Dap could invoke to strengthen his position is not honored at Mission. The three films together—*Daze, Untied,* and *Looking*—make for an excellent program on the issue of negotiating identity, individual and collective, in spite of invisibilized histories.

School Daze is a musical. It does not operate like an old MGM down-on-your-heels/up-on-your-toes sis-boom-bah on a mock set of Claremont College. It is not "good news" on campus that *Daze* is singing and dancing about. More is at stake at Mission than whether Grady (Bill Nunn) makes a touchdown. The college is being held hostage by the "old money" robber barons. A wake-up call occurs in a scene in which the chairperson of the board of trustees (Art Evans) advises the president of the college (Joe Seneca) to squash the student-led divest-now campaign because the venerable personages who finance the college will not tolerate being told where they may or may not invest their money. Actor Evans laments, "Why won't our people support our institutions?" At the time of *Daze*'s filming, Cheney and Fisk were being bailed out of serious financial difficulty.

Lee, to make a wake-up call about intracommunity self-ambush, chooses an enshrined genre of the dominant cinema, musical comedy, whose conventions were not designed to address an embattled community's concerns. Much of the tension on screen derives from his effort to link two opposing discourses: will the ideological imperatives of Lee's agenda subvert the genre, or will the ideological imperatives of the genre derail his agenda? The linchpin is the cinematic rhetoric (framing, choreographed moves, delivery of choral ensemble, costuming) surrounding the fraternity that links the generic conventions (say, spectacle) to the critique of community divisiveness. The story is grounded in Afrocentric modes and idioms (homecoming events, Da Butt, all-up-in-your-face-isms), as are the devices Lee habitually draws from French bedroom farce, *nouvelle vague,* and Scorsese, as well as from independents who work outside of the industry. "Face," which has become a Lee signature, for example, is the visual equivalent of the oral tradition that resonates in the opening phrase of Toni Morrison's novel *The Bluest Eye:* "Quiet as it's kept . . ."

The rival groups at the college are repeatedly in each other's face. In the scene at the women's dorm when Half-

Pint attempts to get a date, Lee goes beyond using main-stream film devices—talk, shot-response, shot—so that a se-ries of women appear who say, without having to actually articulate it, "Get out of my face." When Dap figuratively gets in Da Fellas' face because Da Fellas prefer to go to the dance rather than keep a vigil in the shantytown, they in turn get in our face: "Lighten up, Marcus Garvey," "Preach, Jesse," "Chill, Farrakhan," "Teach, Malcolm." The close-ups in this scene reconnect us to the history in the prologue, reminding us of what is at stake. The "face" device is re-sponsible, in part, for the intimacy Lee establishes between filmmaker, film, and spectator.

Lee's decision to link old conventions with new ones allows him to deliver pleasure in some of the forms by which dominant cinema keeps audiences addicted to voyeurism, fetishism, spectacle, mystifying notions of social relations, and freakish notions of intimate relations. The mix also al-lows Lee to present characters in their milieu and to address socially relevant issues, both of which the dominant cinema rules out. What is lost in the mix is the opportunity to artic-ulate a radical Black discourse. What is gained is the oppor-tunity to position several types of spectators.

Since the test case of television's *All in the Family*, com-mercial success has depended on the ability of an entertain-ment industry product to address a polarized audience. White reactionaries seeing themselves on prime time were affirmed in their bigotry. White liberals, reading the show as an exposé, congratulated the inventors of Archie Bunker on their "progress." Many Black people, desperately needing to see any sign of U.S. Bunkerism defanged, tuned in each week to crack and to reassure each other.

Sexist/gynophobes, heterosexist/homophobes, and other witting and unwitting defenders of patriarchy champion Spike Lee films. So do nonreactionaries. So do many progressives. Not because the texts are so malleable that they can be maneuvered into any given ideological space, but because many extratextual elements figure into the response. Hunger for images is one element; pride in Lee's accomplishment is another. That the range of spectators is wide speaks to the power of the films and the brilliance of the filmmaker.

Many spectators are willing to provide the interrogation missing in the representations on screen because of progressive features: ensemble (collective) playing, the mutually supportive affection of Dap and Rachel (Kyme), the themes of color and apartheid, the pro-Afro aesthetic of Da Butt, and the cast mix of veterans, newcomers, and performers known in other media. Many spectators do not view the film as separate from the figure, Spike Lee, behind it, or the emerging movement that figure is a part of.

The message of *Daze* for large numbers of spectators is entrepreneurial, cultural, political, and emblematic of the resurgence of African-American expression by the generation that came of age in the post-1960s era. The mixed-strategy approach in the Lee films has released a voice the dominant industry would prefer silenced—the B-boys. Lee's composite push (T-shirts, books, and sound-track CDs) has helped to create a breakthrough for various forms of cultural expression in the marketplace. His commercial success has helped to create a climate of receptivity for Black film-makers in Hollywood. His preparation of audiences for more active spectatorship is a boon to hundreds of independent Black filmmmakers and videographers working in the independent sector.

The color issue is introduced early in *Daze* in a robust production number called "Good and Bad Hair" ("Straight and Nappy" in the casebook). The two groups of sisters encounter each other in the dormitory hallway; neither will give way. Jane, a blonde with green contact lenses, accuses Rachel, a brown-skinned sister with a short 'fro, of having eyes for her boyfriend, Julian. The others, meanwhile, are cracking on one another's weave jobs, kinks, and attitudes. The close-up is held on the two actresses, Kyme and Campbell, in each other's face. Their cohorts call one another Jigaboos and Wannabees. The face-off triggers a production number in a beauty parlor called Madame Ree Ree's. There the women sing and dance a *femme de guerre* to a 1940s-style big-band swing composition with fallout lyrics.

The Rays and Da Naturals encounter each other several times. The behavior never varies; they sling color-hair insults, but nothing develops. With the exception of a pained remark Rachel makes to Dap after she has a run-in with Jane, no attempt is made in the film to explore, say, the cost of this proracist pathology. Such an exploration could have occurred in three scenes involving Rachel and her roommates (Alva Rodgers and Joie Lee), but instead they discuss "men are dogs." And it could have also occurred in one scene involving Jane and the other Rays, but instead they plan a party for the frat brothers.

Colorism is reintroduced as a subject in scenes between Rachel and Dap. Dap does not support Rachel's plan to pledge Delta. "They do good work in the community," she argues. Dap, a campus organizer, is opposed. Sororities are as bad as fraternities, he maintains, although he's helped his cousin Half-Pint pledge. Dap's denunciations include charges of color prejudice. She accuses Dap of being equally color-struck, belligerent as he is about light-skinned folks. She teases him too about his claims of being pure African. When he won't relent, it occurs to her that his attraction to her may be PR-motivated. "Having one of the darker sisters on campus as your girlfriend is good for your all-the-way Black nationalist image," she says and exits. Although Dap and Rachel get together again, no further mention is made of her charge.

Not verbally stated but visually presented, color caste combined with gender and class operate in the story of Daryl/Half-Pint. He has working-class origins and middle-class ambitions. The viewer's attention is frequently called to the fact that he is brown-skinned, short, and spare by his placement among light-skinned and husky fellow pledgees and among light-skinned and "healthy" sisters. To "graduate" from a less-privileged caste to a more-privileged caste as a member of the reigning fraternity, Half-Pint perseveres in a grueling regimen. The pledgees wear dog collars and chains; they get down on all fours and bark like dogs; they gobble Alpo on command from pet bowls; they drop their pants to be whacked with a mammoth paddle. Half-Pint is singled out by the president of the campus chapter, Julian/Big Brother Almighty, for taunts about his "manhood." To enter G Phi G, the pledgees will be branded. We see Julian's huge, ugly scar of a "G" during one of his scenes with Jane.

The seduction and corruption of Half-Pint culminate in his participation in sexual treachery engineered by Julian. It is gender coercion—"You're a pussy." "Only a Gamma man is a real man and a real man ain't no virgin"—that drives Half-Pint into the men-as-predators/women-as-prey brotherhood. His supremacist-warped agenda to flee his social origins led him to G Phi G. The extravagant attention that the movie gives the frat forces in terms of production and design makes the seduction and corruption of Half-Pint plausible.

The depiction of the fraternity's abusive order and of Half-Pint's ordeal makes a good argument for men engaging in the feminist enterprise of dismantling patriarchy. But what is made more visible in the film is the vested interest men (and women) have in an order characterized by male power, prestige, and prerogative.

The topic predictably raised in postscreening discussions by spectators who identify with Half-Pint is society's standard of male attractiveness. Art Nomura in his video *Wok Like a Man* tackles the implications of the Euro-American standard of height, weight, and aggression for

Asian men. On-screen and off, one way to become attractive is to have social power or prestige through male bonding, most usually in terms of a shared sexist socialization to despise and exploit women.

Alien standards of beauty internalized at great psychic cost by African-Americans are taken up in Ayoka Chenzira's provocative short *Hairpiece: A Film for Nappy-Headed People*. The politics of color links such works as Julie Dash's *Illusions,* Denise Oliver and Warrington Hudlin's *Color,* Henry Miller's *Death of a Dunbar Girl,* Maureen Blackwood's *A Perfect Image?* Shu Lea Cheang's *Color Schemes,* and Ana María García's *Cocolos y Roqueras.* The politics of female representation is treated in Sharon Alile Larkin's *A Different Drummer.* And the complexity and subjectivity of women's experiences is the forte of Zeinabu Davis, Camille Billops, Michelle Parkerson, and Barbara McCullough. These issues are central to discussions about the presentation of Jane (Tisha Campbell). The bases of her characterization are classic features in the construction of the feminine: narcissism, masochism, and hysteria. Her seductive display at the ball singing "I Don't Want to Be Alone Tonight," her ambition, and her voluntary sacrifice ("I did what you told me, Julian") are classic she-was-asking-for-it features of femicidal texts.

Uplift the Race informs us that in the original script the frat members entered the Boning Room and ran a train on Jane. Apparently, the thinking behind this particular wake-up call went like this: Isn't it a drag the way men get over on women and how women allow themselves to be ripped off, so let's sock it to this character Jane to protest the unfair situation. Yeah, right. But the appearance of intended meaning (protest) fails to mask the constructed meaning (punishment).

When the Lee films are programmed together, a disturbing pattern emerges. Posters of naked women nailed to the wall in Joe's place of business in *Joe's Bed-Stuy Barbershop: We Cut Heads* reappear in *Mo' Better Blues* as pictures the musicians pass around while telling one of the guys he should dump his white lover and get himself "an African queen." They hand him pictures of naked Black women. In *Daze,* a male character says "pussy" in one scene, and in the next the Gamma Rays say "Meow." A more frightening continuity exists between the gratuitous attack of the woman on the stairs in *Joe's;* the rough-off of Nola in *She's Gotta Have It,* an act assuaged by her term "near rape"; and the scapegoating of Jane in *Daze* after she appears in a porno-referenced sex scene with Julian.

Jane is drawn in the conventional pattern of sexual iconography that hallmarks the industry. Gender issues receive no better treatment in *Daze* than in usual commercial fare. But the possibility, and perhaps the intent, were present. The repetitive and exaggerated attention that Lee gives to statements like "a real man," for example, beginning with the first entrance of the frat and the pledgees, sets us up for an exploration that is merely sketched by the comparison-contrast between Julian and Dap—their styles of leadership and how they maintain intimate relationships. What a "real woman" might be is never raised, and little attention is given to the characterizations of female characters.

It was not necessary, of course, to have the frat brothers run a train on Jane. Their presence outside the door and their readiness to go in and "check out how Half-Pint's doing" are suggestive enough of gang rape, particularly after the earlier command was given to Half-Pint to bring "a freak" back to the dorm. It will take another kind of filmmaker, perhaps, to move to the next step and illuminate the homoeroticism-homophobia nexus at play in gang rape and in the kind of surveillance engaged in by the frat brothers, and in the kind of obsessing Mars, Jamie, and Childs engage in about each other through Nola in *Gotta*. Dap's character doesn't articulate the simple wisdom that gay-hate and dominance aren't really crucial to male development. Dap jams his cousin, but he welcomes Julian into the inner circle of the final wake-up call in the film. Would that there had been as much attention paid to human values as to production values.

The antiapartheid theme is introduced in *Daze*'s opening scene. It is the first wake-up call. "We're late," Dap informs the student body assembled around the administration building. Other universities have been pressured to divest, but Mission hasn't. Dap urges the students to take action: to march, to disrupt classes, to stage a sit-down, and, if necessary, to close the school down. He is drowned out by offscreen chanting—"It takes a real man to be a Gamma man and only a Gamma man is a real man." The frat marches the pledgees onto the turf; they disrupt the rally, seize the space, and disperse the crowd. Within seconds Dap and Julian are in each other's face; in the background, visible between the close-up of the two actors, is a "Free Mandela" banner. Virgil (Gregg Burge), the student council president, steps in between Dap and Julian and breaks them up. A similar scene occurs during the homecoming parade when Julian takes exception to the introduction of a political banner by Da Fellas at traditional festivities. Virgil steps in again and breaks them up. In pay back, Dap and Da Fellas disrupt the Greek Show and bogart the step contest. We assume that their performance will reintroduce the anti-apartheid theme. It does not. Instead it reasserts an aggressive machismo ("Daddy Lonnnngstroke . . ." "Get back or we'll kick your Gamma ass . . ." "When I say Alpha, you say punk").

A link, though, is made between South African apartheid and the U.S. sharecropping system. It occurs at the top of the longest, most emotionally varied sequence in the film. This sequence is an audience favorite. Dap insists that Da Fellas help him defy the ban issued by the administration. Booker T (Eric A. Payne) 'lows as how he's not risking being expelled by continuing in the divest-now campaign. He's the first in his family ever to go to college; his family "slaved" to get him there. Dap tries to get him to see that the situations are related, that apartheid is international. Da Fellas walk, fed up with Dap, who speaks of the campaign as a personal mission and of their participation as proof of their loyalty and friendship to him (shades of Julian's "Do you love me, Jane? Well, you're going to have to prove it"). He murder-mouths them as they exit. Sulking, he hurls a dart at the board. There's a knock on the door. Dap opens it. Piled in cartoon fashion against the doorjamb are Da Fellas. "Do revolutionaries eat Kentucky Fried Chicken?" Grady wants to know.

At Kentucky Fried Chicken, Jordan (Branford Marsalis) leaves the table in search of the salt. A shaker is on a table occupied by local working-class brothers. A local in a cap (Samuel Jackson) is relating some off-the-wall anecdote about how he had to get some "bitch" straight. (A few sisters in the audience suck our teeth. We've been assaulted thus far by "freak," "pussy," "tits and bootays," "meow," "bitch"—and the night is still relatively young.) Jordan asks for the salt. The locals look him up and down and continue to talk. Dap calls Jordan back to the table. The local in the cap calls over in falsetto, "Is it true what they say about Mission [limp wrist] 'men'?" This is the umpteenth antigay remark. Dap suggests they leave; Da Fellas grumble but get up. (Members of the audience holler because Da Fellas are leaving behind all that chicken!)

In the parking lot Dap leads Da Fellas to the car. Edge (Kadeem Hardison) does not want to retreat; he's ready to throw down. In seconds the two groups are lined up in a face-off. The guy in the cap lets it be known that the locals are sick and tired of college boys coming on their turf every year and treating them like dirt. On-campus distinctions between Jigaboos and Wannabees are of no importance to the locals; all college types are Wannabees and ought to stay on campus where they belong. "On account of you college boys, we can't get jobs, and we were born here," the actor Jackson says, cutting through the artifice of the staging. The actors strain to stay on their marks, adding to the electrical charge of the scene. Stuck, Da Fellas go for the short hairs. Dap cracks on the " 'Bama country ass" locals' shower caps and Jerri curls and casts aspersions on their manhood. Jordan chimes in with "bitch" here and "bitch" there. The local in red leather (Al Cooper) endures it all with a stony gaze. His partner (Jackson) resumes his assault—"You're all niggers, just like us." He and Dap are face-to-face. No student council president is present to intervene. Dap steps in closer and says, "You're not niggers." There's a helpless quality to the delivery; there's a vulnerability to the moment. What is at stake for the entire community that refuses to wake up is sounded here. The scene shifts.

Da Fellas are quiet and reflective in the car. So are spectators in the movie seats. Monroe (James Bond III) breaks the silence: "Do we really act like that?" Dap swears it's a case of mistaken identity. Jordan launches into a "I'm Bennett and I ain't in it" routine. Grady has no sympathy for "losers." He is challenged on the class issue. Things are about to disrupt, but Monroe makes a cornball remark that gives them an out. Da Fellas, relieved, pound on Monroe while Booker T maintains a grip on the steering wheel. Spotting Julian and Jane, Dap jumps out and jumps right in Julian's chest, saying Julian better make sure that Half-Pint gets into the frat. We've now seen Dap blow the opportunity to develop political clarity three times: with Rachel, when she challenges him on the color question; with Da Fellas, when they suggest that one of the reasons they won't back him is his personality; with the locals, when they let it be known that the debate between the Greeks and campus revolutionaries has no explanatory power in the lives of most Black folks.

The film's finale begins moments after Half-Pint beats on Dap and Grady's door to announce that he is now a "real man." The next scene takes place in hazy yellow light. Images are stretched. Movement is slowed down. In a wide-angle close-up, Dap shouts "Waaake Uuuupp." Fishburne here displays his vocal register in the exact way that Esposito has done in previous scenes. Does this signal concord between the two male groups? The college bell is ringing. The entire school rises and goes to the quad. Julian gets out of bed where he's been sleeping with one of Jane's sorors (Jasmine Guy). He is the last to arrive. The camera adopts Julian's point of view as he moves through the crowd toward Dap. Actor Esposito has a particular expression; it may imply that the character has become aware of his ability to change. As the camera ascends, Dap and Julian turn to us and Dap says, "Please, wake up."

Within weeks of its release, *Daze* became the subject of extravagant claims by folks who'd seen it and loved it, who'd seen it and not liked it, and who hadn't checked it out yet but had their ear cocked to Communitysay: *School Daze* is going to do more to increase enrollment at Black colleges than an army of recruiters could; *School Daze* is going to outshine "A Mind Is a Terrible Thing to Waste" campaigns for gift-giving to Black institutions; *School Daze* is going to revitalize our fraternities, and brothers are going to be stepping all over Harvard Yard. By summer—without recourse to stats or surveys and frequently without recourse to a screening of the film—Peoplesay dropped its prophesying tone, and the statements rang with conviction.

Conversations in neighborhood movie houses focused briefly on the apartheid theme and the range of contradictions treated in *Daze*. Most of the excitement had to do with Lee's original impulse to make use of his experiences as a Morehouse College undergraduate. Aysha Simmons, former Swarthmore student, recalls that despite passionate dissatisfaction with the film's sexism and heterosexism, the overwhelming feeling within her circle was envy: "We envied the social life of a Black campus." Elvin Rogers, formerly of the University of Pennsylvania, echoes Simmons: "The hazing practices were horrifying, but after seeing the movie we wanted to enroll in a Black college."

Communitysay's claims weren't far-fetched. Many Black colleges and organizations actually did raise funds in a direct way with screenings of *Daze*. And Black Greeks did commence to step all over the quads at Princeton, Harvard, and Yale. And although the various federal agencies and foundations that commission studies of Black colleges and universities can't support a causality theory, preliminary reports from the United States Office of Education, the United States National Center for Education Statistics, and the

Carnegie Foundation do show an unprecedented spurt in Black college enrollment, in Black student enrollment, and in gift-giving in the past two-year period. And according to television newscasts during the Thanksgiving holiday of 1990, the Atlanta University complex has been over-whelmed by applications from transfer students and first-year enrollees. In all probability, the 1990 report from the Research Department of the United Negro College Fund will tell the tale more precisely.

The rest of the story is for the audience to report. The Lee films insist on an active spectatorship by the kinds of questions they pose. *School Daze* asks, So what are we going to do about this color/class thaang? Or as the student coun-cil president demanded to know at the homecoming parade confrontation, "What do you want to do—kill each other?"

Special thanks to a number of friends for good talks: Louis Mas-siah; Cheryl Chisholm; Mantia Diawara; Clyde Taylor; the screen-ers of the Scribe Video Center in Philadelphia and the African American Culture Institute of the University of Pennsylvania, and the Black Student Association at the University of California at Santa Cruz (Oakes College); students at Howard University, Spel-man College, Knoxville College, the University of Ohio in Colum-bus; Mrs. Beatty's senior English class at East Austin High in Knoxville, Tennessee; the sisters with the cassette player at the laundromat on Chelten Avenue and Pilasky Street in Philly; and the brothers with the VCR at the Metropolitan Pool Hall near the Intervale Avenue El in the Bronx.

HOW SHE CAME BY
HER NAME

An Interview
with Louis Massiah

I think of this gathering as an inquiry into culture as well as an inquiry into the possibilities of what it means to be fully human as we come to the end of this century. If the problem or the question of the twentieth century is the color line, then the question in the era we are going into is really how can we be fully human? The struggle is between forces of inhumanity that push us further into alienated states against forces that really work for humanity, work for us to gain greater understanding of each other, understanding our possibilities in the world. It's really in this context that I locate Toni as a force for humanness, helping us to try to realize our human potential. As a writer, as a teacher, as an organizer, as a media-maker, Toni has made remarkable contributions to world literature, to the independent Black film movement, and also to political movements around the country. Toni's strength comes from her clarity, her ability to understand and define essential issues of our time.

I would like to start by asking Toni Cade Bambara how she came by her name.

I earned it, and I worked hard for it. I've had several names. When I was an undeclared music major in college, my name was Tonal Cadence, or occasionally Tonal Cadenza or Tonal Coda. When I was in the psychiatric community, my given name, Miltona, was changed to Miltown. At my fiftieth birthday celebration in Atlanta I was given a new name and in a very serious manner. My feet were bathed, my head was anointed with oil, and a group of young women called Sisters in Blackness gave me the name Hanifa. For the last five years I have been trying to get comfortable with that name, but whenever I look at the name there are two scenarios that unfold, neither one of which I can get with. One is Hanifa on horseback dressed as a man during the Crusades, brandishing a sword and shouting "Death to the Infidels!" In my postmenopausal journey toward wise womanishness, this is a little bit too martial for me. The other Hanifa is Hanifa the Hidden, moving from safe house to safe house, trying to get to the waterfront in order to sneak aboard a ship and get away from the mob of mullahs who are out in the street brandishing swords yelling "Death to the Blasphemer!" since Hanifa the health worker has been speaking publicly on the rape of the young children who wind up in her clinic. For the most part I've been living my life out loud, so I don't think I need that lesson in particular. So, for five years I have been trying to get comfortable with the name Hanifa because I take it very seriously when a sector of the community that names me "daughter, mother, sister" takes the trouble to find some other name to call out some other aspect of me that they see.

I was born with the name Miltona Mirkin Cade. My mother informs me that my father, Walter Cade II, intended to have all his children named after him. My brother became Walter Cade III, but when it came to Walter Mae or Walterina, my mother put her foot down. So my father then named me after his employer in that great plantation tradition. Those of you of my generation who grew up in Harlem or who are older than I am can remember hundreds of people who came up on the Dixieland Express to work on Colonel Black's plantation, also known as Chock Full O' Nuts, and how those workers always named their first- or second-born after Colonel Black or his wife, Page. Every time I run across a Page, I ask, "Did your folks work for Chock Full O' Nuts?" Once a season Colonel Black would have his namesakes and their families up to his estate in Tarrytown, near the Rockefellers. There would be watermelon and fried chicken and stuff. He would sometimes hand out a savings bond to his namesakes. Milton Mirkin, the person I was named after, was not forthcoming with any savings bonds or any watermelons. I didn't even know the man, except I think I met him once. It is just a shred of a memory, which I will share.

Whenever I come through the garment center or whenever I see a really well-made Milano straw hat, I get this little memory. Or whenever I see the film *Klute*. Whenever I am in a place with clothing racks and tailoring tables, I get this memory. I am walking down the aisles between tables, and I am around four years old. I have on patent-leather Mary Janes and frilly socks. I have on my navy blue swing A-line coat with brass buttons, and this most wonderful red Milano straw hat with a satin sash tied at the side. I am trying to hold my daddy's hand, but he is using his hands to talk. There is a white man way at the end of this aisle of tables wearing big pants and standing astride like he's somebody. My father's voice is not familiar to me, and as we walk to the White man my father gets smaller and smaller. So I let go of his hand and step away from him. He turns to look at me and I pretend to loosen the sash on my hat. This is just a shred of a memory, but I bring it up by way of indicating what my relationship to that given name was. At some point, around kindergarten age, I accosted my mother, who was trying to take a bath. I was leaning against the hamper, and I announced to Mother that my name was Toni, and it was not short for Miltona, it was Toni, period. She was very indulgent and said, "Yes, sure, Honey." I guess like any other kid, I was always coming up with names. Whenever you get a new doll, you start coming up with names, and sometimes the names are too wonderful for your dolls, so you take them for yourself. I don't know where the name Toni came from, although in those days there was Toni home permanent. In second grade I did have a Toni doll, which had legs that didn't move, it didn't do anything, but you could comb the hell out of its hair, set it with sugar and water, and the staples would hold!

My friends and my family began calling me Toni, but at school it was still Miltona, which I tried not to answer to. I tried to make people call me Toni. Years later in the fourth grade, I am in Brooklyn and there is a singing star named Toni Harper who is singing a song called "The Candy Store Blues." Once again I struggled to make this name my own. In the fifth grade we moved to New Jersey; I got possession of my school record, and with ink eradicator and a nib-point pen I did some choice forgery, but I didn't do it completely, so there were still papers and cards with the name Miltona Mirkin Cade, so I was still struggling with the name. By the time I got to college, it was all over. It was Toni Cade.

The Bambara is in many ways more complicated to talk about, but I'll give the short version. It's 1970 and Mom and I are in Atlanta, which was where she grew up, and she is trying to find her mother's grave, and I am toting around an African art book. I am also "tumbling big." For the last few months I had been trying to find a name for this child. I hit on Bene as a middle name. Jane Karina and Barumba kept giving me these complicated Harero names that I couldn't spell or pronounce or remember without calling them up. Bene, which means "child of," became a middle name. Then Karma, which was her first name, was on every-body's lips: "This is your karma, this is my karma." So I said, "Karma!" Then there was the problem of the last name. I didn't know what "Cade" meant, but I always liked Cade. It was short, but not too blunt, kind of mysterious. It wasn't "Johnson." I felt very at home in the name Toni Cade. So I am looking around for a name, but I didn't want to change the name completely because I wanted people from kindergarten to remember me.

I have always been very fond of the Chiwaras. The Chiwaras are made by the Dogon and the Bambaras. I tried out Dogon first: Karma Bene Dogon. Well, that sounds like, "Karma Bene, well doggone!" That didn't work and Toni Cade Dogon definitely did not work! Then it became Bambara. Karma Bene Bambara. That worked. Toni Cade Bambara—the minute I said it I immediately inhabited it, felt very at home in the world. This was my name. It is not so unusual for an artist, a writer, to name themselves; they are forever constructing themselves, are forever inventing them-selves. That's the nature of that spiritual practice. Maya An-gelou changed her name. Toni Morrison definitely changed her name—Chloe Wofford?!! Audre Lorde changed the spelling of her first and last names. It's not all that peculiar. So that's where my name comes from.

As a very young child growing up in New York City, you did something that most of our parents told us not to do. You talked to strangers.

Yes, and I went into their houses too.

Could you talk about what gave you the freedom to talk to strangers, and who were some of those people you talked with?

We lived on 151st Street between Broadway and Amsterdam, which is a very long block, and there were thousands of families on that block. There were also thousands of families in my building. Many people kept their doors open, which I thought was wonderful because I was very nosy! There was a family up on the fifth floor, and I used to pass their door going to the roof. There were thousands of relatives in this apartment, and if you stepped in or even looked in they always said, "You want something to eat?" And I would say, "Yeah." They would feed me things I would never eat at home, like liver and onions on a biscuit made with water and lard! They were wonderful people except that they beat their children. They beat those children!

There were also some "ladies of the night." (That's what my mother used to call them.) They used to lend out their back room to Black longshoremen who were attempting to organize against Murder Incorporated. I used to hang out and listen to them. There were lots of meetings and rallies going on in that period. I was born in 1939, and the radical thirties were still spilling over in the forties. There was still that notion that an active political life was a perfectly normal thing. People had to organize against the crackdown forces which, in those days, was the police, the FBI, Immigration, the Draft Board, and the Mob, which are pretty much the crackdown forces today, except people don't acknowledge Mob participation too much.

I went to P.S. 186 on 145th and Broadway, and I would walk to school along Broadway. As people were cranking out the awning in the morning, I would say "Hi" and stop and talk. Of course, I would be late to school, always. When I came out of school, I would come around the Amsterdam Avenue way, which was very exciting. There was the Brown Bomber Bar and Grill. There was Walker's Barbecue. There were hand laundries that used to keep J. A. Rogers pamphlets in the window and would sometimes stick them in your laundry and charge you for them. There were wonderful barbershops, and the men would come out and do all that male choreography; hoisting their pants and the like. They would have hats, and gold teeth, and they would talk. I would always stop and eavesdrop. Sometimes they would recognize me as the kid who turns in at 151st Street where the brewery is. Sometimes they would send me on errands. They'd say, "Hey, you little honey, when you turn in, you know that house next to the brewery? Walk up the stoop, knock on the right-hand window, and tell the lady we are going to bring the petition around." So I became this little messenger. Also on that block was this wonderful beauty parlor where *everything* got discussed. I mean *everything*! So I definitely used to lean against the window, and sometimes I would slide in and sit down and listen to stuff. That beauty parlor is not there anymore. A Dairy Queen is there now, with the most wonderful sign that says:

THERE WILL BE NO LOITERING.
THERE WILL BE NO PROFANE LANGUAGE.

THERE WILL BE NO CREDIT.
CURTESY OF THE MANGLEMENT.

I talked to people who seemed interested in me. Because we came from a tiny family (my mother was an orphan, and my father was the son of a runaway), I was always looking for grandmothers, because I didn't have any, and everybody else had some. People had grandmothers with them plus grandmothers down South to go to. This seemed extravagant to me; I wanted some. I wanted uncles and cousins, which I didn't have, so I began adopting people in the same way people adopted me. I had relatives, so to speak, that had never met my mother. They were just people in the neighborhood who thought I was interesting, who wanted to talk to me, or who recognized that I was available.

To answer your question as to what made me able to do that, I have no idea. Loneliness impelled me; curiosity keeps me doing it.

You dedicate The Salt Eaters *to your mother for giving you the literal space to create. Could you talk about your mother as an influence in your artistic development?*

My mother had put herself through school wanting to be a journalist with the *New York Age,* but instead got married and went into civil service. I always think of her as a shadow artist in the sense that that is her take on things. I have been trying to encourage her to be a mystery writer because she really has that kind of suspicious mindset! My mother was not a house-proud woman, but she had a thing about these bookcases that she bought in Macy's basement, unfinished furniture division, and every spring she would spread the paper, get a rag, take the books out, dust them, and then she would repaint these bookcases a sparkling white. I would look at these books, and one of the books was a little, skinny, flat, black book with a little bronze insert, *Bronzeville,* by Miss Gwendolyn Brooks. It had pictures of children, so I kind of thought it was mine. I used to read it and take it to my room, but it wasn't my book, so I would bring it back and put it in the bookcase. I would hear the name Gwen Brooks because I lived in Harlem, and Harlem was a very rich, wealthy society in the sense that we had everybody. The Robesons had moved back in 1936. Camilla Williams was vocalizing up in the Harlem Y. Everybody in the world went to the Countee Cullen Branch, and to the Arthur Schomburg Collection (which is where I met John Henry Clarke). I would look at a poster of Gwen Brooks, and I liked her face. I like her name, Gwendolyn Brooks. It sounded very ordinary, and it sounded like it was possible to be a writer and to be ordinary.

Also in Mom's bookcase was Langston Hughes's *The Big Sea.* The jacket had come off, leaving only the yellow book, so I didn't see his picture, and I didn't know for years that Langston Hughes was the Mr. Langdon who used to come into the library and talk to us. When I was in the fifth grade, I was going to school in the Bronx, but we lived on Morningside Avenue, and though the Mount Morris library was not the closest branch, it was the most interesting be-

cause those ladies really knew books; and they were interested in making you read. If you were taking out two books,
they would recommend a third. Langston Hughes lived di-
agonally across the street, and he would break three rules
that endeared him to me forever. First of all, he would come
into the library and would not take off his hat. Not because
he was rude, but because he was loaded down with a briefcase, portfolio, a satchel of books: he was coming to work.
He had great hats. He had a Borsalino that I would really
like to have. The second violation was he would come into
the children's section. As you know, in those days age borders were very strict and they were heavily patrolled. If you
were little, then you went over here, and you listened to Sunday school stories; if you were a grown-up, you were over
there listening to the senior choir. If you were in the movies,
you were in the children's section, roped off with that lady
in the white dress with the flashlight to hit you with and
keep you all in check. The rest of the movie house was for
the grown-ups.

It was the same thing with the library. So, Mr. Langdon
(as we thought he was called) would come into the children's
library, would stroll along the windowsill; looking at the
sweet potato plants stuck with toothpicks hanging in the
wide-mouth amber jars, and he would comment on them.
We would always be looking at him thinking, Is he the
stranger our parents always warned us against? Was he the
pervert we had to watch out for? What was he doing in
the children's library? Then he would come and sit down
with us and spread out his work. He was always very careful

about space. If his book hit yours, he would say "Excuse me." I can't tell you how rare that was in those days. Nobody had respect for children or their sense of space. Well, he would be writing, reading, and pondering, and then he would look up and break the third rule—he would talk. He would ask us what we're doing. What kind of homework we have. Do we think it is intelligent homework? What was on our minds? The man was a knockout!

So, why I dedicated *The Salt Eaters* to my mom: I can remember any number of times my mother, unlike other parents, would walk around us if we were daydreaming. If she was mopping, she would mop around us. My mother had great respect for the life of the mind. Between working her two jobs, she would put one foot in her stocking and would go into this deep stare. She too had the need for daydreaming and for talking with herself. She didn't get much of an occasion with a mouthy kid like me.

I was writing stories long before I learned to spell. My father used to get the *Daily Mirror* (which my mother thought was an antilabor paper), and there were very fat margins, so I would scribble in the margins. When I had someone captive, like my mother in the bathtub, I would read this scribble-scrabble to her and she would listen. Essentially, it was my mother's respect for the life of the mind. She gave us permission to be artists. After my first aptitude test I was made aware that I was a freak in some way. In those aptitude tests they would say. "If you have a half hour to spare, would you build a wagon, take apart a clock and see how it works?" etc. They never said, "Daydream, just sit in a window and stare. Conjure up characters and plot stories." They never said that. My mother made it all very casual. My brother was something of a prodigy in terms of art and music, and so her thing was to give us access. To give us access to materials, to museums, to libraries, to parks. We figured that one of her motivations was that she had been kind of shy about going to these places, but she became emboldened as a mother. We always had equipment. We had no furniture or much in the way of wardrobes, but we had drawing paper, paints, and raffia to make mats. We had books and a piano. In the fourth grade I went to the Modern School run by Miss Mildred Johnson, sister of James "Dark Manhattan" Johnson. She was very mean, very yellow, very strict, and very snooty. She would look down at me coming in there with hand-me-down clothes. I didn't come in a cab like most of the other students. The other kids would talk about going up to Martha's Vineyard for the weekend, or going to Sugarbush to ski. They went to Europe and to the Met. They were Black people, but they were not my people. It was confusing. We would take our early lessons in French, and in the afternoon we were learning about the medieval guilds of Europe. I was totally out of it. But Miss Francis, my teacher, wrote a report home and said, "She's making a very difficult social adjustment, but she evidences talent in creative writing."

Where did you learn your first political lessons? Who were you listening to?

The radical thirties were not over with in the early forties, so there were people running around the neighborhood
setting up meetings and rallies. And I lived in Harlem with
Black bookstores, such as Micheaux's Liberation Memorial
Bookstore—"the home of proper propaganda"—and with
Speakers' Corner. I do not think a community is viable without a Speakers' Corner. If we can't hear Black people speak,
we become captive to the media, and we disacknowledge
Blackspeak. Our ears are no longer attuned to any kind of
sensible talk. I knew that Speakers' Corner was valuable, because when we left Harlem most people seemed to be kind
of airheads. They were not raising critical questions. There
was no street culture. They were stupid compared to
Harlemites, who were sharp and cynical. My kind of folks.
Everybody spoke at Speakers' Corner, from center to left.
You didn't have too many right-wing jerks getting up on
that soapbox. Who would speak were people like the
women from the Sanctified Church, and they might talk
about the research they were doing on the Colored People's
Conventions of the Reconstruction era. Trade unionists, definitely, talking about the need for a Black coalition, which
we have now—the Coalition of Black Trade Unionists. The
members of the Harlem branch of the Communist party
might give an analysis of candidates running on the ward
level, city level, or national level. Members of the various
Socialist parties would get up and talk about the state, the
circumstances, conditions, and status of workers throughout the world and why there needed to be solidarity, etc. The
Abyssinians (now called Rastas) would get up and talk

about African civilizations and why we needed to support Haile Selassie. Temple people (now called Muslims) would talk about how they were catching hell back in Chicago and Detroit from the government. Why stateside Black folks needed to be in solidarity with West Indians and East Indians coming into the community. West Indians would get up and speak. Folks would talk about how the Puerto Ricans were coming into the neighborhood, and we ought not be xenophobic. The U.S. government was bringing truckloads of Puerto Ricans into Harlem in 1948, which was around the time of the Nationalist party formation, which is why they were bringing in people from Puerto Rico to break that independence movement up. Speakers on the corner would explain all that. Then the Puerto Ricans would get up and speak, and people would try not to laugh at the accents.

So Speakers' Corner made it easy to raise critical questions, to be concerned about what's happening locally and internationally. It shaped the political perceptions of at least three generations. It certainly shaped mine, and I miss it today. There is no Speakers' Corner where I live. There is no outdoor forum where people can not only learn the word, hear information, hear perspective, but also learn how to present information, which is also what I learned on Speakers' Corner: how to speak and leave spaces to let people in so that you get a call-and-response. You also learn how to speak outdoors, which is no small feat. You also have to learn how to not be on paper, to not have anything between you and the community that names you. So I learned a great many things, and I am still grounded in orality, in call-and-response devices, and I do not deliver papers. I am frequently asked to give a paper at a conference and I refuse. I say that I don't do papers unless I am being paid to write an essay that is going to be published somewhere that I know of. But I am not doing a talk and a paper. People then ask me to give a talk. Well, I can do that. I prepare as hard as anybody else in order to be able to make eye contact with people I am talking to. One of the reasons I do that is I am very shy and I don't like being shy, so I make a point of wrestling with that, and one way is to constantly remove any kind of camouflage or any kind of barrier that exists between me and the community that names me.

My mother gave us the race thing. She also encouraged us in an interventionist style. At school we were not to sing "Old Black Joe." We were not to take any shit, and we were to report back to her any stereotypic or racist remark. This was difficult because shit was happening all the time. For example, I had a really fascist teacher in the third grade, Miss Beaks. She did all sorts of things that were really out. I wrote a story once called "The Making of a Snitch." It was published when I was in high school, and it's about the period of the late forties when, as Gerald Horne would say, "the National policy shifted from Blacks as inferior to Blacks as subversive." We were constantly getting pressure in that McCarthy period. When anything weird went on in school, the teacher would grab one person at a time and take him or her into the cloakroom and encourage and bribe the person to rat on classmates. I wrote that story, and many years later I rewrote it when I ran into the classmate who had been made into a snitch in those early days and then turned up in the late fifties as a government agent. He was working the crowd in front of the Hotel Theresa when Malcolm (who was like our mayor) was there, certainly the appropriate person to welcome Fidel to Harlem.

In those days teachers set traps for you. There was this kid Michael who sat three rows over. We used to walk home together because he lived one block from me. He was a very quiet kid, very repressed. The teacher would always lure him into saying something so that she would be able to call his mother to school. His mother would come and strap him with a Sam Browne belt. Most parents would come and beat their children in front of the class. When I would hear at meetings or at Speakers' Corner about the brutality of slavery, I began to connect this as behavior learned and carried over, and I would hope that there would one day be a rehab camp. I still think that. What do we do with snitches like Earl Anthony, who had been a friend of mine, and now reveals himself in a new book as having been a government agent all those years when he was with the Panther party? What do we do with people like that? If you believe in transformation politics, or transformation psychology, you feel that they can change. But we don't have rehabilitation centers to send them to. When I was in Laos in the summer of 1975, in Vientiane City, at the last moment of liberation they sent the generals to the Plain of Jars, which had been carpet-bombed, to share the hardships of the peasants, to live with them and to turn the Plain of Jars into a green haven. The generals went to school six hours a week, learning Marxist-Leninist doctrine, and they shared the hardships of the peasants. I found those kinds of camps in Vietnam, in North Korea, in China, and in Cuba. It's dodgy to set up a system like that because it can get, in a split second, totalitarian and inhumane, but we very much need something because we have so many walking wounded and defectives, not only agent types, but also people who are still stumbling around from the sixties who never were embraced quite enough, who got assigned things to do and then got left hanging, and are still walking blasted.

When did you first realize the possibility of your writing, and when did you begin to think of yourself as a writer?

I never thought of myself as a writer. I always thought of myself as a community person who writes and does a few other things. I always get a little antsy when people limit me as a writer. In terms of scribbling, I've always been writing, so long as I could find paper—not easy during the war. My mother always had gorgeous legs, and my father had a very proprietary pride about her legs, so no matter how bad the market was, or how bad the budget was, she always had black silk stockings. These stockings came wrapped around a rectangle of paper. I couldn't wait for my mama to get her gorgeous legs into another pair of stockings so I could get that paper. I became something of a community scribe. People would say, "Hey, you little honey, run down to Miss Dorothy's house and help her write the letter to her nephew in the Navy." "Run up the way and tell them what happened at the meeting." "Hey, write this down." When I lived in Atlanta, I was a community scribe in the sense that people would hail me, "Excuse me, you the writin' lady?" "Yeah." "Pull in here into the gas station. The man wants to sell his Ford to this guy here. Can you write a contract?" "Sure." "Here's a paper bag and a pencil. Get to it." In return they would give me my inspection ticket stamped. People in the neighborhood would knock on my door. "You the writin' lady? Listen, the telephone company has screwed me again. Can you write a nasty letter?" Then they would pay me with Jell-O with fruit in it. Sometimes they would wrap up a dollar, which had been folded and folded and tied in a corner of a handkerchief. Take you a year to unwrap that dollar. So, I got paid as a community scribe and got trained as a community scribe very early.

When I came back from Cuba in 1973, I began to think that writing could be a way to engage in struggle, it could be a weapon, a real instrument for transformation politics. Let me take myself a little more seriously and stop just having fun, I thought.

Let me talk about my mother as "hero." There is a scene of a woman turning a school out in the title story "Gorilla, My Love," and I once did an article for *Redbook* on Mother's Day which was about my mother at school. In 1946, the United Nations was established in New York and everyone was very proud. They would drive us crazy in school with these assembly programs about the goddamn United Nations. We would have to draw posters for various campaigns about the United Nations. Very generic and very dull. Children holding hands around the globe. So we're drawing one day, and the teacher falls asleep. I am drawing the children around the globe, but now I want to give them color because my children are Chinese, Indian, and African. You know those school crayons, big and fat, but no matter how hard you pressed you could never get any color out of them. I did not want my children looking streaky and mud-colored. I wanted them to look cool. So I thought that if I got the coffee grinds out of Miss Beak's coffee cup, I could maybe get the right color. So I went up to her desk and woke her up to ask if I could have the coffee. She woke up like a bear. The first thing she said was, "What are you doing out of your seat? You take yourself too seriously in general and in particular." Well, I could handle that. But then she started really blowing like a hurricane, talking about "as ugly and crummy and lousy as these crayons are, they are good enough for you people because who the hell do you think you are? You are just poor colored children." Well, this was too big for me. This was a case for Mother. My mother had a turning-the-school outfit. She had a serious Joan Crawford hat and a Persian lamb coat. She wore one of two favorite suits—either an aquamarine suit with a cherub cameo, which I didn't like, or my favorite suit, a da wine, red, wide-wale corduroy, and, of course, her gorgeous legs in the silk stockings. And some I. Miller outlet opera pumps. She was bad! Now, she would stride into the class and lay out the first law: "My children are never wrong, so you cannot be right." All the children would be so delighted because here was a woman come to champion her child, not humiliate, beat, torture, and terrorize everybody and make everybody throw up. The teacher would say, "Can we talk outside?" My mother was not moving. She also had this scary pocketbook. The click on it was like the cocking of a shotgun. Mom allowed how she was a substitute teacher, and she had pull with the Board of Education, she knew everybody, so "your ass is mine." She would start working her thing. She would be working the dimple in her chin, arching one eyebrow and getting this flinty edge to her very articulate voice, and the teacher would be coming apart. The second law: "You apologize to my daughter and you apologize to the class." The teacher would look at me and finally get my name right (the name my daddy gave me). Then she would turn to the class and try to present some lame story about how the coffee gave her nightmares and she ran amuck and lost her mind. My mother would be saying, "Apologize now or I'll meet you down at 110 Livingston Street." We would laugh at the teacher. Michael would not laugh. He never laughed at any so-called authority figure. He knew what would happen, but we all laughed at her. Then my mother swiveled on her I. Miller black suede opera pumps and moved out of the classroom with the sleeves of her Persian lamb moving like regal robes. Mother was therapeutic.

When do you find your tribe?

Well, I felt very at home in Harlem as a child. I spent the first ten years of my life in Harlem. I had skates and got around a lot and met a lot of wonderful people. I met this one woman who had a tremendous influence on my writing. Dorothy McNorton lived across the street from us when we lived on Morningside. She taught me critical theory . . . another story for another day. In Mildred Johnson's school I did not feel at home, but it did teach me a lot about class. I think by the time I got to college I was hanging out in the Village. I began to identify my people as artist types, even though I was a biochem/premed major at the time, and those people were definitely not my people and that lifestyle was not mine. Like being up late at night in the stinky, smelly lab eating weird food out of a vending machine. I would try not to drop and break any test tubes because that was thirty-five cents, and we were on a really tight budget. I felt much more comfortable with art majors and hanging around the art department, so I used to model for art classes.

That lifestyle was more my thing. I liked the smell of linseed oil and turpentine, mainly because one of my spirit guides comes to me that way, namely my mother's mother; that is, her "visitations" are heralded by those odors—she painted. I also liked the theater group. Working so seriously on these dumb plays. I loved it! So I hung out with theater folk and art folk. But these were white people at Queens College, and they were not my people either. There were a couple of political types there, like Ellie Hakim, who started *Studies on the Left,* a journal still around today. This was the height of the McCarthy period, from 1955 to 1959. We had quite a collection of people at Queens. The granddaughter of Robert Ingersoll, the niece of Alexander Woollcott. But hanging out in the Village I got a little closer understanding of who my people were, as I was always looking for a job and I was underage. In the Village I would go over to Montmartre's Spaghetti House and offer to wash the pots. I would take a big soapy pot and go out in the backyard with the pots because they shared the yard with Café Bohemia. That way I could hear the George Wallington Quartet, who practically lived there. Then I went over to Mona's on the corner of Sixth Avenue and MacDougal, right across from Tony Pastor's. My job at Mona's was to get the exotic dancers cabs. Tango, for example, would shake-dance and sit on the laps of sailors, just do her thing, then rip off the wig and bra and, of course, she's a dude. People would get really angry. So my job was to keep a cab at the curb. I would get paid two dollars a night for this.

Another place I worked a lot was the Open Door, where we used to go to hear Miles. I didn't go to hear Miles; I went to see his wardrobe, because he had gorgeous clothes. He always played into the drapes and showed complete contempt for the audience. In the Village I began to run across designers and theater people, artist types, bohemians who had some politics and kind of knew what was happening. But it wasn't until the sixties struck that I really finally felt at home in the world. I finally reconnected with a lot of things from childhood that I had lost. I had lost an edge somewhere while doing those college years, hanging out in Flushing. I always take Harlem as my standard of a viable community: a Speakers' Corner, a place where politics are discussed and where there is critical response so that you do not become captive; a Black bookstore so you do not become captive to schools and other indoctrinating institutions; a library in case you can't get to the bookstore; a park to sit at and talk (also, the park can be where Pop Johnson and his cronies sit to create community sovereignty; they can check out who is coming up the walk); you have got to have a screening room of some kind so you can know what our cultural workers are doing with our image and our voice; you have to have a press to get the word out.

Harlem became my standard, and very few neighborhoods fit this. When we moved to South Jamaica, for example, I thought my brain would atrophy. The only thing that came close to a truth-speaking vehicle there was the movie marquee on Merrick Boulevard. The guy who would slot the letters in had a real serious thing about Black stars. So you would get *Casablanca* starring Dooley Wilson, *Pinky* starring Ethel Waters, *Island in the Sun* starring Dandridge and Belafonte, *Spartacus* starring Woody Strode. That was about it, though. Not enough to keep the mind alive.

Going into movies, how are movies part of your development, and how do you begin to interact with them?

Growing up in Harlem, we had five movie houses in our neighborhood. There was the Dorset, where we saw Boston Blackie and the Three Stooges. That was on Broadway. On Amsterdam, it was the Washington, where we saw sepia movies and second-string things. There was the Sunset and the Regal on 125th Street, where we saw race movies. That's where I saw Herb Jeffries in *Bronze Buckeroo*. On Broadway and 145th Street, there was the RKO Hamilton, where we saw first-run Hollywood movies, as well as a vaudeville show, as well as a bouncing ball sing-along with the corny songs. I was always in the movie house. I liked movies, and I would sit there and rewrite them. Most of the time the stories were stupid because none of the women ever had girlfriends. I used to think, Well, no wonder. No wonder Barbara Stanwyck is getting thrown off the cliff, or Lana Turner is getting shot, or Bette Davis is having hysterics. They don't have any girlfriends. When the story was really dumb, I would start looking at the scenic design: I like that ashtray; I wonder where they got that color. Oh, the clothes in *Mata Hari*. When I first said to myself, I'm going to make movies when I grow up, was in the Apollo. In the Apollo between shows, would be these god-awful shorts with petrochemical eye-stinging colors that blurred outside of the outlines. They were about such really fascinating subjects as the tin can industry. I used to think, Damn, when I grow up, I'm going to make really great shorts for the Apollo. I didn't understand that they were deliberately chosen to get you out of there. They are called "chasers." So you would get up, get out, and the people outside on line could come in and a new show could start. I didn't know that. I just thought somebody didn't have any taste and were buying these really awful movies. That was the first conscious notion of wanting to become a filmmaker.

Then in 1964 I refused to go to work. I'm hanging down in the Village in the early morning. I walk by the Greenwich movie house and the guy is up on the ladder putting up the letters and it says, "Two African films by Ousmane Sembène." I thought, Sembène, I've been reading Sembène. I go over and look at the glossies and they are playing *Borom Sarret* and *La Femme Noire*. I had never thought about African movies. So I went in to see them, and I stayed and saw them again. I figured I might not see them again, and also my friends haven't, so I have to memorize every shot, and then I'll play it out for buddies. Now *Borom Sarret* really resonated with me because I was working on a story called "Sanitary Belt," as in "Cordon Sanitaire," about that hedgerow built as a barrier between European quarters and native quarters. I was playing around with the notion of belt in general, conveyor belt, on the line, worker in the factory, warehousing of Africans, etc.

In Sembène's film there is this Cordon Sanitaire, and that sparked me. I came out of there very late at night. I was in there all day studying those movies. I was studying every frame because I did not think I would ever see them again. It was then I thought I might go to Africa and become a filmmaker. Then in 1970, shortly after my *Black Woman* book came out, and shortly after Chester H. Higgins, Jr.'s first book of photographs came out, we met each other up at the Studio Museum; and we decided to take the film course with Randy Abbott and Ngaio Killingsworth. I wanted to learn editing. Everybody else wanted to go out in the street with equipment. I knew that a film is made in the editing room, and I wanted to be in there. I studied editing under Ngaio and Randy, and we had lots of footage to play with because everybody went out in the street, shot stuff, and gave it up. I could have made fifty movies with all that footage. I was up there having a wonderful time at the Studio Museum learning editing. Of course, by 1970 we'd heard of the

UCLA rebellion, the Watts films, Charlie Burnett, and that whole crew. We heard about the overturning of the school curriculum at the film school. They wanted to make films out in the streets, in the community. I thought that was fabulous.

On the East Coast there was the war to get WNET on board and for Black folks to get in the door, and there were a lot of documentaries being made. St. Clair Bourne was working as a filmmaker and as editor of *Chamba Notes*. Pearl Bowser was doing a Black retrospective film festival at the Jewish Museum. The idea really began to take hold. Then I moved to Atlanta in 1974. Louis Bilaggi Bailey and Richard Hudlin (kin to the Hudlin brothers) were programming independent Black films, and every once in a while a filmmaker would come through and we would show films at my house because I had a big old sloppy house and I didn't care if you moved things around and dropped things. Bailey founded the Atlanta Annual Third World Film Festival, an attempt to program films from around the world. The Festival became a genuinely international event when Cheryl Chisholm took over as director.

I began programming with the notion that eventually I would get around to making movies, would back myself into it. Then I came to Philadelphia and met Louis Massiah, founder-director of the Scribe Video Center. Louis had just come back from Mali. He had done a lot of videos and was thinking about another one. I suggested he tackle the "Move incident" as a community-voice video. He called me up and invited me to come down and do the narration. I thought,

Narration . . . great. I sit in a booth, like Ernest Hemingway with *Spanish Earth,* and I watch the film, jot down notes, and then record. He didn't tell me that I had to write the script, help him devise the film, *and* narrate! Which was wonderful, actually. So now I am based at the Scribe Video Center in Philadelphia and helping to develop filmmakers. I work as a production facilitator for Louis's project called Community Visions, where we aid community-based organizations to explore video as an instrument for social change. I also teach script writing there, and every time I teach a workshop I write a script to make sure I know what I'm talking about. By now I've got this huge folio of scripts, which ends all excuses, so this spring I will start working on a couple of films.

We are missing the writing, which is absolutely essential. Could you talk about the genesis of The Black Woman? *How did that come about?*

In 1968 I was teaching at City College in the SEEK program.

What was the SEEK Program?

The SEEK program was "Let's get these colored people in here, let them fail and flunk out so we don't have to be bothered with them again." But a number of us managed to get up there. The attrition rate at City College was something like fourteen percent, and in the SEEK Program it was less than nine. We were very serious. There was me, Addison Gayle, Barbara Christian, Audre Lorde, June Jordan, Larry

Neal. It was a heavy bunch of folk up there at that time. Three people got on my case. One was Francine Covington, a student I greatly admired, and a woman I greatly admire today. I loved her style of confrontation. She would say to me, "You've been saying this, that, and the other. Why don't you do a book, damnit?" That made me think.

Then Dan Watts, editor of *The Liberator,* where I did book reviews and so forth, said, "You have an interesting take on things. You ought to write a book." Then Addison Gayle would say, "I heard you deliver eight talks. Why the hell don't you write them down and get them printed?" I thought, Oh, a book about Black women. That would be great. I had read a piece by Rudy Doris about women and leadership and SNCC, so I talked to the women in the Panther party, women in CORE, women in SNCC. They were writing position papers and taking the brothers to task for their foolishness and shit. I wanted to get some papers out of them and put them in a book. But the women said, "No, this is in-house stuff. We are not interested in going public." I thought that was a shame and I said, "I'll wait." So, from 1968 to 1969 I am waiting for this call. Then I began looking around for an agent, and I found Cyrilly Abels, an old European-American leftist woman. We began going around to the publishing houses and I began running into a lot of people I used to go to school with, white folks. They are saying things like, "I've seen fabulous manuscripts from Black women, but they wind up on the sludge pile because there is no market for Black women's works." So then I got this idea: Never mind the papers from the Panther party women;

let me do a book that will kick the door open. I know there is a market for Black women's work out there because I know 800 million Black women all by myself. Nikki Giovanni gave me a poem, Alice Childress gave me a story. I put together this anthology that I felt would open the door and prove that there was a market. Sure enough, within the second month the book came out, it went into a new edition. That book was everywhere. There were pyramids of *The Black Women* in every bookstore. All I knew in the beginning was that it had to fit in your pocket and it had to be under a dollar. I didn't know anything about publishing, but I stuck to that. After it came out, a number of startling things happened. My attention at that time was on kicking the door open so that other Black women's manuscripts could get a hearing, and they certainly did. People then began calling me to do lectures and workshops on women's issues. I didn't know anything so I had to study a lot and call up a lot of people. Alice Childress was very good to me in those years. She was one of the first people who walked up to me, put her hands on my shoulders and said, "You have done something valuable. Now, watch out." That was very valuable. The Harlem Writer's Guild gave me a party and I thought that was going to be the end of it. But no, then came all these urgings to be a particular kind of person, an expert, a spokeswoman. I was having trouble being a public person.

Next, I did an anthology called *Tales and Stories for Black Folks* that came out in 1971. What I love about that book is that my students are in it. I was teaching at Rutgers in those days, and one of the things I always tried to make clear to students was "Do not write term papers for me. Make sure they are useful for somebody else as well." People began to write position papers for organizations in their community. A number of people were working at the storytelling library hour, so they wrote stories. I thought that the stories were great and I published them in the book. That book didn't stay in print very long. I was at the Livingston campus of Rutgers then, and everybody on campus had a copy of the book.

What was the impact of Gorilla, My Love *on your life?*

One of my good girlfriends in those days was Hattie Gossett. In those days we were all piecing a living together. Hattie said, "Hey, let me be your agent." She told me about a woman up at Random House named Toni Morrison who was very interested in my work. I said, "Oh, yeah?" She said, "Put together a book and I'll sell it." So I pulled out a bunch of stuff from under the mattress, from the bottom drawer, the trunks, and I spread all this stuff around and I thought, Ooh, a collection. I thought I would put together stories that show my different voices. It looked good, but it looked like ten people wrote this thing. I went to the library and read a bunch of collections and noticed that the voice was consistent, but it was a boring and monotonous voice. Oh, your voice is supposed to be consistent in a collection, I figured. Then I pulled out a lot of stories that had a young protagonist-narrator because that voice is kind of consistent—a young, tough, compassionate girl. Then I changed my mind because the salesmen at the publishing house will think my book is a juvenile book for a juvenile market only. So I put some adult stuff in.

Then at that time I was writing a play called *The Johnson Girls,* which we performed on the *Soul!* show with Audreen Ballard in the role of Inez. Now it is becoming a film with Barbara O done by Iverson White. I decided to adapt the play as a story, and that became one of the stories in *Gorilla, My Love.* Miss Morrison didn't touch anything. She sort of floats a few ideas at you and whispers in that gentle way. Then you go home and think, Oh, brain surgery! Let me rewrite. The book came out, and I never dreamed that such a big fuss would be made. "Oh, *Gorilla, My Love,* what a radical use of dialect! What a bold, political angle on linguistics!" At first I felt like a fraud. It didn't have anything to do with a political stance. I just thought people lived and moved around in this particular language system. It is also the language system I tend to remember childhood in. This is the language many of us speak. It just seemed polite to handle the characters in this mode. I never knew how to answer, so I would just let people talk about the book. I began to learn what was in that book and what was so different and distinct about it.

You have traveled extensively around the world. You have been to Cuba, Sweden, Vietnam, Laos, India, Nigeria, Jamaica, Barbados. You have often traveled as a delegate. What is that experience like, and why is that important to you?

When you are member of a delegation, you have responsibility before you go, while you are there, and when you come back. Before you go, you want to contact your constituency and find out what they want to know about that country. Also, what kind of solidarity they wish to express with the people of that country, and what sort of materials they would like to send. For example, when we went to Cuba, we took diaphragms, blood plasma, and penicillin. When folks went to Guinea-Bissau, building materials. To Brazil, mops, because none of the maids have mops. In the spring of 1975 I was part of a delegation called the North American Academic Marxist-Leninist Anti-Imperialist Feminist Women. It used to take us ten minutes to introduce ourselves. We were invited by the Women's Union of North Vietnam to come as a delegation and to do what delegates do, like raising critical questions such as: What was the infant mortality rate before the Revolution? What is it now? What was the rate of literacy before the Revolution? What is it now? Who were the people on the bottom strata, and what position do they hold now? What are their prospects for the next ten years? I was always interested in the personal stories and I would ask, "Who were you then and who are you now?" We were invited in the spring to go to Vietnam, but they had the victory in the spring, which was unexpected, so the Women's Union needed to go around and visit the socialist camp and thank people for their solidarity during the struggle. So we were put on hold. Many of us had already quit our jobs, sublet our apartments, turned off our phones, etc. I sat down and wrote, and that became *The Sea Birds*. Most of those stories had not been published; been hanging around the house, and they were completed during that spring and summer.

In Vietnam we were also interested in bringing back things for our constituency; we would have to give a debriefing and a report of some kind and had to shape it in some palatable way. Children gave us cards to give to the children here expressing solidarity. When I got back, one of the tasks I had was to deliver this information to my constituency. I decided to do it the way I knew how to do. I wrote a short story in seven sections. I would read a section, then we would have music, somebody would get up and read the greeting cards that the children had made. Then I would read another section based on stories I had been told, then someone would show some slides and posters, then I would read another section. It went on like that. That story line became the title story in *The Sea Birds Are Still Alive*. Very oddly the first time I ever heard it on radio, the person read it, and then had music, then read it, etc. I thought it must really lend itself to that kind of orchestration.

You were in Atlanta when you were writing The Salt Eaters—*could you talk about that?*

The Salt Eaters, like many works, started as entries in my journal. I was trying to figure out as a community worker why political folk were so distant from the spiritual community—clairvoyants, mediums, those kind of folks, whom I was always studying with. I wondered what would happen if we could bring them together as Bookman brought them together under Toussaint, as Nan brought them together in Jamaica. Why is there that gap? Why don't we have a bridge language so that clairvoyants can talk to revolutionaries? So I began thinking about it and jotting things down in my journal. Then the entries got very long; then they threatened to turn into a story. I had hoped that the story would be a short story since I don't have staying power. It was going to be about either a Mardi Gras society or a samba school. This society, for some kind of festival, would elect to reenact an old slave insurrection. They do so, and all hell breaks loose because of the objective conditions in that area. I thought I could pull that off in seventeen pages. I began working on it and it got to be a novel. It was very difficult sledding because I was writing quite beyond myself in a number of ways. I was writing that book in 1981 so I could kick cancer's ass in 1993. That book taught me how to get well. If I hadn't written it, I'm not quite sure I'd be sitting here. I was writing beyond myself in that sense.

Also in the sense that I was stretching, reaching, trying to do justice to that realm of reality that we all live in but do not acknowledge, because the English language is for mercantile business and not for the interior life. The only time you see that realm rendered is in science fiction. I was trying to find another way to do it, and I think I did. So I was writing beyond myself in that sense. When I look at that book now, I realize I'm not there yet. I don't understand it yet. It resonates, it chimes in my bones, but I don't understand it yet. It was very hard work. It is a breathless book. When

Morrison got ahold of it, I thought that she would take care
of it. "Ahh, she'll fix it." She didn't touch it. She said, "This
is fine." I said, "Really?" She said, "Yes." I waited for her to
whisper at me, I waited for her to drift some stuff across my
brainpan, but she didn't, she left the book alone. Or, rather,
she whispered so softly I didn't know what was prompting
the rewrites.

When the book came out, there was a weird reaction
to it. Some reviews were very favorable but totally unin-
formed. Some reviews were not favorable but informed. I
got wonderful mail from people who said, "Thank you for
breaking this ground because I want to write like this, but I
don't want to write science fiction. I like this alternative reality. Thank you." Other people wrote, "'The Yellow Wallpaper' room taught me that I needed to get well. *The Salt
Eaters* taught me how." I got letters from various people
who are now friends, from the Asian community, the Chi-
cana community, who picked up on the Seven Sisters—
Women of the Rice, Women of the Plantation, Women of the
Corn, who said, "We must all get together and create a
Seven Sisters collective. We must do an opera." I am continually haunted by the Seven Sisters. In the late fifties I wrote
a story called "The Talking Stick." It was about a study
group called the Seven Sisters. In *The Salt Eaters* the Seven
Sisters are a performing troupe. In a bunch of things I am
doing now, called *Goddess Sightings,* the Seven Sisters are a
network of people in North America, South America, and
Central America, and they get together to do things like
reimagine America. *The Salt Eaters* was usable, apparently;

I kept finding quotes from it everywhere. People started quoting sections of it in their speeches. I would find quotes on greeting cards—which nobody paid me for. Carole Parks, with permission, used it to create a conference calendar with quotes for each month. Other people drew maps of the landscapes and the worlds in it and turned them into T-shirts for which I was not paid. Then folks started teaching it. Charles Frye taught a course in ethics in the philosophy department at Mount Holyoke and this was the required text. He called me up and asked me to come speak. I am not a silly woman, so I said, "If you want to conduct an intelligent discussion, you call Eleanor Traylor. I don't know nothing about the book. I'm still reading it." I am still catching up with the wisdom of that book.

In particular, and in general, how has motherhood and how has Karma, your daughter, affected your work?

It is very hard to answer. One of the things that Karma did very early in life when people would call me was to say, "She's busy. She's out of it. She is staring out the window. But she's working." They must have said, "Well, this is important." She would say, "Is it important to you or important to her?" I said, "I like this kid. I'm keeping this kid. This kid understands." Then they would probably say something she didn't like, and she would hang up and say, "Some people are so rude to children." Karma gave me permission to write, in the sense that she would not disturb me if I was in my particular chair, at my particular table. She would move around me and take care of things.

There was a period too when I went utterly mad in the eighties in response to the Atlanta missing and murdered children's case. That manuscript too started as journal entries and then developed into pieces that I did for the newspapers, and then I finally realized that I had a novel on my hands, and I didn't want it. One of the reasons I didn't want it was because I knew too much, and I thought if I could reconstruct the real case, and know the difference between this and that highly selective media-police-city-hall-fiction on which someone got convicted, how safe am I? Everybody in the world was doing research for me. People from *Newsweek* and *60 Minutes* would call me up and ask me, "Do you have another angle on this?" I would look in my notes, I would look at something I hadn't researched yet, and I would say, "Yeah, why don't you check out this and get back to me." I didn't have to leave my house. As a result, I stopped going out, I stopped bathing, I stopped washing my hair, I became this lunatic. My daughter would tap me every now and then and say, "Ma, you look like hell." Then it was "Mother, get it together." She was thirteen at the time, and she took what little money was left and enrolled in the Barbizon Modeling School; the idea was to make money as a runway model, pay the bills, and keep us going until I found myself again. She has been a tremendous support in writing. If your children give you permission to write, that's heavy. I am now in a period of recovery, and so is she, so our talk is very interesting. She was remarking the other day that she had no idea that all the skills that she had developed taking care of my sorry ass, that these were marketable skills.

It was Cheryl Chisholm down in Atlanta who hired her to do some work for the film festival that called on many of those homemade skills. She is very good at cleaning off desks, booking your trips, getting people off the phone, blocking people at the door. She is really a good caretaker. When Julie Dash sent out an SOS, Karma went in there and took care of Julie and helped her get the book out. People praise her and she looks at me and shrugs, "Well, it's just what I did with you."

What's the present phase, particularly in light of your bout with cancer in 1993?

For several years I had been stuck—spiritually, financially, psychically, physically. Finally my intestines were blocked. I knew I had been blocked because I couldn't feel my spirit guides around me. I would meditate and get rocked by earthquakes and thunderstorms and all kinds of stuff that never happened before. I was not growing as a creative person. I was putting that kind of sacred practice on the back burners, wrenching my way away from a path I knew I was supposed to take. I knew that I had cancer. So when the doctor told me I had cancer, I already knew.

Now I am in the process of recovery, physically, financially, psychically, spiritually. I am coming through it slowly, mainly by trying to get down to those chambers where I work when I am at my best. No matter what the work is, there is a place I can go to when I am in touch with the best of myself, and I am connected with the most powerful something or others—spirit guides—let's call them angels, if you

like. I also have a tremendous feeling of attachment to
friends all over who are the people who got me out of that
bed and got me well. I was talking to my surgeon the other
day, who was, as usual, praising himself about his scalpel. I
pointed out, once again, "Your scalpel is only a physical
manifestation of the love and affection of my friends. They
got me off the table." When I was in bed, just whipped, but
I had something to do, I would reach everywhere for energy
and nothing would happen. But all of a sudden I would get
this surge of energy, and I would be up, walking down the
ward, giving away my flowers, talking to people, giving orders. Then someone would call, and I would find out that
they had been at a prayer group at that moment, or two or
three people had lit some candles at that moment to send me
some energy. So I am in the period of recovery, and please do
light candles for me because I need some help. I am trying to
write things I have never written before, again writing beyond myself. I am doing a series of things called *Goddess
Sightings*. Some of them are stories, some of them are obviously scripts for video or film, and one of them will be an installation and performance piece as part of Miss Morrison's
Atelier project at Princeton. I am going to do a garden of
goddesses and film it.

Can you talk about your voice lessons?

One of the aspects of my recovery is that I am taking
vocal lessons, which have enabled me to free my voice on
many levels. I always thought I lived out loud, but I didn't.
It also is helping me breathe on many levels. My teacher is a

yoga teacher as well. I decided to take lessons after I came back from the National Black Arts Festival in Atlanta. I had the best time down there. I went down there for a gig, and I just stayed on. When I came home, I felt, Why can't we all feel like that all the time? I was told that when I stopped chemo I might go into depression; it shapes your week, getting ready for it, recovering from chemo, defending the immune system, etc. So I needed to be into something before I started. Well, I was always threatening to take singing lessons. So I have been taking singing lessons. We do drills, breathing exercises, I sing, I do yoga, I do German lieder and Italian arias and Cole Porter. It is very much a part of my recovery.

Are there any questions?

Q: What does the expression you use, "Sam Browne belt," mean?

It is a thick, ugly, Texas ranger belt. It is mean and fascist, and it hurts bad. Michael's mother was a severe little woman who wore severe clothes, and she would beat that boy with that belt.

Q: I wanted to ask about your expression in dance and movement.

In reclaiming the body from the biomedical syndicate as well as from the naturopathic types I have been dealing with, the best way I know of recovering the body is movement. It is only when I am dancing that I inhabit all of my body. When I was in academia, that life would drive me up into my mouth, and all of me would be huddled behind my teeth, and I would have to remind myself that I have this space to stretch out in. When I am totally in my body, I know it, because when I run into people, all of me remembers them. My thigh remembers them, my mind is everywhere, and also I feel gigantic. When I walk down the street, I feel very large, physically as well as spiritually. I feel like everybody is a friend of mine and everybody is just wonderful: "God, it's going to be great when we finally take over and be in charge of this yard. Kente cloth in the Oval Office, deviled eggs on the menu, peach cobbler on the lawn." I have no idea what movement I will get into because my girlfriend Arlene said to me, "So-and-so, the African drummer, is going to be at the Center." I said, "So what?" She said, "I'll pick you up at ten o'clock and we'll go." I thought we were going to watch. Around nine-thirty she called and said, "What are you wearing?" I said, "I've got my pajamas on." She said, "We're going to the dance class." I said, "Are you serious? I am lucky I can walk." Anyway, I got into my tights, the leg warmers, and I went to the dance class.

Now, even when I had been in the best of shape and thought I was a dancer, I never could get through a class. I am flashy and have a lot of presence and style, but no technique. People put me in the front line in the beginning because I am a quick study, but after about fifteen minutes I begin to flag so they put me in the back and I start falling apart. This class was fast; they had some serious drummers. They were reaching that tempo when you get scared—the horses are coming! The drummers kept coming up to that threshold rhythm and I kept getting nervous. Do you know what I mean? Trance drumming to summon the loa. I am trying to dance and it was awful. It was just pitiful. Miss Dunham would've shot me. I am not sure what movement I will go into now. I have done Alexander technique, I've done Nikolai technique, I've done gymnastics. My daughter has done tae kwan do and the like. I'm thinking maybe I'll go that route. In Philadelphia there are any number of us who are doing movement, such as Sandy Clark Smith and Denise Sneed, so I will check with them.

Q: Political concerns have always been a big part of your life. Have you felt any personal disorientation from what has happened in the world in the last few years in terms of the collapse of some of the models we looked up to? Do you still feel in terms of your own sense of what struggle has to be for us here in this country, do you feel that sense of struggle is still very much intact and has not been destabilized by any of these developments?

Yes, I'm disoriented and yes, I do think it has been destabilized, and what I have done in response to it is to close in. I don't do nearly the kind of work I used to do. My arena is very limited. I am still doing draft counseling; I work with women from the Persian Gulf thing. What I am always telling them is that they have to do a video and get their stories out. If I can't do it in video, I don't want to do it. If there is any work that people call me for, if it doesn't involve video I won't do it, because I need to focus and not get too scattered. I think it is because of a lack of courage; there is nothing noble about it, so don't clap. When I go to places or meet people I assume are still struggling and find out they are not, it is very depressing, so I just stay where I am with like-minded people. I can affect and create some value where I am.

Q: I have noticed that none of the African-American films that I have seen have been taken from great American literature. How you do feel about films made by Whites about Blacks?

They are ugly; we don't need them, we have our own genius. *Nothing but a Man,* despite the stupid title, is an exception.

Q: How do you feel about Hollywood films in general?

I don't feel anything about them. I don't have to because I am very deeply steeped in the independent sector. I don't have to go get mugged all the time. I go to movies constantly because I am a film nut. But I go to see them to train myself in film, to look at what are the conventional practices, and what do they mean ideologically or politically, and how to avoid them. When I go to movies to enjoy and to blossom, I'm going to independent films, in particular independent Black films, but also independent Asian films, the independent films that are being conducted in that sector away from the industry, that do not take the Hollyweird model as the protocol, but rather are striking out for something else, for a socially responsible cinema. That's where I am. I don't have many expectations from Hollywood. They can tolerate certain kinds of criticism, but they do not tolerate another vision. If you have a different vision, you need to be moving in the independent sector.

Q: Are there any films that you want to recommend?

Sankofa and the Du Bois documentary called *W. E. B. Du Bois: A Biography in Four Voices,* and also *The KKK Boutique Ain't Just Rednecks.*

THE EDUCATION
OF A STORYTELLER

Back in the days when I wore braids and just knew I knew or would soon come to know *everything* onna counna I had this grandmother who was in fact no kin to me, but we liked each other.

And she had this saying designed expressly for me, it seemed, for moments when I my brain ground to a halt and I couldn't seem to think my way out of a paper bag—in other words, when I would dahh you know play like I wasn't intelligent.

She'd say, "What are you pretending not to know today, Sweetheart? Colored gal on planet earth? Hmph know everything there is to know, anything she/we don't know is by definition the unknown."

A remark she would deliver in a wise-woman voice not unlike that of Toni Morrison's as I relisten to it. And it would encourage me to rise to quit being trifling.

As I say, we weren't blood kin but I called her Grandma Dorothy or Miss Dorothy or M'Dear (I was strictly not allowed by progressive parents to call anybody Ma'am or Sir or to refer to anybody as a Lady or a Gentleman or—the very worst-of-all-worst feudalistic self-ambushing-back for one's political health—refer to a fascist pig dog rent-gouging greedy profiteering cap as a "landlord").

Miz D called me Sweetheart, Peaches, You Little Honey, Love, Chile, Sugar Plum, Miz Girl, or Madame depending on what she was calling me for or what she was calling me out about.

One day, I came bounding into her kitchen on the sunny side of Morningside Park in Harlem, all puff-proud straight from the library—and I stood over her with my twelve-year-old fast self watching her shuck corn over the *Amsterdam News* and I then announced, standing hipshot, a little bony fist planted on my little bony hip and the other splayed out sophisticated like I said.

"Grandma Dorothy, I know Einstein's theory of relativity."

And she say, "Do tell," shoving the ears of corn aside and giving me her full attention. "Well do it, Honey, and give me a signal when it's my turn to join in the chorus."

Well, straightaway I had to *explain* that this was not a call-and-response deal but a theory, "an informed hunch as how the universe is put together in terms of space and time."

"Uh-hunh," she says, "well get on with it and make it lively, 'cause I haven't tapped my foot or switched my hips all day."

So I had to *explain* that this was not a song or a singing tale . . . but a theory.

And she say, "Uh-hunh, well, Sugar, be sure to repeat the 'freedom part' two times like in the blues so I'll get it."

"The freedom part," I mumble, kinda deflated at this point, and sort of slumping against her ladder-back chair.

"Sure," she says, "the lesson that I'm to take away to tell my friends 'cause you know uneducated and old-timey women tho' we may be, we still soldiers in the cause of freedom, Miz Girl."

So I just go ahead and slump on down in the chair she's pulled out for me, and I say, voice real feeble like, "Grandma Dorothy, relativity is not one of them fables, ya know, with a useful moral at the end. It's not one of them uplift-the-race speeches like they give on Speakers' Corner. It's a ahhhh . . ."

"Hmm, Chile," she says, giving me a worried look like she's real concerned about my welfare. "What kind of theory is this? Is Br'er Rabbit in it, or one of them other rascals I dearly love?"

"Miss Dorothy, Mr. Einstein, one of those white guys from Europe, I don't think he know from Br'er Rabbit."

"Uh-hunh. Well, Sugar Plum, am *I* in it?"

"Ahhhh." I'm about to give up on my whole program for self-development at this point. But she, Miz Dorothy, is not concerned with my distress. She has tugged her dress down between her knees, dug her heels into the ruts in the linoleum, is leaning over, her wrists loose against her kneecaps, and she is just rattling on, encouraging me about the many ways I can tell this theory—in terms of air, earth, fire, and water, for example—or in terms of the saints, or the animals of the zodiac, or the orishas of the voudou pantheon, or as a parable assuming my scientific/progressive mother would allow her children (us) to read the Bible and assuming I could remember a parable that might have enough similarities to the theory blah blah blah.

Finally she says, "Well, let me hush, Precious, and you just go on and tell it however Cynthia would tell it or one of your other scatter-tooth girlfriends."

And I come alive at that point—jump up switching hands on hips.

"Well, my girlfriends don't know it. Cynthia don't know it and Rosie don't know it and Carmen don't know it—just I know it."

And she say, "Madame, if your friends don't know it, then you don't know it, and if you don't know that, then you don't know nothing. Now, what else are you pretending not to know today, Colored Gal?"

It was Grandma Dorothy who taught me critical theory, who steeped me in the tradition of Afrocentric aesthetic regulations, who trained me to understand that a story should be informed by the emancipatory impulse that characterizes our storytelling trade in these territories as exemplified by those freedom narratives which we've been trained to call slave narratives for reasons too obscene to mention, as if the "slave" were an identity and not a status interrupted by the very act of fleeing, speaking, writing, and countering the happy-darky propaganda. She taught that a story should contain mimetic devices so that the tale is memorable, share-able, that a story should be grounded in cultural specificity and shaped by the modes of Black art practice—call-and-response but one modality that bespeaks a communal ethos.

I would later read Fanon on the subject—"To speak is to assume a culture and to bear responsibility for a civili-zation."

Later still, I read Paolo Freire, speaking on activist ped-agogy, engaged cultural work. "The purpose of educational forms is to reflect and encourage the practice of freedom."

While Grandma Dorothy was teaching me theory, and the bebop musicians I eavesdropped on while hanging around fire escapes and in hallways were teaching me about pitch, structure, and beat, and the performers and audiences at the Apollo and the Harlem Opera House were teaching me about the community's high standards regarding expres-sive gifts, I was privy to a large repertoire of stories.

As told by women getting their heads done in beauty parlors, or stretching curtains on those prickly racks on the roofs, by women and men on Speakers' Corner—the out-door university on Seventh Avenue and 125th Street in front of Micheaux's Liberation Memorial Bookstore—men from trade unions, from the Socialist party, the Communist party, the African Blood Brotherhood, the National Negro Congress, women from Mary McLeod Bethune clubs, the women's department of Sanctified Church, women of the Ida B. Wells Club, from trade unions, Popular Front organizations formed in the mid to late thirties.

Representatives from the Abyssinia Movement whose membership grew as a result of political mobilization in 1935 in support of Ethiopia's struggle to oust invasionary forces from Italy and Mussolini.

Representatives from the temple men—what we called Muslims in those days.

Stories that shaped my identity as a girl, as a member of the community, and as a cultural worker.

Two types of stories struck me most at the time. One, about women's morality. Now, outside the community and in too many places within the community, "women's morality" had a very narrow context and meant sexual morality. One was taught not to be slack, sluttish, low-down, but rather upright, knees locked, and dress down.

But in the storytelling arenas, from kitchen tales to outdoor university anecdotes, "women's morality" was much more expansive, interesting, it took on the heroic— Harriet T. and Ida B. and the women who worked with W. E. B. Du Bois, the second wife of Booker T. and the Mother Divine of the Peace and Co-op Movement, and Claudia Jones, organizer from Trinidad who was deported during the Crackdown, when the national line shifted from "blacks as inferior" to "blacks as subversive" and wound up in a stone quarry prison and wrote "In every bit as hard as they hit me."

These women were characterized as "morally exemplary," meaning courageous, disciplined, skilled and brilliant, responsive to responsibility for and accountable to the community.

The other type of memorable tale bound up in these women heroics was tales of resistance—old and contemporary—insurrections, flight, abolition, warfare in alliance with Seminoles and Narragansetts during the period of European enslavement; the critical roles men and women played in the revolutionary overthrow of slavery; and in the Reconstruction self-help enterprises founded, the self-governing townships founded, the political convention convened and progressive legislation pressed through; and in days since—the mobilization, organization, agitation, legislation, economic boycotts, protest demonstrations, rent strikes, parades, consumer-cooperative organizations.

One tale heard in girlhood that I do believe informs me, transforms me, is still told today in the islands off the coast of Georgia and the Carolinas. A tale about that moment of landing on those shores not as in very old times when we came as invited guests of the leaders of Turtle Island territories, those days when we came in ships with spices, gold books, and other gifts of friendship and solidarity, visiting the Cheyenne, the Aztecs, the Zapotec, the Aleuts.

Not then, but later.

In that terrible time when we were kidnapped, herded in ships, and brought here in chains as enslaved labor.

The tale goes:

And when the boat brought the Africans from the big ships to the shore, those Africans stepped out onto the land, took a look around, and with deep-sight vision saw what the European further had in store for them, whereupon they turned right around and walked all the way home, all the way home to the motherland.

That's the story version. The historical events on which the story is based, on which a cycle of stories is derived, is used by numerous writers and independent Black film- and video-makers. Paule Marshall in *Praisesong for the Widow*, and Toni Morrison in *Song of Solomon* and *Tar Baby*, Richard Perry in *Montgomery's Children*, Julie Dash in her film masterpiece *Daughters of the Dust*. And are documented in ship's logs and journals, and bodies of correspondence written by numerous European slavers.

"The ship foundered off the coast and much of the barreled cargo was lost. The Africans stampeded and went overboard with the horses. Many drowned, some reached the shoreline and were never seen again, but most of the Africans who reached the shallows returned themselves to the depths weighted down within their irons. And the sight of hundreds of men, women, and children, holding themselves under as the waves washed over them, drove onlookers quite mad indeed.

"And when we saw what was further in store for us, we turned right around and walked all the way home to Africa."

OR

"And there on deck, we looked to shore and saw what was further in store, and we flew away to Guinea."

OR

"They took one look and were struck blind by the abomination, and when they hit the depths, they hung on to the horses till they reached land—and till this day, you can hear those Blind African Riders thundering in the hills, thundering in the hills."

OR

"And when the horrible news grazed the ear of the goddess, she turned, and in turning, the hems of her skirt swept the sands in patterns meter neter nu, and swiftly running across the savannahs on newly bruised feet, streaking red across the outdoor altars burning, tearing bark from the trees with her teeth, rising, ripping roofs from the homes with her nails, whooping, tumbling birds bald and beakless from the clouds shrieking, she was chasing the ships, chasing the ships from the tropic of Capricorn to the Horse Latitudes.

"And there on deck a girlchild in one yard of cloth bent back over the rail of the ship; across her throat an arm as stout as the mast of a man who would brand her or break her, pressing out her breath, wood splintering into her spine, hate poring into her pores, her eyes lifting to the red eye of the twister; then up she rose, from the fingers that clutched and claimed, up from the rust of the anchor chain, up from the nick of seashells in the salt museums, up past the sails that snapped like teeth, she bore her bronchia to the gusts, and was swept up in the skirts of Oye Mawu, blowing all the way home, blowing all the way home, all the way home, blown home."

Grandma Dorothy, in an effort to encourage our minds to leap, would tell us, "Of course we know how to walk on the water, of course we know how to fly; fear of sinking, though, sometimes keeps us from the first crucial move, then too, the terrible educations you liable to get is designed to make you destruct the journey entire. So send your minds on home to the motherland and just tell the tale, you little honeys." And my mama—not one to traffic in metaphors usually, being a very scientific woman—would add, "Yeah, speak your speak, 'cause every silence you maintain is liable to become *first* a lump in your throat, then a lump in your lymphatic system."